In Light of Recent Events,

In Light of Recent Events,

Amy Klinger

THE
STORY
PLANT

The Story Plant
Studio Digital CT, LLC
P.O. Box 4331
Stamford, CT 06907

Copyright © 2022 by Amy Klinger
Library of Congress Control Number: 2021951936
Cover design by Eli Scheer

Story Plant trade paperback ISBN-13 978-1-61188-323-7
Fiction Studio Books e-book ISBN-13: 978-1-945839-61-0

Visit our website at www.TheStoryPlant.com

First Story Plant Paperback Printing: March 2022
Printed in The United States of America

For my parents

1: outside

In the New Jersey suburbs where I used to live, the ranch and split-level houses were packed shoulder-to-shoulder for blocks on end. I had developed a habit of taking strolls just after the sun set, spying through these literal and symbolic windows into other people's lives. Each bulging bay was a giant TV screen featuring mostly mundane, modern living. The hanging up of a coat in a closet, the orbit of someone setting silverware around a table, the delivery of clean laundry from bedroom to bedroom. And of course, the television—the actual television—remote controlled, flipping through syndicated sitcoms, past commercials to the local news stations, and back again.

Sometimes the things I witnessed were not so mundane. Like the time I sat on a bus stop bench watching a remarkable fight between a blazing-angry blonde in silky blue pajamas and a stocky, basketball-coach-of-a-guy, bald and brooding with arms folded tightly over his chest. Her face was contorted and fierce as she circled him like a raptor, until a spring snapped and he stood abruptly, shouting back at her. That was when she picked up a palm-sized object from the table and winged it right through the side window, startling the neighbor's dog into a barking fit. Seconds later, the man blasted out the front door and down the concrete steps. He paced in the driveway, fists pressed to his hips in rigid triangles at his sides. There was nowhere for me to hide, and he spotted me sitting under the streetlight at the bus stop at a time of day when there were no buses stopping. I offered a tight, sympathetic smile and a weird kind of wave. He let out a long, slow sigh, then with a bitter laugh, shouted to me, "She hates when the pasta's not al dente."

And though I never tipped the scale to become a peeping tom (I didn't even own a pair of binoculars), I will admit that at least twice over the course of the three years that I lived in my quiet condo, I happened to inadvertently witness the coupling of a young couple in the second-floor apartment that could be seen from my bathroom window. But (a) both times, I was in the middle of brushing my teeth, not actively being intrusive, and (b) their lights were on, their blinds wide open and she was bent over the windowsill like the farmer's daughter in the hayloft. So, while I didn't necessarily turn away from the scene (and I may have turned out my own lights so as not to be spied in return), I don't think their lack of discretion should damn me to classification as a pervert.

My interest in other lives was not kinky, just curious. Seeking out those everyday moments of poignancy or grace, silliness and tenderness, explosive scenes like the shattered window or quiet moments like someone slowly turning the blinds closed for the night.

Though not a skill most human resource professionals would actively seek in an employee, I found that the ability to likewise sit quietly and observe in the workplace provided a subtle advantage that seemed evolutionary in nature. Because really, at its most basic, an office (such as the one in which I worked) was a living demonstration of the pack mentality, whereby every interaction was filtered through the lens of perceived status. And status—whether bestowed by one's title, office size, or number of subordinates—mattered. When you took the time to look and listen before exposing yourself in a meeting or at the nearly empty coffee pot in the break room, you were better able to navigate the complex social maze of cubicles. This applied to the go-getters as much as the coasters. I fell into the latter category.

Pseudo-voyeur, coaster, technically single young woman with a slight case of ennui and an undersized sense of ambition, this was me circa 1996. And it only mildly troubled me. After all, the vast majority of the world's population led quiet, not particularly remarkable lives. Odds were, I would never be a Publisher's Clearing House sweepstakes winner, but it was just as unlikely that I would be struck by lightning.

What I hadn't counted on was the kung-fu kick of coincidence. The chance encounter. That notorious butterfly effect that sets in motion a series of actions and reactions that make complacency a joke. Or at the very least, irrelevant.

Regardless, at that time, as long as I had a reliable paycheck that afforded me a comfortable home and the ability to take a nice vacation once a year, I found little to complain about, and even less to strive toward.

And I had found a kind of kindred spirit in my administrative assistant who, like a pain-in-the-ass younger brother, was equal parts exasperating and entertaining. We were part of the Economics Department in the Business Division of the College Textbooks Unit of Preston House Publishing. Like me, Pooter was not wired for climbing the corporate ladder. But while my strategy was to blend into the background as an undistinguished, mildly effective middle manager, Pooter's was to channel a sort of harmless con-man who succeeded by being exceptionally helpful to everyone but me. I, he assured me, was too clever to fall for that kind of ingratiating behavior.

Together, we formed a kind of Wonder Twins alliance, facing off against corporate America with the sheer force of our own skepticism of things like leadership training and wellness initiatives. We might have been cogs in the wheel, but we were not just along for the ride.

Or were we? This was my disheartening thought as I sat beside the Xerox machine while it doled out printed pages like a blackjack dealer. Moments later, the copy room door was hauled open.

"I just saw your note and came straight here," Pooter said, pretending to be out of breath. My expression read unimpressed.

"Sorry. It's Melita's birthday and a few of us took her out to lunch. And the waitress was really slow. And there was construction. Both ways—"

I put up a hand like a traffic cop telling him to stop.

He picked up the cover page from the top of one of the stacks. "I thought Hollister was already out the door?"

"It was, but there was a missing figure that screwed the pagination."

I pulled a completed manuscript from the output tray and began inserting the corrected pages. He nudged the finished pile sideways so he could slide up onto the table.

"Really, Pooter, don't stress yourself. I'm sure you could use a break."

"Speaking of, I have to leave at three o'clock today," he said.

"Because a four-hour day is just too much?"

"I have to pick up my nana in the city."

Ignoring him, I set the Xerox to do another run.

"It's Thanksgiving," he said. "You're cutting out early too.

"My boss isn't here. Yours," I said, my hands pointing to my own shoulders, "is."

Pooter held his finger up and cocked his head. "Hold on, shh..."

"No, I won't shh."

He shushed me again. I listened for a hint of whatever he was hearing, but all I could make out was the copy machine.

He started nodding his head to the mechanical beat. Standing abruptly, he hunted around the room, eventually picking up a ball point pen and a broken pencil. Taking one in each hand, he started to drum on the table. It was a galloping beat.

"Do you recognize that?" he asked.

"No."

"Dum-duhduh-dum, duh-duh-duhduhduhduh-dum."

He repeated it a few times then stopped, anticipating that I would have figured out what it was he was toying with. When I still showed no sign of comprehension, he began to sing while drumming in time with the rhythm of the copier: "We're on the road to nowhere, come on inside."

His singing was on key, but thin and awkward. I was embarrassed for him, but Pooter was not embarrassed. Rather, he was completely enamored with the discovery of music in the machine.

He was nearly dancing now as he continued drumming and singing the song louder. I was not going to let him see me laugh. He gestured to get me to sing along.

"I get it Pooter. Can you shut it, please?"

As if the needle on a record had been lifted, he stopped. "What?" he said. "It's not like there's a painful symbolism in the office copy machine playing 'Road to Nowhere.' Am I right?"

Along for the ride. Road to nowhere. Asleep at the wheel. Choose your favorite inertia idiom.

"It's more about your shitty singing," I said and tossed a crumpled title page at him, which he deftly swatted away.

"You clearly underestimate the brilliance that is David Byrne," he said. "Technology is the heartbeat of modern meaninglessness."

He jettisoned the marker. It popped in, then out of a mug featuring a sleeping basset hound and the words "Wake me when it's Friday."

"Oh, by the way," he said. "Rigid is looking for you."

Bridget only sought you out when there was a problem. And generally, the degree of unpleasantness with which you had to deal was directly proportional to how long Bridget had to wait for you to address said problem.

"You didn't think to tell me until now?"

"Don't worry. I told her you just were catching a light snooze in the supply closet."

I handed him the remaining insert pages. "Just get these done and bring them to A.J. Today. Before you leave."

The office population was already thinning. Several desk lights were off and the white noise of phone conversations and drawers opening and closing had become muted.

If there was going to be an upside to an encounter with Bridget, it would be the possibility of seeing Dan before we headed out for the break. That hope was snuffed out seeing his door closed and light off when I reached her desk.

Seated straight-backed before her typewriter, Bridget Knutson gave the impression of a concert pianist.

She was focused and fluid, modulating her tempo, clack-clacking with force, halting with dramatic pause, leaning her head forward or to the side on particular points of emphasis. It was best not to interrupt, so I stood patiently, hands folded.

Bridget's desk was a masterwork of organization: color coded files with typed labels, a polished steel cup holding six lethally sharpened pencils, and a tightly packed, perfectly edged Rolodex. Off to the side, there was a dust-free computer that she never used because it was "sinister," and a framed photo of her prize-winning corgi, "John Carlo."

Without breaking her typing stride, she said, "We have a problem."

"Okay," I said.

She stopped and turned to face me. "The approval sheet for the Metcalf manual cannot be processed."

I mentally rewound my steps in getting signoffs from the various approvers. "Does this have to do with Franny being out?"

"She needs to sign it. I won't even bring it to Dan until she does."

I took a breath. Freakin' Rigid. "Bridget, she's out for another week and a half. If Dan will just sign off, we can at least start pre-production. Then when she's back—"

As if summoned, the elevator doors opened and presented Dan, his tie loosened, hair wind tousled. As he came toward us, I could feel my ears heat up.

"There is a process, Audrey," Bridget admonished. "If Dan approves, then Franny makes changes, you're going to get everything all knotted up."

"I understand, but Franny saw an earlier version and was pleased with the general direction."

She simply shook her head the way a teacher disappointed by a cheating student would do.

"You both look displeased," Dan said when he arrived.

I jumped in first. "I was hoping to get your approval on the Metcalf manual before heading out for Thanksgiving. That way we can start pre-production on Monday."

Dan looked at Bridget, "That's not OK?"

She heaved a sigh. "As I told Audrey, she needs to get Franny Pike's signature first."

He looked at me for further explanation, but I knew he would defer to her. He outsourced all his administrative thinking to Bridget, relying on her to keep him sheltered from things that mentally taxed him like appointments and processes. In many ways, Bridget functioned as Dan's boss rather than the other way around.

"OK," I said. "I'll figure it out."

"Good." He smiled. "You having Thanksgiving with your family?"

"Yeah. My brother and his wife are coming in from Texas. My sister and her kids will be there, and my dad and his girlfriend. It'll be a little weird. I mean nice, I'm sure. You?"

"Patricia is in Switzerland, so I'm going to visit my folks in Minnesota," he said. There was something slightly adorable in the way he referred to his parents as "my folks."

Bridget resumed her typing. "My sister, John Carlo, and I will be enjoying some vegetarian lasagna and ice cream sundaes."

"That sounds like a delicious alternative," I said, trying to appear more gracious than I felt.

Dan flipped through the message slips he had picked up off Bridget's desk. "Well, I hope you both have a nice time with your families. I'll see you Monday."

"See you Monday," I said, and hovered a bit until he disappeared into his office.

Looking back, it is quite possible that at that very moment a particularly colorful monarch butterfly, whose effect would soon be felt, was taking flight from Los Angeles to Newark.

I turned to leave. Bridget held out the unsigned approval sheet. "Don't forget this."

2: Long Distance

The cemetery spilled over the top of a low hill. If it were a painting, the view might have been called "Pleasant Suburbia," a panorama of cul-de-sacs, squat ranch houses, above-ground pools, and a couple of tree-lined parks with ponds and playgrounds and ball fields. It was a prime real estate spot, and I always thought that someday, the town would go full-*Poltergeist*, letting some fast-talking developer bulldoze the graveyard to put in a McMansion neighborhood. Except the owners would be tormented by ghosts of people like my mom and Mr. Nygaard, the town pool manager—ghosts that would do things like tuck sheets into super-tight hospital corners or blow whistles if you ran down the stairs.

That Thanksgiving morning, it was all crooked tree lines and sepia tones. Our shoes crunched on the brittle grass as we made our way to the south side of the cemetery—me, my dad, my sister Bobbie, and her twelve-year-old twins, Charley and Fiona.

It was almost five years since my mother died. We chose that day to come together as a family, mostly because that's when we were all together (apart from my brother Kenny who lived in Texas and never came home). But maybe we went then because Thanksgiving was her holiday.

My mother would start days ahead, cleaning and shopping, chopping, blending and baking. Tupperware

containers of all sizes and shapes multiplying in the refrigerator, their lids labeled with her narrow, flowery
script: "sausage", "broth", "croutons", "crans". She was
manic during the week—a superhero, handing us bat-
ter-covered beaters to lick, a banshee when she caught
us stealing from the containers.

My father had one job on that day: keep the kids
out of the way. Meanwhile, my mother would tornado
through the house, an unpredictable force picking up
errant socks and dropped tissues between caramel-
izing onions, arranging centerpiece flowers and pol-
ishing my grandmother's silver. Bobbie, Kenny and I
would spend a lazy morning playing Monopoly or reading in the family room, all of us lounging in our pajamas, glancing up at the television occasionally to mock
the Macy's Thanksgiving Day Parade commentators.

My mother would rebuff our offers of help, even
while stewing in her martyrdom as the frazzled cook
and event planner. Or when we did assist, our efforts
would be redone for having put too many toothpicks in
the pyramid of cubed cheese or failing to fold napkins
properly.

But with the first doorbell ring, followed by a steady
flow of nearly a dozen cousins, a switch was flipped, and
my mother transformed into the most genteel of host-
esses, laughing off the week's frenetic effort with a casual wave of her hand.

The last Thanksgiving she prepared was in 1990, just
over a year before she died. In the Thanksgivings that followed, my brother and other relatives scattered to other
parts of the country with new families and traditions of
their own. So for the last few years, my father, Bobbie, her
soon-to-be ex-husband Doug, the twins, and I had gone
out to dinner to an old colonial inn that featured an "authentic, Pilgrim-inspired" menu.

This was to be the year that Thanksgiving returned to the Rohmer family home with Bobbie meticulously recreating Mom's menu, using her grease-splattered and note-scrawled recipe cards. Everything was to be the same, according to Bobbie. The exception, of course, being the absence of our mother and the presence of Joyce, Dad's girlfriend of several months.

At the cemetery, we passed headstones with names of families whose descendants still lived in town: Van Sykle, Mortimer, Winther, and (ever our favorite) Richard "Dick" Payne, whose grandson Everett was now the school superintendent.

My father had chosen a south-facing plot since it afforded the most sunlight. My mother had been a summertime sun worshipper. You could tell what time of day it was by the ever-shifting position of her lounge chair on the patio. I supposed that all things being equal, when selecting a burial plot, opting for the sunniest was a good strategy to encourage visitors.

Though on that day, when the sky was locked in flat, steel-colored clouds, it afforded us no actual warmth.

The headstone was simple but elegant in its own way, polished linen-colored granite cut with her name, Dorothy Rose Rohmer. While my brain, over time, had settled into understanding that my mother—what remained of her physical, living presence—lay in that rocky earth beneath our feet, I felt a terrible wrench in my gut every time I saw the adjacent plot reserved for my father, the headstone engraved with his name, but the year of death a looming TBD.

That day's pilgrimage was as awkward and weird as every other year. Dad began as if he were placing a long-distance call then handing over the receiver so the rest of us could talk.

"Hello, Dot. It's us: Audrey, Bobbie, Fiona, Charley, and me. Kenny and Loretta send their regrets..." The wind seemed to carry his voice away and behind us. "Kenny had a work emergency and couldn't get away. No grandkids to report about, but they seem to be doing very well financially. And as you can see—"

(I lifted an eyebrow at Charley, as if to say, "Did he really just say, 'As you can see?'" She smirked behind her mitten).

"We're all just fine."

Whether due to the cold or the holiday, the cemetery was empty but for a man in a dark overcoat and a girl roughly the same age as the twins. They were down the hill from us near an outcropping of shrubs. His hands rested on her shoulders as he leaned down to speak briefly into her ear. She looked up at him, said something. God, I hoped it wasn't her mother.

My father continued, "The twins started junior high this year. They're getting tall, like your side of the family."

A not-so-gentle nudge to their backs from Bobbie drew a semi-synchronized, "We miss you, Grandma."

"And you'll be proud to know that Bobbie gathered up all your Thanksgiving recipes so we can have a real meal at home this year. It'll be a little like you're here with us." There was a wobble in his voice. He waited a beat then said, "Audrey, would you like to talk about how things are going at your job?"

"Oh. Sure," I said. "There's not much to tell. We have a new book on tax codes coming out in January. And they've made some good menu additions in the cafeteria that I've been enjoying—new soups, a noodle dish."

Bobbie chimed in, "Why don't you tell us all about your mystery man."

"I'm not—"

"You don't have to hide it," Bobbie said.

"There's no—"

"That was an expensive silk tie I found in the couch last week," Bobbie said, rocking on her heels.

"Or," I said, "maybe you could talk about why Doug's not here today."

"Girls!" my father snapped. "Do you think your mother wants to listen to you two bickering on the one day we all visit?"

Given the choice, I bet she would. Just like we would have given anything to be on the receiving end of the laser-eye smackdown she would have given us for snarking at each other in this setting.

But clearly, we all had things that we didn't feel the need to trouble our ghost-mother with. Like Joyce. Now would have been the perfect time for my mother to show up, rising from the grave like the ghost of Thanksgivings past to rattle her chains and wheeze-moan: "Not...good...enough." Really, it's the least she could have done on that dreary day.

"The twins are shivering," my dad said looking at them. They had been leaning into each other to keep warm. Nearly perfect mirrors of each other, it sometimes took me several seconds to process which one I was talking to.

"Why don't you all start back to the car," he said. "I'll come in a minute." He picked up a small stone, kissed it and set it on top of the headstone where a couple others already rested. The rest of us did the same. Then Bobbie set down a pot of brick-colored mums.

Walking back along the path, I put an arm around Fiona who seemed neither comforted nor bothered by the gesture. Since her parents separated, she had become somewhat emotionally opaque with me, and I wasn't very good at probing. Charley had always been more able to roll with changes, even as a toddler, and she bounced along, cheerful as ever, even in a cemetery.

I heard Bobbie's quick footsteps behind me. She grabbed my arm, pulling me to a stop. Fiona drifted off with her sister toward the car.

Bobbie's voice buzzed in my ear, "Did you see him?"

"Dad? What'd he do?"

"Not Dad. The guy in the coat. With the kid."

I turned around and craned my neck, but Bobbie held me firmly. "Yeah, I saw them."

"You know who it was, right?" I shook my head.

"That was Jamie."

I turned around again. "Keefner?"

She nodded, eyes big.

"You think that was James Keefner?" I asked.

"Yeah. I do. His dad died last summer. And his mother was buried down in that part. It has to be him."

"I doubt it."

"I'm telling you." She took a breath. "It must be so weird for him to be here." She waited a beat and then said, "Would it be crazy if I went over and said hello?"

"If it's him—and I doubt it's him—it's kind of a private place, don't you think? And it's not like he'd remember you."

"I bet he would. If I mentioned Kenny."

"It's a cemetery, Bobbie. People are entitled to a little privacy."

She pouted when I pulled her along. But neither of us could resist turning around to see if we could catch a glimpse of the man over the hill.

Kenny and his wife Loretta had been planning to make the trip from Houston. But just the night before, Kenny called to explain that a flock of geese had died in a tailings pond owned by the mining company he worked for; he was block and tackling the environmentalists and wouldn't be able to make the trip.

"Rude," Bobbie said.

"I'm sure he would have come if he could."

"You always let him off the hook." Trading her cemetery clothes for sweats and an apron, she was standing at the counter cutting carrots and turnips into narrow spears for roasting. She pointed a sharp knife at me. "He hasn't been back since the funeral."

"It's not like he hasn't met Joyce." I was seated at the kitchen table peeling and quartering potatoes. "Did you know Joyce and Loretta chat over the phone sometimes?" I added.

This comment drew a scoff from my sister. As the one closest to our mother, Bobbie was viscerally opposed to Dad getting serious about Joyce. Or, really, about anyone. Bobbie had cast herself as Dad's protector and general hovering presence. She fussed over his every trip to the bank or the grocery store, envisioning car accidents, muggings, a hard fall off the curb. And she became excessively agitated about silly things like him not getting the proper savings for the coupons he clipped every Sunday, or the newspaper delivery landing in the street instead of the driveway.

When Joyce—the co-worker of a friend—came into Dad's life, he started needing Bobbie less. "I don't know what her end game is, but I have no doubt she's trying isolate him from his family," Bobbie had said one evening when I was over for dinner, though I could find no evidence to support the claim. In fact, it seemed to me that Joyce over-invited us to participate in their weekly goings-on and activities.

Then she said, "And don't you find it strange that she never married? There's got to be a reason."

As a thirty-five-year-old, single woman with no viable prospects on the horizon, it was hard not to bristle at the suggestion that being unmarried indicated an inherent flaw.

While I was certainly not thrilled by Joyce's presence in our lives, I couldn't find significant fault with her apart from her being a little overly sweet. Her enthusiasm for things like Broadway musicals and tropical fish felt a little too...enthusiastic. And her total lack of cynicism made me feel like she would never really understand my father who, though soft-spoken, had a sly, dark sense of humor. Daughters' opinions be damned, Joyce didn't seem to be going anywhere.

"Girls!" Bobbie's sudden shout to the twins startled me.

Fiona appeared in the doorway; her head slumped low on her shoulder as if weighed down by the bulk of her new braces.

"I like your new mouth metal, Fi," I said.

She closed her lips over her braces and tossed off a masterful eye roll before turning to her mother. "What."

"Please give a quick iron to Grandma's tablecloth and napkins. They're in the linen closet by the bathroom." Unlike our mother, Bobbie demanded full participation in the Thanksgiving preparations.

"I just brought up the extra chairs," Fiona said. "Charley needs to get off her butt. She's been watching TV with Grandpa all morning."

"I don't care who does it, just make sure it gets done."

Fiona disappeared from the doorway as quickly as she'd appeared. From the top of the stairs to the family room, she shouted, "Char, Mom says to come up and iron stuff. Now!"

A muffled protest came back, which launched a counter protest, and so on.

Bobbie had told Joyce to come by at two o'clock, which would allow us some mental space before getting the meal underway. But it was noon when Joyce opened the door and announced herself. Bobbie met her in the entryway.

"Oh. We weren't expecting you until later this afternoon."

A bottle of wine wedged under her arm and a foil-covered casserole dish in each hand, Joyce delivered an unreciprocated cheek-to-cheek air kiss. "I decided you could use a hand."

I reached out to take the wine and one of the dishes. Joyce held the other out to Bobbie so she could remove her coat.

"And did I forget to mention we were all set with food?" Bobbie said more than asked.

Running interference, I called downstairs, "Dad, Joyce is here!"

"I know," Joyce said. "But these are some of my favorites, and I just had to share. The one in Audrey's hand is a Mexican chile-cornbread stuffing that's just a little spicy. And that," she pointed to the dish in Bobbie's hands, "is bourbon, mashed sweet potatoes with candied pecans on top. Absolute heaven!"

Taking back the sweet potatoes, she squeezed past Bobbie and headed for the kitchen. Over her shoulder, she added, "Oh, and I left a key lime pie on the porch to keep cool."

Bobbie's eyes went wide as she hissed at me, "Lime is not a fall flavor!"

After all the preoccupied anticipation of the Thanksgiving dinner, it was uneventful, perhaps even a little politely dull. Though the smells, flavors, and dinnerware were weighed down by nostalgia, the circumstances so little resembled those of our past that it seemed to relieve the pressure for everyone, even Bobbie, who brightened and relaxed into the praises she received for a perfectly executed menu. The only quick flare of tension came when Charley announced that she liked Joyce's stuffing better than the "regular" kind. While Joyce basked in the glow of the compliment, Charley gave an impish side-glance at her mother—a gauntlet thrown that seemed to mark a new era of what Bobbie would later refer to as the "hellion years."

Belts loosened and napkins tossed like surrender flags on the table, the twins gathered and carted away the dishes and serving bowls. Once the table was mostly cleared, I took ownership of the dishwashing, grateful for a respite from conversation.

My father, Joyce, and Bobbie retired to the living room with glasses of Scotch. Dad casually mentioned that he could really go for a cigar, but the protest coming from every room was unanimous and so vocal as to make him grumble about "too many women in this house."

After the dishwasher was loaded, the pots washed and the pans dried, the twins and I re-stacked the China safely in the cabinet and fit each piece of antique silverware in its place in the velvet-lined box. We shoveled the leftovers into plastic containers, sorting enough for each of the households to have roughly two more meals.

The twins peeled off, one to the TV, the other to the phone. From the living room came a thread of conversation about Bobbie having seen Jamie Keefner at the cemetery.

"Kenny was good friends with him in high school. He used to come over to play basketball and ping-pong, hang out in the basement."

Joyce murmured something I couldn't catch.

"I know!" said Bobbie. "I've been kicking myself all day for not going over."

The conversation seemed to lull, so I slam-dunked the dishtowels into the washing machine and went to join them. Bobbie had sunk deeply into the rose-colored easy chair that had been our mother's. Dad sat on the couch beside Joyce, his arm curled around her shoulder, fingers playing absently with a silky fold in her sleeve. I wondered if I would ever get used to seeing him using the same intimate gestures he had shared with my mother.

There were a handful of brochures fanned out on the coffee table. Joyce was holding one and reading aloud: *"Sink into serenity at Tranquility Bay. Each of our spacious resort beach houses features two bedrooms, two baths, a gourmet kitchen, and an expansive porch overlooking the sparkling waters of the Gulf of Mexico."*

She looked up when I walked in the room. "Audrey, informal poll: Florida Keys or Acapulco?"

"Dad doesn't speak Spanish," said Bobbie, appealing to me as if I had an actual say in the matter. "And there's lots of crime outside the resorts."

Both Bobbie and Joyce were looking at me, waiting for an answer. I suddenly felt the small burden of their expectations, each of these women trying to snatch whatever scrap of loyalty she could away from the other. I looked at my father whose expression was obscured by his glass of Scotch.

"I've heard good things about the Virgin Islands," I offered as I sat down on a hassock that belonged to a chair that had long since been removed.

My father pulled his arm from around Joyce and leaned forward, resting his elbows on his knees and touching his fingertips together as if holding a fragile Christmas ornament.

"Girls, when Joyce and I are on this trip," he paused. "Wherever we end up," he paused again. I knew what was coming. "We're planning on getting married."

From downstairs, we could hear the canned laughter of a TV sitcom. Bobbie was tight-lipped and blank-faced. I had to manufacture some enthusiasm for both of us quickly before it became especially awkward.

"Wow, congratulations you guys," I said trying to put an exclamation point in my voice. That was all the opening Joyce needed. She stood up and launched a full embrace at me, whispering to the side of my head, "Audrey, I know no one can replace your mother, but I am so certain we're going to be closer than ever."

I tossed a pointed look at Bobbie, urging her to say or do something. Begrudgingly, she pulled herself out of the chair. Arms held out, she said to my father, "Tying the knot. Good for you guys."

She and I switched partners and hugged anew. "I'm happy for you," I said to my father. He gave me a squeeze and the two of us broke away quickly.

"I know it's a little strange," said Joyce, "to be doing this without friends and family around, but we wanted to keep it quiet and low key. We'll all celebrate with a nice dinner when we get back. We promise."

Reaching the limits of our public displays of (dis) affection, we returned to our seats.

Joyce settled back under the wing of my father's arm. She kissed the back of his hand.

Bobbie said, "I still think Florida is the best choice. Dad, remember that trip to Disney?" Ah, nostalgia would be her emotional shield.

He seemed grateful for the conversational detour, explaining to Joyce, "We took a sleeper train from here to Orlando when Bobbie was, what nine? Kenny would have been eleven, Audrey was just in Kindergarten."

"Disney World is amazing!" said Joyce.

"Except Audrey got the flu on the train ride down," said Bobbie.

"What a mess, poor thing," Dad said. "The fever and puking and crying. Dottie was up every hour with her. I thought they were going to kick us off the train in Georgia."

"She was sick the whole trip," said Bobbie.

"Oh, no," Joyce said with a sad face at me. "What did you do?"

"We had already bought the admission tickets. And they weren't cheap."

"They left me in the hotel with a cranky old French lady named Claudine," I said. "And they all went off and had a great time."

"You see?" said Bobbie. "Look at those eyes. She's still bitter about it."

It would be no use explaining that at this stage in my life, I was over any resentment about having missed out on Thunder Mountain. But better to have them think otherwise than explain that the shadow in my eyes came from the strangeness of hearing my father speak of my mother without hesitation just minutes after announcing his plans to remarry.

"Well," I said, "the leftovers are sorted and labeled. I'm going to head home."

"Come on, Audie, sit back down. We'll pour another round," Bobbie said.

Bobbie wanted me to stay as a buffer, but I just wanted to go home, enjoy the just-washed smell of the bedsheets and start a new crime novel that I'd picked up.

"I can't. I have to let the neighbor's dog out while they're away. They just put in new carpet, and I don't want anything to happen to it."

None of this was true. In fact, pets weren't allowed in my condo complex, which Bobbie knew since she kept telling me I needed to move so I could get a dog. Instead of calling me out, she looked at me coolly.

My father stood up. "Well, Happy Thanksgiving, sweetheart. Thank you for all your help." He gave me a forehead kiss. Joyce held her hand out for a squeeze.

"Congratulations again. It's great news, really."

"See you later, sister," Bobbie held her hand up for a high-five as I passed. I shouted good nights to the twins and got a reply from one of them.

As the screen door sighed to a close, I felt the hunched presence of our house like an old, sad-eyed dog. The split-level with a crumbly brick stoop. Ageless, olive-green vinyl-siding. The halo of a netless basketball hoop still hanging over the garage. The walls inside held our family history. Cruel fights and heartbreaks, silly secrets and daredevil tricks that could have killed us. It seemed plausible that remnants of every moment were still trapped inside, like murky cigarette smoke that had seeped layers-deep into the paint and plaster.

From my car I looked at the facade and could see the same incandescent light spilling onto the same hedges trimmed every fall to the same height they've been for the last forty years. Maybe it was time for a fresh take.

3: Lawn Art

Six years earlier, on a swampy-humid summer morning, my roommate at the time (a divorcée with whom I only interacted to sort out the monthly bills) answered the phone. I could hear her in the kitchen saying I was still asleep, but yes, Mrs. Rohmer, she would give me the message and yes, she would make sure I knew it was important.

I had been summoned home by my mother without explanation other than the fact that I needed to be there in an hour. It was an unusual request, both the insistence that I come, and that I be there at a specific time, my mother knowing schedules were not a strength of mine. I left the house, unshowered, uncombed and a little out of sorts.

Bobbie was already there when I arrived. She was standing just beyond the reach of the lawn sprinkler, shading her eyes against the sun and yelling at me, "Don't park in the driveway." She waved her arms. "The driveway. Don't park in the driveway!"

I stopped mid-turn and rolled down the window, questioning. She held her hands up, "It's what Dad said."

I backed up and sidled my car beside the curb.

Joining Bobbie on the walkway, I asked, "Where are they? Why are you standing out here?"

"Mom doesn't want us in the house yet. Dad was pulling some weeds when I got here, but then he went inside," she said. "He was kind of snippy about it, like I'd done something wrong. Have I done something wrong?"

"No doubt," I said.

The young family living in the Schmauders' old house came outside. We watched as they packed up kids, cooler, and swimming gear in three trips before they shut everyone in the car and backed onto the street. The mother gave a quick wave while the son in the back flipped us off.

"Little turd!" Bobbie shouted after them.

The neighborhood was noisy that day with a yawing chorus of lawnmowers. Two driveways down, a guy in long Bermuda shorts, shirtless, was at work on his vintage Mustang, the car's open hood a giant alligator about to devour him. Bobbie looked at her watch and huffed. "I have to take the twins to a birthday party at noon."

When my father finally came out of the house, he did, in fact, have a cloudy, scowling look on his face, and he nodded to me in an uncharacteristically curt greeting.

"Where's Mom?"

He motioned with his hand toward the house, and just then, like a game show curtain rising to reveal my prize, the garage door began to open. From the shadowy backdrop of old paint cans, rakes and a tool-scattered workbench, a dark-helmeted figure astride a silent motorcycle emerged. It was my mother, toe-stepping her way out onto the driveway.

Bobbie looked at me. I looked at my father. My father looked at the sky, the mailbox, his sneakers. When my mother had arrived beside us on the walkway, she flipped up the visor on her helmet, and was big-grinning, relishing the baffled looks on her daughters' faces.

"Check it out, girls!" she said.

There was a brief pause as I mentally drew straws with Bobbie over who would respond first. "Wow, Mom," I said. "What's this?"

"It's a 1982 Honda CB250."

"I mean—"

"She means what are you doing with it?" Bobbie jumped in.

My mother peeled off her helmet and plunked it on the center of the handlebars. "I bought it."

"To ride?" Bobbie asked incredulously.

"No, honey, I'm going to install it as lawn art."

Dad's hands were deep in his pockets, his chin pressed down into his chest.

"Mom," I said. "You haven't ridden a motorcycle since I was a kid, how are you going to handle a motorcycle?"

"I signed up for a class at the Continuing Ed program at the high school. It starts next Tuesday."

She was all eyes and enthusiasm.

"Dad?" Bobbie looked over at him.

"Don't look at your father. This was my choice."

"It's ridiculous," he said quietly.

"It's certainly not safe," Bobbie started.

"Aren't there other hobbies?" I said.

Her expression of enthusiasm flipped as fast as a light switch to anger. She seemed to be scrabbling for words, then finally said: "You know what? You can all...go screw!"

She had to get off the bike to walk it back to the garage, and in so doing, she knocked the helmet to the ground. As it sputtered down the driveway, she bolted after it, dropping the motorcycle with a rough, metallic clank. Chasing down the helmet, she nabbed it by the chin strap just before it skidded into the road. A passing car swerved and honked.

Bobbie and I stood tight-lipped, barely suppressing our laughter as she came back and picked up the bike without even a glance at us.

As she slowly turned the machine around and wheeled it back into the garage, I wondered how we would reconcile this new version of "Mom"—the one who tossed off words like "screw" and who just might be in the market for a pair of leather pants—with the one who folded Dad's underwear with the same care as if they were napkins at a four-star restaurant, who hated facial hair on men and scolded our own "potty mouths" even as grown-ups.

Years later, that summer morning lingered in the periphery of my thoughts when I was alone. Sometimes, I would re-imagine that day with my mother having already taken the motorcycle class, just so she could have had the rich satisfaction of strapping on her helmet, jump starting the bike and riding off down the road, leaving us in a cloud of noise and driveway dust. Because here is what I think. I think that shortly before that sweaty, summer morning, my mother discovered that something was going wrong in her body, and instead of going to the doctor, she decided to buy a motorcycle. And if that was true, it was both the bravest and most cowardly thing I could imagine anyone doing.

It always surprised me, the morning after Thanksgiving, to wake feeling hungry, as if maybe I had eaten so much food that my metabolism kicked into overdrive in my sleep and furnace-burned all that gravy and stuffing and pie.

Not only hungry, but I also woke to find myself unexpectedly energized and motivated to accomplish something. Though the forecast called for chilly temperatures, strong sunlight spilled like an invitation over my hand exposed from under the covers. And so, the previous day's ambivalent mood lifted like a thick fog, ushering in a shiny new morning.

An idea presented itself, tentatively at first and then, not being rejected outright, it took root: a run. I would go out for a run. Never mind that I hadn't exercised in general in over a month, and that I quite specifically hated running. It seemed to be what my body and being were craving—movement, self-propelled; the feel of muscles at work and my heart putting in extra effort. A run, indeed. The start of a healthier, action-oriented self who embraced the things she despised and made them fun and wholly satisfying.

From the way-back of my closet, beneath a pillowcase stuffed with hats and mateless gloves, I dug out a pair of running shoes whose tread had come in contact with the ground no more than six times in their two-year lifetime. I dressed in layers and choked my hair into a ponytail.

The air was unexpectedly sharp when I stepped out. I tried not to feel that I had been duped by the sun and eager blue sky teasing in a very unNovember-like way. I engaged in some half-hearted stretches of the hamstrings and calves, a few butterfly strokes of the arms for warmup. And I was off.

My steps were unhurried. The key was to imagine I was simply fast walking, but not the weird, ass-waggy way—more like I was in a slight hurry to get to the bank before it closed. For a full block, I was pleasantly surprised at how not unpleasant this running thing was.

I nodded to a trio of strangers on the bus bench waiting for their ride into the city. I kept my arms loose and my breath steady using the one breath in, two breaths out technique that my high school gym teacher taught me to help with the side stitches that used to double me over whenever I had to run more than a mile.

But by the middle of block two, my body parts had caught on that there was no "bank"; that we were, in fact, simply, appallingly, running. My knees were confused; my back grimaced. Even my jaw felt pissed off. One breath in, two breaths out. To quell the mutiny, I established a destination: the elementary school parking lot, roughly a half-mile away—achievable without being too ambitious.

I kept my eyes fixed on the pedestrian crossing sign on the other side of the intersection, hoping that it would change to a red stop-hand, allowing me a merciful yet fully justified pause. But the closer I got, the passage remained stubbornly clear: "Come, fast walking person," the sign said, "I'll hold the traffic at bay for you."

Not a full stride into the intersection, a car proceeded to make a right on red. The woman braked hard when she saw me but had already blocked my path. I raised my hands in a "What the hell?" gesture. She shrugged her shoulders, then continued on her way. And just like that, whatever strange and magical momentum I'd had evaporated like the clouds of my rapid breath. I had jogged roughly the length of a football field.

With an odd mix of self-loathing and relief, I walked back to the condo, hands on hips, breathing heavily, pretending to anyone passing by that I had just finished a long, hearty run. I paused at the edge of the walkway that led to my condo. Mrs. Ass was out in a heavy parka and sweatpants tending to the decorative cabbages that she'd planted. After two years as her nearest neighbor, I still didn't know her real name.

I didn't even know what she looked like since every time our paths crossed, she kept her back turned to me. More specifically, her ass, as most often she would be stooped over her perennials and urns of geraniums. I'd never seen her have guests, and she very rarely left her premises (I'd even seen groceries delivered to her door). Her unwillingness to engage with even the barest minimum of neighborly civility made me uneasy, wondering if I had done something to offend her the day I moved in.

So instead of going inside, I detoured around back to my car and got in. I had no wallet, but my keys were tied into my shoes (and probably caused enough drag to be the real culprit behind my aborted run, I reasoned). With no clear destination in mind, I headed out in the direction of the turnpike. Eventually, I decided to stop by my father's house to cook breakfast as an unspoken apology for the abrupt departure the night before.

Though it had seemed early enough to beat the traffic, it became clear that one should never underestimate the siren call of Black Friday sales in the official mall capital of the country. The highway was not in bumper-to-bumper mode, but it was certainly clogged. I reminded myself, I wasn't in a hurry and instead, took the time to appreciate the bordering landscape: the dinosaur jaw of the New York City skyline on one side and the tall Meadowlands' grasses shivering in the wind on the other.

I arrived a little before eight o'clock, slowing down at my father's driveway. But I didn't stop. Instead, I had an idea for a different destination, and wondered if it might not have been my subconscious plan all along.

I drove a series of turns remembered only kinesthetically from my high school years, a time when driving was brand new and exhilarating. In college, I'd had a boyfriend from Philadelphia, who couldn't comprehend the seemingly random layout of our suburban neighborhoods with their abrupt dead-ends and arteries that doubled back on themselves. He marveled at my Zen-like navigational skills as we zigzagged around streets with names like Brook Pond Road, Brook Hill Street, Hill Road, Hillside Road, and Brookside Lane in areas where there were no apparent brooks or hills.

I couldn't help but think how much like mice in a maze we were as kids, finding our way on our bikes to the Twinkies and Eskimo Pies at one friend's house or another.

We reveled in racing around the corners, exploring the dense interior of our turf, bound by the larger, busier streets lined with strip malls and gas stations.

So, it was with a sense of déjà vu that I found myself approaching the house in which Jamie Keefner had grown up: a gray, shingled ranch with an enormous sycamore tree in the front yard. I slowed to about ten miles an hour and gathered a picture in my mind of the skinny teen who used to live there, trying to fuse that memory of him with the giant man on the movie screen, the one in the big shootout in the mountains or the clandestine meeting in the nightclub.

The thing that people don't often think about with celebrities is that they actually come from somewhere. They don't spring forth from the head of Zeus, fully bronzed in beauty, grinning their grins through a set of perfectly white, squared-off, teeth. Like the rest of us, they were born and reared in a specific and real location. They suffered the same kinds of triumphs and humiliations. They had friends and rivals and shitty summer jobs. And even if a celebrity chose to downplay his roots, the people, those of us who knew him, would claim him as our own. A certain pride and satisfaction came in knowing that he had been nourished by our education system, our municipal water, our community standards, our little league, our neighborhood deli. All of it, we knew, left some kind of imprint on his being. To the world, he was James Keefner. To us, he would always be Jamie. A single-name code for the blockbuster star who came from Arlendale, New Jersey.

This was especially true for my family. In Jamie's sophomore year in high school—the year his mother was killed in a highway accident—Jamie attached himself to a small posse of guys that included my brother Kenny and his friends, Pete and Owen.

They were an unremarkable bunch of boys. None of them particularly smart or athletic; they were neither troublemakers nor do-gooders. They had few serious interests, though Kenny and Owen goofed around on guitar and drums respectively, always vowing that one day they would form a band. Pete had some artistic talent, and kids paid him fifteen dollars to paint their favorite album covers—Grateful Dead or Iron Maiden or Yes—on the backs of their denim jackets. This crew of boys was disinterested in the petty politics of high school. And so, when Jamie's previous friends struggled with awkward feelings about what they imagined was his grieving process, Kenny, Owen, and Pete were only interested in playing ping-pong, listening to music, and raiding the refrigerator.

I approached the old Keefner house, but stopped short a block away, pulling to the side of the road. There was a black car in the driveway, but the curtains appeared to be drawn. I sat listening to a CD Pooter insisted I borrow. Trippy and mysterious, it was a compelling soundtrack to my stakeout. If it was James

Keefner's car—and given his alleged presence at the cemetery the day before, it seemed possible—he might make an appearance.

For thirteen minutes I sat, my stomach snarling for sustenance. I thought about pancakes and bacon and was about to retreat to my original plan when the front door opened. I hunched down instinctively, whispering, "Holy shit." Craning my neck, I could just barely see a man in a black coat and gray, knit cap and the same blond streaked girl from the cemetery. They were getting into to the car.

Like a character in a James Keefner movie, I waited until the car pulled out, and gave them a fair lead before starting the engine and following.

I tailed from a reasonable distance as the black car wound knowingly to the closest neighborhood exit and went left onto Parkside Avenue. From there it seemed we were driving to the center of town. I wondered how long I would allow myself to follow them. Would I go to the city? Would I go to the airport? Then what?

The car signaled left, then pulled into a diagonal parking space. I drove past it slowly, but not too slowly. And there was no mistaking that chiseled profile. It was James Keefner.

The next closest parking space was three away from his car. I slid in and realized that my heart was pounding hard, harder than it had during the failed jogging attempt. The black car's door opened and Jamie, in dark sunglasses and the girl who was presumably his daughter stepped out.

There could be only one place they were going. I waited until he opened the door to Ronnie's Bagels and, without allowing myself a moment to reconsider, I got out of the car. I walked a brisk pace to the shop, deciding that I wouldn't actually approach him; I would simply be the person in line behind them picking up some bagels for the family.

One breath in, two breaths out. I went in, a jingling bell announcing my arrival, but no one turned to look.

There was a man my father's age being waited on. Behind him, Jamie had his hands in his coat pockets and was scrutinizing the front page of the *New York Post* on the stand beside a candy rack. His daughter wandered over to the beverage cooler.

The man ahead of us was talking loudly. "I says to him, 'That's fifty bucks I could've spent on a decent meal.' What can you do?"

The man behind the counter was not Ronnie, but rather Amjad who had bought the business three years earlier amid some vocal indignation that an Iranian couldn't make an authentic bagel. It turned out that Amjad made better bagels than Ronnie ever did.

"Hey-ya. Get me some of that scallion spread you got."

"Cream cheese? How much?" Amjad asked.

The man held up his fingers in a smidge gesture.

I fake coughed, started to shuffle a little. Jamie hadn't moved and was still staring down at the newspaper as though willing himself invisible. Amjad hefted a bag of bagels the size of a toddler over to the man. They exchanged money.

"You get the coffee?" the man asked raising the cup in his hand. Amjad waved his hand. It was an exchange I'd seen played by others who had caught on to the shop owner's casual business style, a strategy that won over the skeptics, keeping them faithfully coming back when there was a bagel shop practically every other block.

As he passed us, the man's face was eclipsed by the bagel bag. Then it was just Jamie, his daughter, and me.

"What can I get for you, my friend?"

Jamie pulled his gaze up from the newspaper. His voice was quiet and monotone. "Two breakfast sandwiches, please. One onion bagel with American and tomato and the other, plain with cheese, no bacon."

Amjad went in the back to microwave the eggs. The girl came back to Jamie with a bottle of orange juice in her hand. I may have been silently hyperventilating.

"Uhm. Hmm." I mumbled.

Jamie didn't turn around.

"Excuse me." I couldn't help but notice that his posture sagged a little when I spoke. He turned halfway. "I, uh. I saw you at the cemetery yesterday. I just wanted to say—"

"What are you, following us?"

"No, no. Oh gosh, no. I was there. I just happened to be there with my family." He nodded and turned away again, reaching for the juice.

"I don't know if you remember, but you were friends with my brother, Kenny. Kenny Rohmer?"

He looked over his shoulder at me. "Look, I really just want to get our breakfast and go."

"Sure, of course. I don't blame you. I'm sorry. I shouldn't have, you know, intruded. Privacy. You know. I know."

But then, startlingly, miraculously, James Keefner turned fully toward me.

"Yeah, of course I remember Kenny." He looked at me a moment. It was too much. I looked away self-conscious, catching a horrified glance of myself in the mirror behind the counter: the frizzy ponytail, the heavy layers of T-shirt and sweatshirt. "You look so much like your mother. It's kind of eerie."

Amjad returned holding a cup of steaming scrambled eggs. He got to work prepping the sandwich.

"Yeah. Wow, Kenny Rohmer. That's a long time ago. You must be...Bonnie?" Everybody knew Bobbie. She had fantastic breasts at age fifteen.

"Bobbie. She's my older sister. I'm Audrey. The youngest." His expression admitted he had no recollection of me.

"How is Kenny? He still live around here?"

"No, he's in Houston. But good. Married, works for a mining company."

"And your mom? How's she doing? She was always really sweet to me."

"She died. Five years ago. That's why we were at the cemetery yesterday. We go every Thanksgiving."

He nodded.

"I'm sorry to hear that your father passed last summer," I said.

He nodded again. The girl wandered over to the case that held the coffee cake and cookies.

"Something else?" Amjad was handing over the foil-wrapped bagels.

Jamie held up the juice. "And I'll get a coffee." He turned to the warming coffee pots on the shelf behind us.

"For you, miss?"

It was then that I remembered I had no wallet. "I'll need to think about it." I shifted back to Jamie. "It must be kind of strange being here. I mean, being you being here."

"Yeah. A lot, actually. I hadn't really been back. But I wanted to show Storey the town. And the house needs to be packed up."

He added a splash of milk to his coffee, no sugar. Returning to the counter with a twenty-dollar bill in hand, it was clear that Amjad had no idea that he had a major celebrity in his shop.

"Out of twenty...twelve dollars and twenty-five cents is your change, sir. Thank you very much."

Jamie gave me a curt smile and nodded for Storey to move along. He was leaving. "Hey, can I tell Kenny you said hello?"

"Sure thing."

"And you know if you need any...uh...boxes for packing. I can get you a bunch. I work in publishing, and we use a lot of paper, which comes in boxes."

There it was: the same teenager smirk on the grown man's face. "Probably a big dumpster would be more helpful. But thanks."

Boxes, indeed.

"Take care," he said.

And as he left the bagel shop and stepped out onto the sidewalk with his golden-haired daughter, it felt as if someone had snuffed out the sun.

Amjad was smiling. "You need boyfriend? I have a brother."

4: Leftovers

The break-room counter was wall-to-wall with left-over desserts: three Saran-wrapped tins of pie, a motley mound of brownies and butter cookies, half a stale babka and a greenish brick of a cake that would remain untouched for a week before it suddenly disappeared. Cast out from their former homes, their freshness diminished, flavors flattened, these sweet rejects received renewed affection at the office, where something as insignificant as a *New Yorker* cartoon taped to the refrigerator could precipitate a flow of curious traffic to the kitchen.

By nine thirty in the morning. I had already had one brownie, a chocolate-dipped butter cookie and a sliver of pumpkin pie. I called Pooter's line though his desk was just outside my office. "I'll give you a $30,000 bonus if you get me a cup of coffee."

"I'm busy."

"In that case, I'll fire you if you don't get me a cup of coffee."

"Piss off. I'm not your errand boy."

"I can't go in there again. There's still pie left." He hung up.

Pooter's job interview went something like this. "So, John. Tell me about yourself."

"I can tell you that only my nana calls me John. All the relevant stuff is on my résumé. The rest is, you know...like what? I have a massive music collection."

I had interviewed six other candidates using the scripted questions provided by our human resources department. In return, I got six completely scripted sets of answers ("My weakness is that I care too much about my work"). This candidate was not going to give that kind of interview.

"OK, then, not-John—"

"Pooter."

"Pooter?"

"The bastardization of my last name."

"That's what you go by?"

"There were eleven Johns in my grade."

"What about your middle name?"

"Gaylord."

"Pooter it is."

Clearly, I was going to need a better set of interview questions.

"OK. As a music fan, here's a hypothetical: The Rock 'n' Roll Hall of Fame has room for only one more inductee before it seals up for good. How do you decide who it will be?"

Without a second's pause Pooter said, "Get rid of half the crap that's in there now to make room for worthier artists."

Speaking as if writing in a pretend notebook, I said: "Shows promising problem-solving skills."

We talked instead about the high and low points of the *Pulp Fiction* soundtrack, and that somehow led us to our mutual affection for crispy Chinese noodles dipped in duck sauce.

It later turned out that Pooter's résumé was almost entirely fabricated. He had never been sports editor of *The Wallingford Bugle*, a fictitious community newspaper in rural Pennsylvania. He never coached little league soccer there either. He did wait tables at the Lyndon Denny's but he did not leave voluntarily to "pursue more meaningful employment."

But in the moment of the interview, it didn't matter. Here was someone who seemed able to breathe some life into the everyday.

"Well then, do you have any questions for me?" I asked him.

"Do you like your job?"

"I don't dislike it."

This was true. I never dreaded going into the office. In general, I liked the people I worked with, even if, apart from the occasional happy hour, I didn't socialize with them. And so, Pooter became my partner in apathy, the two of us leaning cynically on each other and smirking our way to the next paycheck.

Desperate for that cup of coffee, I called him back.

"What."

"Get me a coffee, and I'll buy you lunch."

Having worked with him for six months by the time I had to produce my annual budget for the following year, I found that I needed to pad the line item for Meals & Entertainment with roughly thirty lunches at an average of twelve dollars each—a little over $300 a year earmarked for bribing Pooter, most of the time to help me out of a self-inflicted bind.

It nearly got him fired once when I begged him to tell Langdon Herbert—the bestselling author on my list, if not our whole division—that he'd forgotten to give me a message regarding a last-minute cover change. In truth, I received the message, but as the fourth such request in same number of days, the art department would have gutted me with their X-ACTO knives if I'd gone back another time. I never asked the art director to make the change, and the book was printed with the last round's cover. Herbert later admitted he liked it better, but in the moment he wanted someone's head and Pooter took the brunt. Herbert blustered and spat cruel insults of incompetence at him, but Pooter hit just the perfect notes of humility and conciliation. It was precisely his ability to bullshit that made him far better at his job than either he or I expected he would be.

Pooter returned with a cup of coffee and a massive slice of apple pie. "You are a complete jerk."

"That's not really a news flash."

He handed me a fork. "How was your Thanksgiving madness?"

"We went to the cemetery. Bobbie bossed. Joyce was hanging all over my dad. They told us they're getting married. We ate, I did the dishes, then went home. Oh yeah, and then I got up the next day and stalked a major celebrity."

"Hold on, that's a lot of—"

My phone rang. I felt a flush of girlish thrill with the caller ID indicating it was Dan. This is the one-sided conversation Pooter heard.

"Hey.... Yeah, it was a little uncomfortable, but fine overall.... I don't know, I'll have to check my schedule and get back to you.... That definitely sounds interesting. Let me think about it and call you back."

As I hung up, Pooter put his feet up on my desk. "How is Dan-Dan the Handsome Man?"

"Please remove your feet from my desk."

"Did you ever wonder if a person's success can be attributed to his name?"

"No."

"You take a guy like Dan. Daniel Rayburn. It's such a good, clean, reliable name. Nothing sticks out or hits a weird note. A sci-fi hero name. Do you think he'd have made it to editor-in-chief if he were Marvin Peabody?

I don't think so. I swear, my name has always been a stone around my neck, one way or another. Apart, of course, from landing this glorious gig."

I was only half listening. Dan's invitation to dinner and other activities had me mentally scrambling to find an excuse to get out of plans to see *Leaving Las Vegas* with my friend, Julie.

"Let me guess," Pooter said, "Patricia is away, and Dan wants to play."

"Keep your voice down. And get your feet off my desk." I shooed his shoes again. "In fact, I'm sure you have stuff to do."

Pooter removed his feet one at a time and leaned in. "But you haven't told me your celebrity stalking story."

"I haven't got time now."

"Fine," he said. "I want ham and salami on a sub: lettuce, tomato, provolone, oil and vinegar. And onion. And an *Orangina*. And a chocolate chip cookie."

"Forget it."

"I got you coffee. A deal's a deal." He went to snatch the pie from me, but I pulled it out of his reach.

After he left, I tried to read a new proposal but was unfocused. It had been a week and a half since Dan and I had been able to meet. I had assumed it would be another two, figuring Patricia would be home after the Thanksgiving break. So, hearing Dan's voice, warm and magnetic in my ear sent my endorphins flying.

I opened my email and typed to Julie: "I'm so sorry, but I have a cousin who's unexpectedly in the city. I'm going to raincheck on the movie and meet up with her. Hope that doesn't screw your plans too much!"

5: The Fun Quotient

There was a rotation of restaurants that afforded us anonymity, each within a two-hour radius of the office, places off-the-beaten path "upstate" or in western Jersey as was the case with the Iron Sites Inn. A rustic, post and beam lodge, built in the 1940s as a hunting club, it seemed entirely plausible that the only thing that had changed over the years was the hairstyles of the waitstaff. Dan and I had happened upon it in the summertime on a drive back from eastern Pennsylvania after our first weekend away together. We savored the fading summer as we traveled a scenic route through the countryside scattered with restored colonial farmhouses, tin roof barns, old cemeteries, and rusty junkyards.

Three months later, the fading leaves had fallen and there was a light dusting of snow on the ground. As I waited for Dan to arrive, I sipped a rum and Coke beneath the unimpressed gaze of a mounted elk head, its age showing in the spotty bare patches on its neck and a dusty cobweb stretching between the antlers. Around the big dining room were a few couples and one large table celebrating a great-grandfather's ninetieth birthday with a giant cake boasting as many candles.

The main attraction of the restaurant and the one that kept drawing us back was the big bay window that afforded a view of the field where deer would appear just after sunset to graze in the tall grass, oblivious of the trophies of their ancestors that decorated the walls just a few hundred feet away.

A pair of does were meandering over when Dan arrived. I nearly jumped out of my chair, eager to throw my arms around him in a way I had to suppress every day when we were at work. His return embrace was warm and genuine, our kiss was brief but emphatic.

"I'm sorry to be late. Warren was hammering us on our revenue projections." He removed his jacket and sat down. "I'm not sure what he expects. The numbers are the numbers. Just because he doesn't like them doesn't mean they aren't valid."

Though I was a few layers lower in seniority, I liked when Dan talked to me as if I were a part of that world. I had barely seen Warren Dumont, our vice president, let alone been in the same room with him, but from all I'd heard, he sounded like a man who wielded his authority like a caveman with a club.

Dan reached for my hand, not letting go when the waiter arrived to take his drink order. And though we ran virtually no risk of being recognized this far away, the gesture felt dangerous and meaningful.

He pointed out the window after the waiter had gone. "It's dinner in the field too." We could see two more deer had joined the earlier pair, though the light was waning, and they were nearly shadows.

"How was your trip back home?" I asked.

"Nice. My dad's stress test came back fine. I think his blood pressure just spikes when my mother's around."

The waiter brought Dan's Scotch, a basket of warm rolls and a tiny dish with flower shaped pats of butter.

"And you?" he asked. "Thanksgiving with your dad's girlfriend, how'd that go?"

"Fiancée."

"Oh?"

"They're eloping. Though I guess it's just considered getting married if it's not secret."

"You OK?"

"I am. It wasn't a huge surprise, and I really do understand that it's probably a good thing for him. It just feels weird that they're going off to Florida or somewhere, and then coming back as husband and wife. It's like, 'Can you pick me and your stepmom up at the airport?' It's fine that he's getting married, but I don't have any use for a stepmother."

He brought my bent fingers to his lips and kissed them sweetly. "You may someday."

Infidelity notwithstanding, being around Dan made me feel like I could be a better person. He opened the space for me to be kinder in my thoughts, softer around the edges. Most of the time, I was grateful for the redirect, but in this moment, I preferred to keep those particular emotional barriers intact, so I changed the subject.

"So, get this. Friday after Thanksgiving, I went to get bagels to bring to my dad. I'm waiting in line; the door opens and in walks...James Keefner and his daughter." (I may have taken some liberties with the details.)

"The actor?"

"Yeah. He grew up in my hometown. Was actually friends with my brother in high school."

"I read somewhere that he grew up in this area. Did you talk to him?"

"A little, but he was trying to keep a low profile, so I just gave him his space." (In any case, it was what Audrey with the soft edges would have done.)

The food arrived in all its carnivorous glory: a juicy, almost rare ribeye with fat fries for Dan and venison

51

medallions in a pan sauce for me. I averted my eyes from the twilight grazers out the window.

"Hey," he said. "I don't want to talk shop for more than a minute, but Bridget is arranging travel this week for the AAP conference coming up." He paused. "I know you were planning on going, but I'd like to suggest that Pooter go instead."

I set my fork down. "Why?"

"Two reasons. One, I suspect he's ready for a little more responsibility—" I tossed off a skeptical look. "And two," he paused, "I think there would be too many opportunities for you and me to be careless."

"Getting careless was precisely what I was looking forward to," I said flirtatiously. I had daydreamed of a high-rise hotel room with a dazzling panorama of the Vegas Strip. There would be champagne and room service, smoldering gazes in a smoky casino.

"I know," he said. "And I really want to be away with you too. But we shouldn't take that kind of risk."

"Shouldn't?"

"Can't. Won't." The period to the end the discussion.

I pushed at the limp, watery green beans on my plate, hating them. It was the prior year's trade show that had marked the first time Dan's orbit had crossed into mine.

A group of eight of us from Business Texts had flown to Miami. I was a last-minute addition to the trip when Daria, my boss, went into premature labor and had to go on long-term bed rest.

It was my first trade show and so I went with a certain eagerness, fortified by my dry-cleaned dress pants and a crisp, new stack of business cards. I was fully prepared to network, attend panel discussions and make good impressions on my colleagues. And all those things were completely possible. But I quickly learned that a three-day conference was a little like a high school field trip where many of the businesspeople, ordinarily bound by office rules of decorum, were almost giddy with the respite from professionalism and, let's be honest, distance from their significant others. There was schmoozing during the day; boozing in the late afternoon, dinner and evening; and the nights were ripe for hook-ups.

Had I hitched my neophyte wagon to a different group, say the Science and Technology Division, things might have gone differently, but I followed the lead of my cohorts, Dmitri Lloyd and Carly Fury, who on the plane ride actually talked about Miami's "fun quotient" compared with the previous year's conference in Minneapolis.

And so, it was on the second night of the conference that I joined the pair in crashing a lavish party hosted by a major media company that owned a handful of publishing houses.

About an hour into the event, I went to get a fresh glass of wine. When I returned to the spot beside the massive display of fruit, Carly and Dmitri were gone, giving me the distinct impression that they no longer required my company. I plucked a handful of grapes from the stack and scanned the room for them or any familiar face, and found myself locking eyes with a nice-looking guy with shaggy, brown hair, tortoise shell glasses, and a welcoming smile. He looked like a writer.

His name was Kyle Quinn, a development editor for high school English texts. Talking shop with Kyle, I learned that the "dead white guys" were now having to give up a greater share of anthology space to writers who were African American, women, or African American women. On this and other points of literary education, we seemed to be on opposite sides of opinion: he lamenting, I applauding.

We ate a little, drank a lot, including a handful of pretty, pink cosmopolitans. There were some foggy, fairly stupid conversations including one about the 3,000th edition of Dante's Inferno, "Now Featuring Six New Hell *Bolgias!*"

"Number Ten: Stupidity," he said, "To this torment are condemned the bungee jumpers, pro-wrestling fanatics, and chronic mis-spellers of the underworld."

"Careful, I think the Eleventh Circle is reserved for the Judgmentalists."

"That's totally not a word."

And on it went until it became clear that most of the partygoers had gone elsewhere and the bartenders were no longer serving, though these most likely occurred in reverse order.

"So, Audrey."

"So, Kyle."

"What do you say we raid the mini bar in my room? I'm a five-minute walk from here."

I had figured on another hour or more before having to determine if I liked Kyle enough to hook up with him, or even if I liked him at all. I was suddenly irritated with Dmitri and Carly for abandoning me, leaving me to chart my night solo, in an obvious state of inebriation, which had only gotten inebriated-er.

"Let me go hit the ladies'. I'll meet you in the lobby."

The lights in the bathroom were interrogation bright, and my eyes couldn't focus, like I was riding a very slow merry-go-round. Knowing I was near the tipping point between comfortably drunk and queasy, I cold-soaked some paper towel and laid it on the back of my neck for a moment.

Back in the lobby, Kyle was standing beneath a tall palm spotlighted from below. Beside him was a shimmering water fountain wall that chattered like gossip. I walked slowly, deliberately, trying to look as if I had total control over the heels I was wearing, though I suspected it had the exact opposite effect.

Kyle offered a steadying elbow. "Ready?"

I tightened my grip on my purse as if it might keep me from swaying. "So, I actually think I'm going to pass on the mini-bar invitation."

Over Kyle's left shoulder I spotted Dan, who at the time, I knew only as "Dan Rayburn, Editor-in-Chief" of our division, a tall, athletic looking guy in his early forties who seemed at the same time approachable and completely intimidating; I had never exchanged more than a polite smile with him.

He had just stood up from a table in the hotel bar, where he and three other executive types were shaking hands, concluding some type of business.

Kyle moved in front of me, blotting out my view of the bar, and reached a hand to my waist. "I don't believe you turn into a pumpkin this early."

"I had one cosmo too many. I'm just going to crash for the night."

"Well then, why don't I come tuck you in?" His other hand reached into my hair and toyed gently with the dangling earring there.

"Look, it's been fun hanging with you, but I—"

"We'll keep it totally casual."

"I don't think—"

"Come on, what's a quick screw between strangers?"

I pushed his hand away, irritated and ill-feeling. "Don't be a dick," I said.

"Oh, I see. You play the tease all night and that makes me a dick?"

I put my hands up defensively and took a step backwards, "Good night."

He turned and headed toward the exit before yelling over his shoulder, "You stupid cunt."

In that moment, Dan and his crew had stepped into the lobby, and from the direction of their gaze, they unquestionably caught the tail end of the interaction. In fact, they, the desk clerks, check-in guests, anyone within twenty feet would have heard Kyle.

Fixing my eyes on a square tile on the floor, I took a moment to remove my earrings and slip them into my purse. I willed my gait steady over to the concierge and, though my hotel was just a few blocks away, I asked him to call a cab to take me there.

The next morning, from the depths of a thick, sludgy sleep, I was awakened by a couple arguing just outside my door as they passed on their way to the elevator. I pried open one sticky eyelid and saw it was 6:07 a.m. Dmitri and Carly had been planning on meeting for breakfast at eight o'clock, and painful though it was, I forced myself out of bed so I could revive myself with some coffee and a bite without having to see them.

The shower was hot and sharp as needles on my skin, but it helped cut through the fog and fatigue so that by the time I reached the hotel buffet I had a mild appetite despite a pulsing headache.

I scooped a small mound of stiff scrambled eggs onto my plate and added a couple triangles of dry toast. Disinclined to make another trip through the buffet, I poured myself two cups of coffee and sought a quiet corner in which to sit. But there at the centermost table, like the fucking dining-area ambassador, sat Dan Rayburn. I swore and was just about to abandon my tray to go find a vending machine when he looked up from his newspaper and smiled in my direction. I glanced behind me, sure he must be greeting someone else. When it turned out no one was there, he gestured for me to approach. I swore again.

"You're up early," he said. I would remember these as the first words he ever spoke to me.

"Noisy neighbors," I said. He arched an eyebrow.

"Oh. Not that kind of noisy. Just regular, checking out noisy."

My brain begged my mouth to stop sending words out into the world. He gestured to my double coffees. "You meeting someone?"

I shook my head. "One for each eye."

He laughed a genuine laugh. I made Editor-in-Chief Dan Rayburn laugh.

"Rough night?" He could have been acknowledging the hangover at the moment or the embarrassing scene with Kyle, or both. "Have a seat." He motioned to an empty chair. "My seven-o'clock cancelled."

Such was my penance for avoiding Dmitri and Carly that morning: making small talk with my boss' boss, fighting the urge to lay my head down on the cool table while drinking coffee through a long straw.

At this point, Dan was so prohibitively unattainable that it didn't even occur to me find him attractive; he was simply a nuisance that morning. And he later explained that asking me to join him was simply the gesture of a benevolent overlord (my words), who was taking the opportunity to converse with a member of his underlings (again, my words) that he'd only known as a name on the paycheck he signed. As such, the conversation was polite, but mundane as we each told our origin stories of finding our way to Preston House. He via the finance world, having previously been an analyst, and me after having done three years of steady office work as a temp, during which I honed one of my few talents: typing seventy-five words per minute.

We talked about my boss, Daria, what an earnestly nice person she was, and did I know that she had performed on Broadway as a kid in the musical Annie? I didn't. Bosses were sometimes total mysteries like that. I wondered what quirky secrets Dan Rayburn had.

Having downed my coffee and scant breakfast, I felt only moderately better, so I bowed out after about thirty minutes, saying I needed to dress for my morning shift in the booth. He thanked me for the company, and I didn't see him again the rest of the trip.

Back at the office, Dan and I were sometimes in meetings together. When we passed in the hall, one of us would offer a "hello" or "how's it going," but our worlds didn't really intersect again until five months later at a retirement party for Lorena Gallego, Dan's previous administrative assistant.

The gathering was held at El Torito, the nearest and most favored of our happy hour haunts. Nearly every Thursday after work you could find a half dozen or so employees there, gesturing with Coronas and playing darts in the corner.

Given the free appetizers at the party and the fact that Lorena had worked in the Social Sciences Division for six years before coming to our department, the turnout would be significant.

At these kinds of department-wide social gatherings, you could tell a person's level of seniority by the timing of his or her arrival. Officially, the party was set to start just after five o'clock, but only the editorial assistants would be there at 5:05 p.m. And they would stand pressed together like high school freshmen in the cafeteria, keenly observing and developing strategies for navigating office politics. Next to arrive at roughly 5:25 p.m., would be the assistant and associate editors. They would gather in the opposite corner with their backs to everyone else until the senior editors, the marketing, design staff and others arrived—then and only then would they start to mingle. And when the department heads joined forty-five to fifty minutes after everyone else, there would be a perceptible shift in the attention of the room: space would be accommodated, drinks offered, and conversations within their earshot would become a little more refined.

When I arrived at Lorena's party (between the associate and senior editors), Pooter was standing with the cluster of editorial assistants, one elbow on the bar and a beer in his other hand. We nodded to each other as I peeled off to join the conversation between Renny Culpepper and Carly Fury. The waitstaff bustled through the crowd delivering overloaded nachos and cheap margaritas, while reggae music floated down from hidden speakers (El Torito was favored for its mood, not its authenticity).

Lorena was surrounded by a handful of people from her old department, many of whom I recognized from the staff cafeteria. She was speaking animatedly about her plans. Though about ten years short of retirement age, she and her husband had sold their home and most of their possessions to purchase a fully stocked motor home so they could travel around the country, spending much of the year at the national parks, while settling at one for the summer as camp hosts.

A master of diplomacy, who had equal parts grace and wit, Lorena had always seemed to me to be the most undervalued member of our team. Now the center of attention at her own party, she seemed different. Or maybe it was that we seemed different to her, as if we were already people she remembered from a recent past.

By the time members of the executive team arrived on the scene, most of us were into our second, some a third, drink. The door swung open and admitted Dan, Liza Batista from Social Sciences, and a red-haired guy from Finance I knew only by his nickname "Wags." They made a raucous entrance, Wags having delivered the punchline to a joke just as they walked in.

Though he tried to be casual, Renny shifted his position to be in direct line of Dan just so he could provide a personal update on one of his projects. Renny had ambitions. I had heard him boast that during his interview (having previously set a record for being promoted from editorial assistant to assistant editor in a mere three months), Dan asked him where he would like to be in three years' time to which Renny quite earnestly answered: "Sitting behind your desk." He and I were stark contrasts not just in that way, but also in the way he rhapsodized about his particular discipline: business law and financial regulation.

I downed the rest of my beer as an excuse to duck away from the meet and greet. Gesturing toward the bar, I asked, "You guys want anything?"

Carly declined while Renny said, "Might want to keep it in check, Audrey. You don't want to make a bad impression on people here," he leaned his head toward Dan who had moved on to join Lorena's circle.

I patted him on the arm, "You're so good, Renny."

Moving upstream against the crowd, I made it to the bar and ordered a couple of Dos Equis, deciding to deliver one to Pooter, "Just 'cause." I handed it off like a relay race baton and moved over to the side as one of the waitstaff rolled out a massive sheet cake with the words, "Bon voyage, Lorena!" written next to a bright blue, buttercream Airstream-shaped camper.

Then the toasts began: one from the HR director who first hired Lorena almost ten years to the day, one from Elaine Zuri, Lorena's lunchtime walking partner and closest friend, and finally, one from Dan that began with an inside joke about the Dewey Decimal System and ended with a warm thank you for the last three years of keeping him and his team (a sweeping gesture toward all of us) in line, at least to the best of our ability.

The party kicked into a higher gear when the staff from a neighboring real estate office that we played against in beer league softball descended on the bar and began intermingling. I hung out on the periphery of one conversation, chiming in when I had something to contribute, but mostly enjoying my buzz and assessing how soon I could make a discrete exit. When I saw Dan leaving the party, I figured a precedent had been set. I lingered another fifteen minutes and then slid my way through the crowd toward Lorena to wish her safe and interesting travels, reminding her to send postcards so we could feel bitterly envious.

Outside, the horizon's pale blue had started to deepen and darken, and a fingernail thin moon hung just above the treetops. I was rummaging in my purse when a seagull picking at a scrap of garbage startled me so that I dropped my keys, and they went skidding under a nearby car. I kneeled on the pavement and (not being in the most clear-headed state) I half tossed my purse after the keys thinking I could use it to drag them out, which is how I managed to get my purse stuck under the car as well. Flat out on the ground, shoes flailing to scoot far enough under to reach one or the other, I heard someone ask, "Is everything OK?"

"Fine," I replied. "Just planting a car bomb is all."

"Do you need help?"

Amy Klinger

"That would make you an accessory." I paused. "And I've already lost one accessory," I said with a snort-laugh.

I managed to grasp the purse strap which enabled me to pull the keys within a finger's reach. Scraping my forearms and knees, crawling backwards and trying desperately to keep my skirt from riding up, I finally emerged from the backside of the car. I brushed off the gravel bits that had embedded in my skin and on my clothes. Dan looked at me as if he were trying to do a hard math problem. I jangled my keys at him. "They ran away."

He shook his head at me. I let out a weighty sigh. "I thought you left," I said.

"My wallet was back at the office," he said. "You're not driving, right?"

"Nnn...o. I..." Across the street the glow of a green and white logo featuring a sea siren beckoned. "was going to get some coffee."

He glanced across the street. "Great, me too."

"It's OK, I don't need a chaperone."

"It kind of appears otherwise."

It actually was a bit tricky to cross between the fast, oncoming cars whose drivers were not anticipating pedestrians at that part of the road. Once on the other side, we had to scramble over the guard rail—another graceful attempt to keep my skirt lowered—and walk through tall, scratchy weeds to the parking lot.

Inside, it was an oasis of rich, jewel-toned colors, heady coffee aroma and a sweeping, big band song that was loud enough to be heard without being obtrusive. A bored-looking barista took our orders—short cappuccino for me, grande Americano for Dan, then we sat down at a round, wooden table. I had no idea what we should talk about.

"You're missing out on the party," I said. "Lorena's going to be disappointed."

"She and I are having lunch tomorrow. Plus, the noise in there was getting to me."

When the other barista called our order, Dan stood to get it. "Do you take sugar?" he asked.

"Just a dust of cinnamon, thanks."

When Dan returned, he set our cups down gently as a waiter would. He took off his jacket—a dark, charcoal gray—hung it neatly over the empty chair and loosened his bright red tie.

"You're like my dad's mailbox," I said.

He squinted at me, an expression that would become a frequent visual code letting me know when I was being cryptic.

"It's this dark gray, cylindrical thing with a red flag..."

"I'm familiar with what mailboxes look like."

"You're almost that exact color combination. The jacket, the tie." I took a sip of sweet, frothy milk. "And the white shirt—"

"Like an envelope," he said.

"Like a letter from the goddamn IRS."

"That's hardly a compliment."

"It could be a refund notification."

Dan grinned and looked into his coffee before taking a long sip. "It's never a refund notification."

And then he did something that changed everything: he unbuttoned the cuff of his shirt and folded the sleeve up around his forearm. The gesture was totally casual, but strangely intimate. I felt a sudden and startling rush of attraction that felt like getting clobbered by a big ocean wave. My ears burned with the realization, and I had to look away, afraid that he would read it in my face.

My feet started fidgeting. I needed to redirect my attention. "So do you know who's going to be your new admin?"

He leaned back in his chair and nodded wryly. "They're moving Bridget over."

I audibly gasped.

"Thanks, Audrey. I feel much better about it now."

Dan was renowned throughout the office for his disdain for things like punctuality and office cleanliness. Lorena had always indulged him by setting meeting times on his calendar thirty minutes early and simply keeping his office door shut when the inside looked like it had been ransacked by vandals. But if Lorena's style had been "enabling mother," Ridgid's would be "indignant warden."

"This could be the best steel cage death match ever," I said.

"I'd put my money on Bridget." He sipped again at his coffee, and then said. "You're pretty funny."

Out of the three words he had said, my ears latched on to just two of them: "You're pretty," and I flushed bright as a tomato.

The barista called another order, and a couple of teenaged girls stood to claim it. As they chattered past our table, Dan pointed up at the ceiling, presumably to the music surrounding us. "That's Odetta. I saw her at a music fest at the shore a few years ago."

"Ha!" I nearly shouted, startling us both. "In '92—I was there too. An old boyfriend of mine's brother was the sound engineer, and he gave us tickets. I'm embarrassed to say I had no idea who she was at the time."

"And Pete Seeger was there too, and a few others?"

"That's right," I said. Though actually, my memory of the day was gauzy and warped from too much weed and beer and sun.

Still jittery and unable to look Dan in the eye, this new coincidence of having been at the same show—perhaps sitting just a row apart—unsettled me even further. If I were the kind to put stock in that kind of thing, I might have wondered if the universe were trying to push us together.

Stupid thing to think, I thought. But my mind, like an unruly child, kept wandering away, and I caught myself imagining sliding my hand across the table, running my fingertips over his exposed wrist, feeling the quiet pulse there and then tracing the round knob of bone at the base of his hand. I downed the rest of my coffee and set the mug down, harder than I intended.

"I'm good," I said. "Ready to go when you are."

"You sure?" he asked, and I nodded. "I'll just finish this then."

As he raised the mug to take the last couple of sips, I stole a glance at his fingers looped through the mug handle, at the tiny hairs on his knuckles, and then at the wedding band there: a barrier to further musing about wrists and pulses.

As he had on the way in, Dan opened the door, letting me go through first. This time because he had pushed it open from the inside, I had to pass by him at a much closer proximity. I felt alert and charged as if instead I'd had a double shot of espresso.

We crossed farther up the road, closer to the office where the oncoming traffic was easier to see. The parking lot still had a good number of cars, suggesting that the festivities were carrying on just fine without us.

Dan and I were about to part ways when I realized something. "Hey," I said. "I have a bootleg CD of that music fest with Odetta."

I hadn't meant for it to be anything other than an interesting callback to the earlier conversation.

Dan said. "I would love to borrow that."

It seemed from that moment, the evening turned into a strange, slow game of "Chicken," the two of us moving toward a cliff, each thinking the other would peel off and return to the safety of our regular lives before we hurtled headlong off the Cliffs of Adultery.

"I think it's in my car."

There were about twenty CDs in my car. The Odetta bootleg (an apology gift from that boyfriend following our first breakup) wasn't one of them.

"Shoot, it must be on my shelf at home."

"Where's your place?"

"It's close, just over in the Sutton neighborhood."

"I pass right by there."

"I could run in and get it for you."

And so it went. As I drove toward home, my eyes kept darting up to the rearview mirror to make sure the headlights of his Audi were there. I told myself over and over that I was misreading the situation, that for nostalgic reasons, he was simply interested in borrowing the CD and nothing more.

When Dan got caught at a red light, I hesitated, thinking I should just keep going and pretend I didn't know he was no longer behind me. I kept on the gas and drove another few hundred feet. Then with flutters in my gut and a vice grip on the steering wheel, I pulled over to the curb, and waited for his car's lights to reappear.

As we arrived at my building, I rolled down the window and pointed for him to take the visitor's spot.

From there, I decided I would let Dan's actions dictate mine. If he got fully out of the car, I would lead the way to my condo. If he stayed in the car, I would run in, get the disc and bring it to him.

He opened his car door and stood half in-half out, looking up at the building. "That's an old building," he said.

"Used to be a school."

"Huh." Then, he stepped both feet out of the car and closed the door, moving to inspect the stonework.

"Hold on, I'll go get the CD and be right back."

That was what I had intended to say, but the words never came. Instead, I flipped through my keys for the right one and started toward the walkway. Dan followed.

As I turned on the lights, I suddenly felt self-conscious, embarrassed of my knick-knacks and decor. The framed Inuit prints seemed disingenuous: I had never been to Canada, let alone Cape Dorset. My grandmother's crocheted blanket with its bright mismatched blocks of red, orange, and yellow were a sentimental comfort on cozy-on-the-couch nights, but it clashed loudly with the more subdued hues and neat angles I tried to imbue in the rest of the living room.

Enough, I told myself. Get the CD quickly and send Dan on his way. "Hang on. I'll be right back."

I was not particularly organized about many things but keeping my CD cabinet in alphabetical order was always an obsessive habit. The Clearwater Festival bootleg was right where it belonged between Captain and Tennille and Color Me Badd.

I came back holding the CD triumphantly over my head. "Here it is." I held the CD out toward Dan. "I don't know why I didn't just offer to make you a copy and bring it in on Monday."

Most people's smiles start at their mouth and work their way upward on the face. Dan's was the reverse; it started at his eyes, where they became crinkly at the corners just before his mouth turned upward in an earnest grin.

He didn't reach out to take the case from me. Instead, he asked, "You don't?"

These were the memories I sometimes got distracted by, playing them over and over in my head like a favorite romance movie.

"Hey," Dan squeezed my hand as the waiter set down the check. "Are you still with me?"

"Oh, sorry." I gave a dismissive wave of my hand. "I just realized that I forgot to tell Kenny about seeing Jamie—James Keefner—when we talked last night. I'm here now."

When the waiter brought the check, Dan held out his hand for it.

"Let me get dinner tonight," I said.

He shook his head. "I'll let you cook me breakfast tomorrow."

I perked up. "You can stay over?"

He smiled.

"Well then, settle up and let's get the hell out of this deer mausoleum!"

Two months after Lorena's party, Pooter pressed me for some explanation as to "what was up." We were having lunch at a nearby pub. He couldn't put his finger on precisely what, but I had become different, distracted, like I was avoiding talking to him. I denied it, though not convincingly.

"Look, if I did something wrong, just tell me."

I tried again to suggest he was imagining things.

"Fine," he said annoyed. "I'm not stupid, Audrey. But if you're going to play it like that, then whatever."

It was a bad idea. I knew it on every level. Yet I reasoned it was better to confide in him than have him private-eyeing around for clues and figuring it out on his own. So, I told him the whole story, and about how

Dan and I had been continuing to see each other when circumstances allowed.

Pooter didn't say much, he just ate his shepherd's pie, picking the carrots out and setting them aside in a neat pile. I filled the conversational space with some of the thoughts that had been rolling around in my head, relieved to finally have someone to talk to about it.

"It's not like I've fallen for him. For obvious reasons, it's not a relationship that's going anywhere. And truthfully, that's totally fine with me. It's just, when we've been together, it's been really...nice, fun." I dived back into my chef's salad, ate a few forkfuls. "Sometimes, I imagine that we're, like, spies. You know? We have these double lives. It's hard having an affair. I feel like—"

"No. It's not."

"What?"

"It's not hard. You know what's hard? Being faithful. Having an affair? That's the easiest thing in the world."

"Oh, you're an expert on relationships now?"

"No. I'm not," he said. "I just know people who have shitty marriages—people who make a promise and keep it. If you don't want to keep your promise, you get out. You don't cheat. Cheating is easy."

I thought about that for a moment. Stepping over that line, once the opportunity was there, I had to admit, had been easy. I put my fork down and folded my hands in my lap. My expression was a mix of sheepishness and a healthy dose of concern.

Pooter threw a scrap of bread crust onto his plate and rolled his eyes. "Don't look at me like that. I'm not going to tell anyone. Just...don't be stupid." He crumpled up his napkin and covered the rest of his lunch. "Or, don't be stupider."

6: Sugar Bomb

The second week of December, the Christmas decorations were at their peak. The neighborhoods blinked and twinkled like Candyland in the early morning on my way to the office. Some of the houses were strict "white-lighters" with strands meticulously looped and tucked into front-yard evergreens, white icicle chains dangling from the gutters, or sometimes just a single bulb candle placed in every window. Meanwhile, their more expressive neighbors went all-out. Flashing red, green, yellow, blue, and white lights framing doors and windows, entwined like ecstatic ivy around railings, in the shrubs, and strings of blinking bulbs not quite placed but perhaps lassoed into the sprawling tree branches.

As a kid, ours was that house on the block: the single, willfully un-illuminated one that might as well have had a big, fat Star of David flying on a flagpole out front, even though we were half-Protestant.

When December rolled around at the Rohmers, Hanukkah and Christmas seemed to cancel each other out rather than compete. When all my friends' families were tearing into morning mother lodes of presents, Kenny, Bobbie, and I were likely to be doing what we would on any typical weekend, reading the funnies, playing board games, and watching TV. Mom might make us waffles or corn muffins as a treat. As for gifts, sometimes we would get a new pair of sneakers, a sweatshirt, or other utilitarian gift; other years, it would be a box of our favorite sugar-bomb cereal: Count Chocula for Kenny, Quisp for Bobbie, Lucky Charms for me.

As a grown up, I wasn't particularly scrooge-like about Christmas, but I sometimes found myself irritated by the season. At work, tinsel and ornaments, Ho-ho-hos and Happy Holidays! spread like kudzu in the break room, the copy room, along cubicle walls, in the elevator. Even Pooter had a battery-operated Santa staged prominently on his desk so that any time someone walked by, the figure would break into "Jingle Bell Rock" and sway its hips side to side. But Pooter being Pooter, he had posed the doll's hands up by its head, so it gave off an unsettling burlesque vibe.

"You were looking for me?" Pooter held up the Post-it note I'd left on his desk. I looked at the clock.

"Sorry, I was stuck behind a school bus on my way in."

"Must have been a very slow school bus."

"They're very conscientious, those drivers."

"They have to be."

"All those kids getting on with their lunch boxes. And then there was the construction...Anyway, you were looking for me?"

"I wanted to see if your calendar was clear for February 10th-13th."

"Hard to say, I'm generally booked with social engagements at least three months out," he said with socialite affectation. "Why?"

"I was thinking you might want to go to the AAP Conference in Vegas."

His eyes widened as if he'd won a scratch ticket, "Seriously? That'd be great! I'll have to brush up on my blackjack. Would we get to see a show do you think?"

"Not 'we', you. There's only budget for one of us, and I've already been. Seemed like a good opportunity for you to get to know the broader industry. Your job will be to man the booth, though, not lose your shirt in the casino. But I'm sure there'll be some downtime in the evenings."

"I'm in," he said. "That's so cool. Thanks for the opportunity!"

Seeing him so enthusiastic eased a little of the sting of Dan asking me to stay behind. It seemed likely that Pooter would actually do a better job than I would at making connections and coming back with useful insights.

He took a step out of my office, then quickly popped back in with a look on his face that I couldn't read: surprise, concern, a hint of amusement.

"What?" I asked.

He stepped inside as a figure passed: a tall woman dressed in a trim, navy, wool coat and heels despite the day's slushy precipitation. With her boy-short, copper-colored hair, she was easy to recognize from the photos in his office. Patricia was on her way to visit Dan.

"Thanks. It's OK. Just close my door on your way out." I added in a whisper, "Call me when she's gone."

On the subject of Patricia, my mind stayed inside a space with a similarly closed door—aware of her presence on the other side, but easy to ignore by simply focusing on the things in my line of sight. Apart from sharing updates on her travel schedule, Dan and I never spoke about her. What I knew of Patricia was only what I had learned before the relationship with Dan began. In fact, it was some of the first gossip I'd heard when I started at Preston House—that Editor-in-Chief's current wife was the former wife of Chasen Baylor, that once-beloved senator who'd been photographed in compromising positions with an underage girl in St.

Barts. And that *Ladies Home Journal* magazine had once done a cover story about her: Patricia Ripley, rising from the ashes of her first marriage and "remaking" herself as one of the world's most sought-after commercial photographers, traveling the world on assignment for clients like Coca-Cola, Lockheed Martin, and Dole. Beyond that, I had no idea how she and Dan met, nor how long they'd even been married.

A little over an hour after Patricia had arrived, Pooter rang. "The chicken has flown the coop. I repeat: The chicken has flown the coop."

"Was the rooster with her?" I asked.

"Negative."

Though I hadn't noticed the tension, I could feel my posture relax a little, the wrinkle in my brow let go. I allowed myself to think about why she had visited. I wondered if Dan had known she was coming. And if so, whether if, even for a moment, he'd considered warning me.

Not two hours later, I was getting myself lunch at the salad bar in the grocery store nearby when I did a double take. I had nearly missed recognizing her in the produce section, the woman wearing that same navy coat and those shoes, a tidy purse hanging at her elbow like a piece of jewelry.

There was a certain way Patricia pushed the cart down the aisle, not really pushing at all, which would require a certain amount of effort. Rather, she and her cart were gliding, as if on a conveyor belt; her shoulders never rose or fell outside their constant level plane.

I watched as she quite nearly caressed the colorful orbs of bell peppers. She was like a tall fairy who, coincidentally or not, caused the spray-misters to spontaneously come on as she passed the purple cabbage heads. She reached out into the spray, then smoothed a dampened hand through her hair.

With the recent James Keefner surveillance experience under my belt, I scuttled back to the entrance and picked up a basket to serve as camouflage as I followed Patricia half an aisle behind.

She held no shopping list. She read labels and turned items around and upside down to find their ingredient lists and expiration dates. Only very selective items made it into her cart.

I placed a bag of lentils in my basket. She added a large bag of rice (organic) and a can of vegetable broth (reduced sodium). I desperately wanted her to pick up something humanizing—Marshmallow Fluff, mold remover, *Monistat*—but the only other items she added were a jar of salsa (mild), a tin of cocoa (imported), and a roll of paper towels (extra thick).

When she paused, I paused, giving fake scrutiny to the variety of Cheerios on the shelf. When she moved to a new aisle, I lagged at a sample table where a cheerful woman in a Santa hat greeted me with a cup of bright blue yogurt. The angle afforded me reasonable cover as I fronted a smiling, nodding face to the woman, while keeping my attention focused on Patricia. She was examining a jar of something. But when she returned it to its place, it must have boxed out some other items and an adjacent jar tumbled off the shelf, landing not so much with a crash as with a quiet crush.

In the interest of remaining incognito, I quickly re-engaged with the sample lady, explaining that there are almost no naturally occurring blue food items in the world. Even blueberries are closer to purple, I said. So, then, I wondered at her, what would compel this yogurt company to try to sell a product that was so clearly developed in a lab? The woman just shrugged and said, "Would you like a coupon?"

By the time I looked over again, Patricia had gone, but the jar remained a shattered blob on the floor and there was no one arriving with a mop. Grabbing the coupon, I made a hasty exit.

I glanced down the adjacent aisle but could only see an elderly man staring in squinty confusion at one of the shelves. I went to the last row, where the sandwich bread and dairy were housed, and there was Patricia, still browsing. As she walked toward me, I was incapable of looking away. My throat tightened and I held my breath when, just for a second, her eyes locked on mine. But it was she who broke her gaze first, dropping her chin to her chest and looking down and away at something near my feet. It was a gesture that evoked something like embarrassment. She knew I had seen her leave that bleeding jar behind.

I walked on, right past her, my posture straight, my expression calm while trying to drum up satisfaction that I had won some sort of competition. Instead, I could only feel ashamed at my own lack of shame.

7: Sounds Like Singing

The sweet and pungent smell of short ribs braising in the oven reminded me of home. Not necessarily my home, but rather an abstraction of home, a Pottery Barn fantasy of a wide white porch and shutter-framed windows, hardwood floors cozied up with round braided rugs and a big family-style table set with vintage China and napkin rings, and oversized wine glasses with identification charms on the stems.

My condo, with its closet-sized kitchen full of chipped dinnerware and hand-me-down pots and pans offered no trace of that domestic glow, but I still felt a distinct satisfaction in presiding over the cooking of a festive meal, oven mitt like a puppet sidekick on one hand and a wooden spoon like a conductor's baton in the other. The potatoes were boiling, and a bottle of Cabernet sat breathing on the counter. I was Hostess with a capital H.

The phone rang. It was my father calling from Key West for the second time that day. The first, shortly after noon, was to tell me that he and Joyce were officially married.

"What's wrong?" I asked.

"Did you know that Joyce and I are closer to Cuba than we are to Miami?"

Receiver wedged between my ear and shoulder as I folded napkins, I asked, "Were you thinking of defecting?"

In the background, I heard Joyce, "Tell her about the sea turtles!"

"We saw sea turtles," my father said, his voice rising excitedly on the word "sea."

"Yeah?"

"And, hey, you should see the robes they give you at this hotel. It's like being wrapped in a cloud."

I had never known my father to speak in similes; for Louis Rohmer things were what they were. I wondered how many piña coladas he'd had.

There was a knock at my door. I looked at the clock. Three minutes to eight and the table wasn't set yet.

"Hey, Dad, I'd love to hear more, but my company just arrived."

"Sure. I just called to wish you a wonderful new year, sweetheart."

"Thanks Dad. It seems like yours is off to a pretty good start too."

"It is. Get this, after dinner, we're taking salsa lessons!"

"Oh," I said, thumbtacking for later the strange contemplation of my father doing the cha-cha. The knock at the door was louder this time.

"Tell her to have a Happy New Year, Lou," Joyce's small voice said.

"Joyce says 'Happy New Year.'"

"Back at her. And congratulations again. I'll talk to you soon."

"Next year!" he said.

Pooter stood on the stoop, bobbing up and down to keep warm. He held out a wrapped bouquet of white tulips and feathery pine branches.

"I think I got hypothermia waiting out here."

"Since you're two minutes early, you may have the honor of setting the table." I traded the bouquet of flowers for one of silverware. "Pretty flowers," I said, tossing the words over my shoulder as I headed into the kitchen.

I sleeved a layer of dust off a vase that had been on the shelf and attempted to arrange the tulips artfully. Then, shifting back to the appetizers, I peeled the plastic wrap off a platter of artichoke dip surrounded by a tidy arrangement of carrots, celery, and assorted crackers. Pooter was setting each piece of silverware neatly in place.

"You look nice," I said. "I didn't think you actually owned an iron."

"I didn't think you were capable of giving a compliment," he said. "We're both full of surprises."

I set a stack of dinner and salad plates on the counter that separated the open kitchen from the dining room. "These too," I said.

"Wow, you say please and thank you at home about as much as you do at the office."

"Your reprimand is noted. Thank you," I said sweetly.

There was an unexpected awkwardness to seeing Pooter in my own space, away from work or happy hour. As if a new line of "personal" had been drawn.

"Do you want a drink?" I asked. "I have beer, wine, water."

The kitchen timer sounded, and I turned off the flame beneath the potatoes. "Beer sounds good."

"Here." I handed him the appetizers. "Bring these over to the coffee table? Please."

I joined him in the living room with two bottles of beer, each with a frosted glass overturned on top.

Pooter sat on the couch; I settled into the chair—a chubby, slip-covered garage sale find that all of a sudden seemed too large for the corner in which it sat.

He grabbed a handful of spiced almonds and popped a few into his mouth. I nudged the remaining ones back in place. A gesture I realized my mother would have made.

He made as if to spit the almonds back into his hand. "Oh, am I not supposed to eat these? Are these decorative nuts?"

I wondered how Pooter and my friend Julie would mingle. Would his sarcasm irritate her? Would she be condescending toward him? Maybe it was a mistake to have invited them together, especially on a holiday that was so loaded with cliché and expectation. And yet, that was precisely why I invited them. These two completely unsentimental friends were exactly the kind of company I wanted. Knowing Dan would be ringing in the new year with Patricia at an elegant dinner party with their writer-surgeon-professor-investment banker friends, there was no way I was going to depress myself at another family-friendly First Night celebration. Or worse, at a bar.

Julie arrived in a flurry of cold air and crinkly paper bags. She'd brought two bottles of champagne and an assortment of muffins and scones for New Year's Day breakfast, the abundance of which made me wonder if she was anticipating staying over.

Julie Lee and I met my first day on the job at Preston House, a day when I had borrowed my father's car, and got on the highway early to avoid traffic and make sure I arrived on time. I remember putting on my signal to change lanes and starting to move when another car approaching from behind, sped up to keep me from getting over. Swerving back into my lane to avoid a collision, I flipped off the driver. It wasn't until I was in the elevator that I realized the woman riding up with me was the same one who had cut me off.

"You really should drive more assertively," she told me.

"I had my signal on," I said fixing my stare on the illuminating floor numbers.

"But you weren't going. So, I did."

"You arrived here, what, three minutes sooner than I did? And look at that, we're in the elevator at the same time."

"Yeah, but only one of us is grumpy about her commute."

When I didn't respond, she said, "I'm Julie Lee. Are you going to orientation? Let's sit together." And with that, Julie Lee decided we would be friends.

I traded her my unopened beer for the Champagne bottles. She reached out and gave Pooter a handshake I knew to be almost painfully firm. "Hi, I'm Julie Lee."

"We've met," Pooter said. "You're in Legal. I sometimes bring contracts down for Audrey."

"Right, of course," Julie said with a winning smile.

I handed her my unopened beer. "I'm off to mash potatoes. Pooter, I assume you can handle the music?"

It was 8:37 p.m., a long way off from midnight. What were we going to do with all that time? What if we had nothing to talk about? I wished I'd made other plans. I wondered what shirt Dan would be wearing. Maybe the dark green one that set off his eyes. Or the one with French cuffs that he reserved for VIP lunches. He would undoubtedly have on his father's Omega watch so he could stretch out his arm and count down the last ten seconds of the year.

Pooter yelled from the living room. "Think you have enough James Taylor?"

Julie chimed in, "Oh man, I used to get stoned all the time listening to James Taylor in my dorm."

"That explains why you don't remember me."

"Precisely why you shouldn't take it personally."

I was relieved that Pooter was opting for charming over caustic. It could easily have gone the other way. It still might, I supposed.

"In any case, I correctly assumed your music collection would suck, so I brought some of my own."

From his coat hanging on the hook, Pooter pulled a small, zippered case from his coat hanging on the hook and started flipping through CDs. He put on a band called Old 97's and tried to get us to appreciate the "awesomeness" of a song whose mix of bluegrass and fast-driving punk managed to pull off a country song set in Queens. When we failed to show the proper amount of enthusiasm, he called us unimaginative, and switched the disc out for a live recording of Billie Holiday in a German nightclub, a better set for dinner.

The short ribs were fall-off-the-bone tender, balanced between hearty and delicate, cooked to the letter of the recipe. I was warmly pleased by their success. The easiest part of the meal, the mashed potatoes were lumpy and lackluster; the beet and apple salad bled into them turning the edges a vivid pink.

Julie had second helpings of everything and poured herself the last splash of the first bottle of wine. Though she was an even five feet tall, she was exceptionally lean and athletic, a twice-a-year marathoner, who almost never failed to do at least a six-mile run before work, even when the roads were clotted with slush.

I often wondered why a textbook, Type-A personality like Julie had the patience, let alone interest, to sustain a friendship with me, inclined as I was toward sleeping in and to putting off decisions. She found it exasperating that I was flatly unwilling to set goals for myself. In fact, over time, Julie had adopted the unsolicited role of motivation coach, facilitating me through the processes of asking for a raise and negotiating my condo purchase, but also helping me feel indignant in certain situations when I didn't have the instincts to do so myself.

But for all that, plus three years of shared meals and girls' night outs, we knew very little about each other's histories and inner lives. So, it was easy for me to keep from telling her about Dan, a revelation that would either end my friendship with Julie or, more likely, the relationship with Dan. And I wasn't interested in divesting myself of either at that point.

Pooter moved the salad around on the plate, making fork-shaped dents in it. "You're not fooling me," I said to him.

"It's not you, it's me. I hate beets."

Julie was opening the second bottle of wine. "I have an ex-boyfriend who said the same thing. Only it was more like, 'It's not you, it's me. I hate you.'" She let out a high-pitched laugh.

Pooter held out his glass. "How could anyone hate someone whose name sounds like singing? Joo-Lee-Lee, Joo-Lee-Lee."

This time her laugh was full of warmth and girlishness. She stood up, "Well, Joo-Lee-Lee is going to the loo."

When I heard the bathroom door close, I said to Pooter, "I can't tell if you're flirting or not."

Pooter took a sip, "Me neither."

"She is so the opposite of your type."

"What's my type?"

I started pulling the dirty dishes toward me.

"Seriously, Audrey, I don't date. So, what's my type? Clearly, she's female. Not likely a serial killer."

"Those are high standards."

Pooter gathered up the silverware. "I could do a lot worse than Julie Lee."

"She could do a lot better," I said flicking a napkin at him.

As the evening carried on, the banter remained playful and easy. Julie kept us entertained with travel stories, like the one about coaching and guiding a blind friend on a five-day hike to the top of Machu Picchu, and another about tracing her roots and meeting distant family members in a small village in South Korea.

But what most engaged Pooter was the revelation that Julie's brother was the lead singer in a funk-rock group called The Cock Asians, a band that was ranked #117 in "Pooter's Top 150 Bands, 1970 to Present".

"The Caucasians?" I asked.

Julie answered, "Yes, but no. The Cock. Asians. It's ok, they're all Asian."

"You've gotta hear them," Pooter said, and he hopped up and bolted to his car, returning a minute later with an even fatter case of CDs including two discs by The Cock Asians. This was all the motivation he needed to officially play DJ, providing Julie and me with a crash course in the "only music worth listening to." He served up old classics in order to highlight just that particular grace note or bass line that took a song from good to phenomenal, as well as songs from virtually unknown bands who seemed to have a disproportionate number of members who had died before they'd turned thirty.

Just before eleven o'clock, it occurred to me that I hadn't been thinking about Dan. Instead, I was genuinely enjoying New Year's Eve with these mismatched friends. We weren't wistful of the fact that others we knew were celebrating with their dates and their spouses, a few that had tucked their kids into bed hours ago. Arbitrary date or not, the pending arrival of the new year seemed to infuse our conversation with optimism, perhaps even offering that proverbial clean slate from which to make changes for the better.

As if reading my mind, Julie sat up and said, "It's time for some champagne."

"It's still an hour to midnight," I said.

Julie and Pooter looked at each other and laughed. "Pooter said you'd say that."

Julie opened the living room window to launch a champagne cork onto the frost-covered grass. Pooter got up with just a hint of sway and joined her. It occurred to me that I might be having *two* overnight guests.

As the champagne flowed, I brought out a plate laden with carefully cordoned pineapple triangles, hulled strawberries, banana wedges, ladyfingers, pretzel rods and lemon pound cake. In the center of the coffee table, I placed a steaming pot of brandy-laced chocolate fondue.

There was something primitive and communal in the way we knelt around the pot, each of us taking turns dipping our skewered morsels of food like sophisticated cavemen. On one of the darkest nights of the year, the Sterno flame was a comforting source of light and heat, even if it was from a can.

Julie ate a chocolate-dipped pineapple slice. "Mmm, I do fondue. Do you?" she said, wiping a drip from the corner of her mouth.

Pooter dipped a slice of banana, which slipped off his skewer and drowned. Instead of retrieving it, he stabbed into a strawberry. He raised the skewer in the air like a professor with a pointer. "Fondue: strawberries. Fondon't: tuna."

Julie snorted, "Ew."

I grabbed a cookie and held it up to my eye like a monocle. "Fondue: Nilla Wafers. Fondon't: pencil erasers."

"Fondue: candied orange peels," Julie said. "Fondon't: put the cost of a cute pair of Italian shoes on your expense account." She slapped a hand over her mouth and then hid behind her champagne glass.

"Oooh," said Pooter.

"It was on a business trip. I needed them for a meeting."

"Well, then." I said, "Fondue: cover your nose and mouth when you sneeze. Fondon't: admit that you've never actually read any of the books you've published."

They both raised their eyebrows at me. "Don't give me that look. That's the development editor's job!"

Pooter grabbed a pretzel rod and tapped his temple, "Fondue: make a fresh pot of coffee when you take the last cup. Fondon't: have a fling with your boss and think no one will find out about it."

With my bare hand, I caught the chocolate drips off a marshmallow that was halfway to my mouth. They burned, which may have been the only thing keeping me from launching across the table to throttle Pooter.

"Oh," said Julie. "Wow, I had no idea you two—"

Her misunderstanding was a gift. I had no choice but to run with it. "Yeah. It was just one date. Pooter and me. Not a fling," I added hastily. "We just had dinner. Once. When was that?"

I shot eye daggers at him, demanding that he follow my lead, or he was so fired.

"Yeah, that was, like, in the fall. We had dinner. But it was too weird," he said. "And like I said, someone was bound to find out. So that was it."

Julie nodded. You could see some skepticism in her expression, which seemed more attributable to whether we did or did not sleep together rather than that we were covering up something dicier.

"So, you two never—"

"No," said Pooter at the same time as I said, "Definitely not."

"Did you see her music collection?"

"He still lives with his parents."

Pooter had the good sense to steer the conversation toward the subject of awkward first dates, and after a couple painfully funny recounts from Julie, Pooter spoke unusually candidly about a blind date he'd had the year before with a woman who, it turned out upon meeting, was paraplegic.

"It was unexpected for sure. I had to admit to her during dinner that I was a little put off that she didn't tell me beforehand that she was in a wheelchair."

"You told her that?" I asked.

"She asked, so I was honest. I said I felt like I had probably been judged for a reaction I might not have had if I had known beforehand." He clarified, "It's not like I said or did anything rude when I met her, but I'm sure I showed some surprise or something in my expression."

"What did she say?" asked Julie.

"She said, 'Well, you didn't tell me you have brown hair.'"

"Not quite the same," I said.

"Her point was that needing a wheelchair to get around is part of who she is. It's just a fact like having brown hair is for me. It was a good conversation. Uncomfortable, for sure. Especially when she asked me point-blank, if the friend who'd set us up had told me she was paraplegic, would I still have agreed to the date? I had to admit that, horrible as it was, I probably would have found an excuse.

"But, I told her—and this was true—if a situation like that were to happen again, I wouldn't shy away from it. She gave me a lot to think about. We met for coffee once but we really didn't have miuch in common and that was it."

The story sandbagged the mood a little and prompted the first real lull of the night. Though we'd stopped picking at the fondue, the Sterno was still burning low, and we each seemed to get slightly hypnotized by its shimmering, blue fire. Then Julie glanced up behind me at the clock in the corner. "Oh my gosh, it's two minutes to midnight! Grab the other champagne and let's take it outside!"

We scrambled, Keystone Cops style, out the door and down the front steps. We clung to each other, Pooter between us, arms around each other's shoulders, as Julie held up her wristwatch and counted down from twelve.

Three-two-one...then we heard the POP-POP! POW! of fireworks in the distance. Pooter worked the cork on the champagne bottle, wedging it between his knees for leverage. When it finally fired off, the cork hit something that broke on impact.

"Oh shit, Pooter," said Julie.

I thought, better that it's one of Mrs. Ass' ceramic pots than her window. We tried and failed to stifle our laughter with our hands. Pooter foisted an overflowing bottle of champagne on me. We took turns swigging and whooping with the honks and toots and clatters from the building across the street. Maybe it was the coupling couple.

I looked up at the night sky; the stars were blocked by dense cloud cover. Maybe it would rain, maybe snow, maybe the clouds would clear. The coming year was equally obscure. And so, among friends, I stumbled my way into 1997.

8: opposable Thumbs

There were four stalls in the women's bathroom nearest my office. I considered the second stall to be mine, having consciously selected it on my first day on the job and never using another, even waiting or leaving the bathroom and returning later if it was occupied. This wasn't a matter of habit; I had strategically determined that it was likely to be the least frequently used of the four, and for some reason, that mattered to me. So, it was not without a small amount of horror that I discovered early one morning that my stall had been defaced.

"You are so shitty."

That's what it said, scratched into the beige paint with a key or perhaps a paper clip. It was on the inside door so that you had no choice but to stare at it during your moment of biological need and have that message stare right back at you: "You are so shitty."

The writing was not big or bold, but neatly composed in compact, straight, evenly spaced letters. At a publishing company, even the graffiti started with a capital letter and ended with a period. No contractions used here, the message was pointed and deliberate. Someone had gone into the stall with a pounding heart, fresh and full of frustration and anger, and took her time to express it anonymously in this public (albeit semi-private) forum.

But for whom was it intended? My first thought went to Liza Batista, the executive editor for Social Sciences who was notorious for her mercurial demeanor and the relentless pace with which she chewed through admin assistants. A smile or kind word from Liza was as rare as her stern admonishments were frequent—and not just to those staffers that she managed, but also to colleagues at her level of seniority.

Just the week before, I had overheard her with someone in her office, "You're useless today. Go home and come back tomorrow when you're ready to use your God-given brain."

It wasn't that she was an angry woman, just focused. But while most people thought she was simply a bitch, I respected her. Her delivery may not have been pleasant, but she always seemed to have a legitimate gripe when she chose to express it. And as part of the senior staff, a woman, one of the few African Americans represented at that level, I thought she was smart for building a steely persona around herself. Few ever endeavored to challenge her.

It could have been any number of women who might have aimed that message at Liza. But then I wondered if, instead, the message was an act of self-loathing. A message by the writer to the writer, a confession of sorts. I read once that keeping secrets causes significant stress on the brain that can only be released by articulating that secret in some capacity. Whether it's unburdening with a friend or on a radio call-in show, the very act of sending the information out of the brain helps re-establish a sense of mental equilibrium. Perhaps the vandal was responsible for a hit-and-run accident. Maybe she was an arsonist. Or maybe she was a compulsive bathroom vandal. Maybe she was simply having digestion issues.

"Maybe it was meant for you," Pooter suggested.

I had told him about the graffiti as we ate sandwiches in my office during what was supposed to be a working lunch outlining February's calendar of events. But there wasn't much actual work happening.

"I don't piss people off," I said. "Certainly not to that extent."

"It's just a little coincidental that the message happens to show up in the one and only stall that you use."

"Until five minutes ago, no one but me knew that was the only stall I use."

"So you think. People can be pretty observant."

"That still doesn't answer the question why someone would write a message like that about me."

"No ideas?"

"None."

"Not one reason? Nothing you've done?" And then I got what he was driving at.

"Yeah well, like my bathroom stall preference," I said. "You're the only one who knows about that. So, unless you're sneaking into the women's bathroom to try and shame me by writing cryptic messages, I'm not too concerned. You're just trying to make me paranoid."

"You know, it is possible that someone has seen you two together. Or caught a lingering glance by the water cooler—"

"We don't do that!"

"Or maybe he told someone who told someone—"

"He wouldn't do that."

"Maybe the whole office knows and you're the only one who doesn't know they all know it."

It felt like a kick to the gut. He must have seen my face fall because he quickly tried to recover.

"I'm just teasing you, Audrey."

"What have you heard? What do you know? Who knows?"

"Nothing, nobody. I swear."

"I don't believe you. I need to know, Pooter. You need to tell me."

"I haven't heard anything. I just carried the joke too far is all. You know me. It's only funny when it's no longer funny."

True words, but I still didn't totally believe him.

"I swear on my nana's life that I have not remotely heard anyone say anything about your relationship. As far as I know, your secret is vault-tight."

Invoking his grandmother carried some weight, but I remained on edge. When I was sure no one else was in the bathroom, I went in and examined every other stall, hoping to find other instances of graffiti, but there were none. And so, I did the only thing that was in my immediate power to do: I changed my stall to number three.

The raccoons were rattling the garbage cans at the house next door. For months, the Cavanaughs had tried everything short of poison to keep the marauders out, putting cement blocks on top of the cans, replacing the aluminum ones with big lock-top plastic bins, bungee cording the lids to the handles. Still, the raccoons' determination and opposable thumbs managed to pry the tops open, and in the morning, the Cavanaughs would wake to yet another wreckage of refuse: banana peels, shredded coffee filters, fat wads of tissues, yogurt containers, undecipherable leftovers—all of it strewn across the driveway. The garbage pick-up crew would simply bypass the scene, keeping to their schedule, and the Cavanaughs would be stuck with both the clean-up and a trip to the dump. There were worse problems in the world, but I sympathized with them.

"Maybe they should arm me with a BB gun," I said aloud.

Dan was in bed next to me flipping through a three-week old copy of *The New Yorker*.

He regarded me over the top of his glasses. "What?"

"Who. The Cavanaughs."

He shook his head, "I..."

"Oh. The raccoons."

"You've named the raccoons?"

"No, the neighbors. The raccoons are in the Cavanaughs'—the neighbors'—trash again. From the guest room window, I'd have a clear shot."

"You with a gun."

"A BB gun."

"You'd break a window with the first shot."

Dan had unexpectedly stopped by earlier with a lukewarm pepperoni pizza and a bottle of wine. I was planning on spending the evening switching out my summer clothes. It seemed like a worthy effort now that fall had come and gone, and we were three and a half weeks away from Valentine's Day. Having the opportunity to further procrastinate on this particular chore wasn't unwelcome, I could just continue to ride it out until the weather turned warm again. But I had a pinch of a wish that he'd called first, if only to fool us both into thinking I might have had more compelling plans on a Friday evening.

It was the third night that week he'd been over. Patricia was out of town for an undetermined amount of time. I had overheard Dan telling Rigid that she had landed a gig for a Japanese cigarette company whose oddly ironic advertising campaign featured extreme athletes doing insane things in amazing parts of the world. That week she'd been in British Columbia attempting to photograph a trio of hot, young snowboarders. Bad weather had made it impossible for the helicopter to take them to their "first descent" peak, and so the crew was on hold, no doubt eating well and enjoying a variety of spa treatments on the client's dime.

"What are you doing on Sunday?" I asked him. "We could go skeet shooting. There's a place—"

"It's winter, silly. And why the sudden interest in shooting things?"

"Maybe I'm looking for a career change."

"As an assassin?"

"At least I'd have a travel budget."

"You're back to this?" He put down his magazine.

"Well, you're keeping me off the trip to Vegas, so why can't I do the San Diego conference?"

"As much as I'd like to, Audrey, I just can't justify it. Warren is eyeballing every expenditure. Plus, I already turned Renny down for his request to go to some tax seminar in Albuquerque. Maybe we can swing something after the fiscal year, but not now."

I barely suppressed my pouting. It had seemed like the perfect getaway plan—a college friend's wedding in San Diego was coinciding with an economics conference at SDSU, which was a great opportunity for scouting new writers.

"Why don't you just take some vacation days?" Dan asked.

"Maybe I will." I said it as if it were a dare. "You know, a guy I dated in college is going to be at the wedding."

"I don't do the jealous thing if that's what you're fishing for."

I thought about Christopher from back then. Tall, thin, barely five hairs on his chin to be shaved. We were great friends that thought we should try to become a great couple, and so we fumbled around once on the rug in my apartment trying not to wake my roommate, but at some point, we just looked at each other and decided we'd rather watch *The Terminator* on cable.

I plucked at some lint on the blanket. "He's bringing his boyfriend, so there's no need anyway."

Dan returned to the magazine. I picked up my book and read the words on the page, but their meaning didn't quite materialize. For the last few days after my conversation with Pooter, there had been a busy part of my brain that wouldn't quiet down.

"Dan, do you think people know?"

"Are we talking about raccoons again?"

"You and me. Do you think people at the office know?"

"Well, have you told anyone about us?"

I made sure there wasn't even a second's hesitation in my reply.

"That's crazy. Why would I do that?"

"Well, I haven't either, so why would you worry?"

Dan's inherent lack of concern over what people thought was something I couldn't imagine for myself. It was the kind of self-confidence that came from being at a constant level of high accomplishment at work and earlier, during his school days. I gathered from stories he was an impressive athlete from a young age, and I knew he was a competent jazz pianist. His parents were still living, still married, and he got along with his siblings, so he seemed to have no family baggage. I doubted he had even had an awkward teenage phase. At a time when all his friends were fumbling around with their big feet and bucked teeth, acne and greasy hair, he was probably just the right height and weight, with his features all in as perfect proportion as they were now.

And if at the office, it was revealed that he was having an affair with a member of his own team, he'd probably get hearty slaps on the back from the old boys, and, at worst, an eye roll from everyone else. Except maybe Rigid who would purse her lips like a church lady and never speak to him again. And Liza Batista who would tell him outright that he was pathetic.

But for me, there would be ugliness. And the irony was that people would assume that I was sleeping with him to further my own career ambitions, when it couldn't be farther from the truth. I wasn't sure exactly what my motivations were, but there were times when I wondered if I was sleeping with Dan because he was a better catch than I would otherwise have merited. And even though I was baffled as to why I had ever attracted his interest; I was also filled with a simple and pure happiness for having done so. Nevertheless, I was always aware that this fling could end in some kind of messiness. And if the affair became known at work, my career there, however mediocre, would be over, but Dan would continue to sail along.

I knew that wasn't totally fair. Whatever the flaws in his marriage, he clearly wasn't abandoning it. He stood to lose more than I did.

"I just wonder if people pick up on subtle signs that we may not even be aware of. What about pheromones?"

He started laughing, "I don't think pheromones work that way." He laid the magazine down on his chest. "Have I done something at work that is making you uncomfortable? Do you feel like I'm treating you differently from everyone else?"

These days, it was hard to think much about the pre-affair Dan without the context of the present bedfellow Dan, but if I were honest, I had to admit that, no, nothing had changed at the office.

"I guess not."

"You just need to get better at compartmentalizing."

"That's hard to do. Especially during really boring meetings."

"Oh?"

"Yeah, like your budget ones. It's like you're talking, but I only zero in on the business jargon that sounds lewd. Like when you say, 'There are lots of moving parts.'"

He took off his glasses. "Really."

"Or 'We've got to drill down.'" I deepened my voice in an imitation-Dan style that sounded nothing like Dan.

He rolled over and closer. "Any others?"

"The word 'spreadsheets' makes me blush."

"I'll need to keep this in mind next Tuesday."

"That wouldn't be compartmentalizing."

He laced his fingers through mine. Pulling me over on top of him, we kissed and teased. I had once dated a carpenter whose hands were scratchy and raw, as if he could use just the surface of them to smooth an edge of pine. Dan's hands were uncalloused, white-collar soft and sensual. Both were appealing in their own way.

With the luxury of a Saturday morning before us and no Patricia looming on the horizon, we took our time redefining the topography of my bed. Later, I listened to the sound of him brushing his teeth while he hummed a scrap of song I didn't recognize. For whatever else I claimed in my mind, here was the realest reason I was sleeping with Dan: it was a lot of fun.

He sauntered back from the bathroom naked. "Looks like your cross-the-way neighbors are at it again."

"Is that why you took so long brushing your teeth?"

He slid back into bed. "Oh hey," he said, "Are you going grocery shopping tomorrow?"

I shrugged noncommittally.

"If you do, would you mind getting me a bag of that Colombian coffee? I can't get it at my place and I'm almost out."

"I wasn't planning on going, but I guess I can. I need to pick up my pills anyway. Assuming that you still want to have sex with me for another month."

"Yeah, that works for me."

"OK, then."

The raccoons had gone. The passing cars on the street made a shushing sound on the rain-wet pavement.

"G'nite," I said and turned off the light.

"What would you do?" Dan asked, "If you got pregnant."

Since the day I started taking birth control at nineteen, I hadn't missed a single pill. I'd never even given a thought to unplanned pregnancy.

"Depends. Who's the father?"

"Are you ever serious?"

I pinched a fold in the sheet and twisted it. "I don't know, Dan. What would you do?"

"I think I'd be OK with it."

His words floated like a helium balloon between us, hovering but not sailing away. "Well, that may be. But it doesn't answer the question."

"No, I guess it doesn't. Sorry," he said. "That was unfair."

"Yep."

"I'm sorry," he said again.

"I know. It's fine. Good night," I said, not wanting to talk more about it.

I rolled over but made no attempt to fall asleep. The strange thing, I realized, was that it wasn't the question about getting pregnant that first hit a sour note. It was the other question, the am-I-going-grocery-shopping question. Simple, casual, nothing inappropriate about it. And yet, as soon as he'd asked, before any mention of a hypothetical fetus, it had tweaked me.

It took some mental digging to understand why. And then, as if I'd picked up a well-wedged stone and found a squirming, leggy thing trying frantically to escape the light of day, I realized that something had been nagging me, not just in that moment, but over the course of the last few weeks since I followed Patricia in the grocery store. I had been bait-and-switched. I was no mistress; I was the misses—the homebody, the sit-on-the-couch-and-read-a-book pal, the cooking-dinner-grocery shopper. Patricia, who whirled about the world and landed back in town for stints to attend gallery openings and celebrity fundraisers, to have urgent, enthusiastic I-miss-you-so-much sex with Dan, Patricia was the mistress.

It took way more verbal restraint than I thought myself capable of to not sit up in bed and shout, "I'm not your domestic surrogate!" I kept quiet, still a little unsure about this revelation, figuring that sometimes a bag of coffee is just a bag of coffee. But then, I reminded myself, a baby is never just a baby.

9: Shellacked

I was moving full tilt about the condo with a breath-less combination of panic and thrill. Bathroom first. I pulled, fluffed, and refolded the towels into neat, hanging rectangles.

Then, unraveling a wad of toilet paper, I swiped out a slug of toothpaste that had been haunting the sink for the last three days. I elbowed a smudge on the mirror, then looked at the shower.

Screw the shower. I closed the curtain.

On the living room chair was a heap of clean but wrinkled laundry that I had intended to fold later that night. I bear-hugged the pile and hefted it to the spare room, where I tossed all of it onto the futon. I went back to collect dishrags, junk mail, empty CD cases, and anything that had been shipwrecked around the living and dining rooms. The futon was the dumping ground for that lot, too, before I closed the door with satisfaction that the bulk of the mess had disappeared fairly easily.

I figured on having seventeen more minutes to minimize the chaos. The call had actually startled me out of an early evening nap, induced by a book about personal finance that Julie had loaned me. When I wasn't immediately greeted with a voice on the other end, I figured it was a telemarketer and nearly hung up. But then the caller, a man, knew my name.

"Is this Audrey?"

I couldn't place the voice. My mind tried to match it to old friends and past flings, but there wasn't enough to go on.

"Yeah. Who's this?"

There was another pause. I started to feel uneasy, wondering if I was about to receive bad news.

"This is. This is James. Keefner. I—"

"Not funny, Dan."

"Wait. What?"

"Wait. What what?"

"I'm in the area," the voice said, "At my dad's old place on Darden Ave?"

"Seriously, knock it off."

"Really, it is me. I ran into you at the bagel shop after Thanksgiving. You offered me boxes?"

My feet froze in place. I put my hand over the receiver in case I gasped, or worse, squealed.

"Oh, yes, of course. I can get you boxes. How many?"

"No," he laughed a little. "I don't need boxes, that's not why I am calling. It's my wife, Chloe, she has an idea for a children's book I wanted to maybe run by you. You said you worked in publishing."

"I...well, I work. It's college books, textbooks, that I work in. Economics—I mean, yeah. Anytime. I would love...be totally cool to talk about her idea some time. Even though."

"I actually called your old house. It's the same number I remembered from high school. Isn't that funny?"

"You talked to my father?"

"I didn't say who I was. Just that I was an old friend."

I still wasn't totally convinced this wasn't a hoax. But no one other than Dan knew the story. I never ended up telling Kenny because I knew it would get back to Bobbie, and she would go ballistic at me for not letting her accost him at the cemetery.

"So how far away are you from your old house?" Jamie asked me.

I sat down on the couch. "Forty minutes, give or take."

"I was thinking, if you're not having other plans, maybe I can, you know, stop by."

My hands were shaking. *What was this epic joke?* "You mean when, tonight?" There was silence on the other end. "Jamie, are you still there?" I asked.

"'Jamie.' I haven't heard that in forever." There was a palpable heaviness coming through the phone.

"I..." he said. "What's not true...is that thing about the kids' book. That was dumb. But I am at the old house, and it's just...and I..." his voice trailed off.

"Sure, Jamie. James," I said. "Definitely. Come over. Do you have a pen? I'll give you directions."

In the kitchen, I emptied the dish rack and let soapy water fill the sink to soak off day-old tomato sauce and other meal remnants. The counters were in fairly decent shape, just a quick wipe-down, and then it was back to the bathroom to work on the other mess: me.

No time for a proper hair washing; a rinse and a damp comb-through would have to do. I set my face with a light flip of a blush brush and touch of lip balm. Ditching the sweats, I pulled out a favorite pair of old jeans from the pile of clothes on the futon and a gray tee that I knew fit well but looked like something I would have thrown on after work.

I went back to the kitchen to put away the dishes in the rack. With one plate to go, there was a quiet knock at the door. My pulse rate shot up instantly. One breath in, two breaths out. I tossed the dishtowel under the sink and smoothed down my clothes as if to calm my frantic aura.

Even through that weird fishbowl lens of the peep-hole, I could see it was clearly James Keefner. He was looking down at his shoes in that same defensive pos-ture he used at the bagel store when I opened the door.

"Hi."

"Hey."

"Come in."

I looked behind him to see if there was an entourage with him. Then, James Keefner stepped over the thresh-old to my home. I couldn't help but think this was just how a vampire encounter was supposed to happen.

"Sorry about the clutter," I said. "I live alone and wasn't expecting anyone. Plus, I'm sure you're used to more sophisticated settings."

"Well, my father's place is no great shakes either."

Either? I flinched.

He stood politely on the mat by the door, looking less fresh than he had at the bagel shop, and certain-ly less polished than in television interviews. His hair was shaggy, but not in a trendy way, in an uncombed way. His eyes looked tired and, I could see, they were showing some faint corner crow's feet. Even still, he was painfully handsome.

"Your coat? Did you want to sit? I'm not sure what..."

"It's fine."

He took off his coat and handed it to me. Soft, dark cashmere. Like an exotic animal in my hands.

"Should I make coffee? Or some food? Are you hun-gry? I can do pasta. Or pancakes!"

He shook his head. "I'm really sorry to come barg-ing in on you like this. I just needed...I just." He swept a hand down over his face. "At the old house... It was..." He seemed to run out of words.

I started walking to the couch thinking he'd follow. Over my shoulder, I said, "After my mom died, I didn't go by the house for months because something as stupid as seeing a bottle of her favorite shampoo was enough to wreck me. I don't know how my dad stayed—stays—there. Especially now."

He was still in the hallway. "Listen, I'm really exhausted with the time difference and everything. Do you maybe have a pullout couch or a guest room? I should have asked over the phone."

Sleep here? Oh. Then I thought of the guest room that had just become my domestic landfill.

"I just need a place to crash for the night and then I'll get out of your hair."

"Yes," I said. "I have a guest room. You'll have to give me a minute to set it up."

"I can help with that."

"No," I put up my hand firmly. "No, no. It won't take much. Just have a seat and pretend you're someplace a little more...posh."

I disappeared into the guest room and closed the door behind me. I had no choice but to shove the entire mess into the closet, which was already well stuffed.

"Mind if I wash up a little?" I heard him ask.

"Of course, bathroom is around the corner on the right. In fact," I paused, thinking about the items in my medicine cabinet, then with an all-clear, I said, "There's a new toothbrush in the medicine cabinet if you need one."

"Thanks, that's great."

Once I heard him close the bathroom door, I darted to the hallway linen closet for sheets and a couple of pillows. Every few seconds, I got another star-struck lightning bolt when I realized that James Keefner was in my home, using my bathroom, about to sleep on my futon. It was thrilling and weird and a little terrifying and very weird.

After I had wrestled the futon flat, I opened the door to the guest room. I was just tucking the sheet under the foot of the mattress when he came in to help. It was like being in the presence of a living hologram. From one angle, I saw James Keefner, *People* magazine's sexiest man of 1993, stunning in full tuxedo on the Oscars red carpet; and then with a turn to his profile, Jamie Keefner, an average, brown-haired kid from the New Jersey suburbs.

Though average didn't really apply, even back then. My clearest memory was when I was about eleven and he a skinny-waisted, shirtless sixteen-year-old, playing basketball with Kenny, Owen, and Pete in our driveway. The slam, slam, slam of the ball on the pavement pulled me from my homework to the window where I watched them. No, not them. Only Jamie. Jamie going up for a lay-up and missing. Him goofing with the ball behind his back. "C'mon Jamie, just pass the fuckin' ball," Pete said. Jamie wiped the sweat above his lip with a fingertip while he slammed the ball at the pavement twice more, took a jump shot and caught nothing but net. He raised his arms high overhead, and I sank low below the windowsill so I wouldn't be seen.

I tossed Jamie a pillowcase.

"Hey, listen," he said. "I know it's going to be hard, but I need to you to promise me you won't tell anyone, not a single living person, that I'm here. Or even that you've seen me."

That was disappointing. "Oh."

"And I should probably tell you something." Maybe this was all some method acting thing he was working on? "You're probably going to hear some unflattering news about me."

"Like what?"

"I don't really want to talk about it tonight. I just need to get some rest."

"OK. As long as the cops aren't going to come beating on my door," I laughed.

But he didn't laugh. I tossed a second pillow onto the bed. "I have to go in to work tomorrow. I'm on standby for my assistant who's setting up at a tradeshow. But you can be here as long as you like. Whatever you need. I can try to sneak out early and bring home some take-out."

"That's sweet, but I won't need to stay." He looked out toward the living room. "Hey, I didn't see a TV anywhere. Is it in a cabinet or something?"

I instinctively moved in front of the closet door, blocking a potential avalanche. "I actually don't have a TV."

He was incredulous.

"It broke about three months ago, and I haven't had a chance to replace it."

"You don't have a TV? Not even a little black and white one?"

I shook my head. He sighed heavily. "How am I going to know what they're saying about me?"

"I have a radio?"

He sighed again, even heavier.

"Are you sure you don't want to talk about it?" I asked.

He pressed his lips together in a straight line and shook his head.

"Right, OK. I'm sorry I don't have a TV for you. Anyway, there's cereal, milk, eggs. Help yourself to whatever in the morning."

"Thanks, Audrey."

There was my name again, coming from his mouth. Where many Jersey friends called me "Awdree", he gave the first syllable more breath and space "Auhdree." No doubt he had worked to lose his hometown accent.

I was sure he'd be gone by morning, maybe even leaving in the middle of the night to find a hotel, somewhere with a TV. But maybe during a time of bad publicity, staying out of the public eye was a good call. And the fact that he'd called me, essentially a stranger, suggested that he didn't have a better option in the area.

Satisfied that he might remain a guest at least overnight, I headed to the bathroom to get ready for what would no doubt be a sleepless night. I pulled a stretch of floss from its reel and was just about to begin cleaning my teeth when I saw it in the bathroom mirror. Beige. Worn out. Pathetic. The one Dan not-so-affectionately called "The Beast." My bra, the most comfortable, unsexiest of all bras in the history of bras, was hanging on the back of the door, one of its lumpy, wrinkled cups pointing at me like a nasty, stuck-out tongue.

It did, in fact, turn out to be a night of minimal sleep. I'd rolled from one side to another and back again, got up to pee, fought the temptation to peek in on Jamie. I put an extra blanket on, took the extra blanket off, tried reading, and eventually dozed around two thirty in the morning. When the radio clicked on three and a half hours later, I felt sludgy, as if I had oatmeal in my veins. When I headed to the bathroom, I was thrilled to see the door to the guest room was still closed.

Freshly showered and wrapped in a thick, pink bathrobe with a towel turban on my head, I stood paralyzed in the hallway, realizing with dismay that all my clean work clothes were heaped in the closet in the guest room. I slipped inside ninja-quiet to grab an outfit and bolt.

But since I was there, I had to look. The world had seen every detail of James Keefner's face on the big screen, but how many could actually claim to have seen him unguarded, slack-jawed and sleep-tousled. Maybe he drooled.

But in the dim light, all I could see was a lump of covers. I heard his slow breathing, just shy of a snore. Dimly disappointed, I got a hand to the closet door-knob when I heard him stir. Panicking, I bolted from the room. Realizing I wouldn't have the nerve to go in again, I plumbed my bedroom closet for an outfit, only to find blouses I hated, a suit I wore once, and summer dresses. Though it was forty-three degrees out, I opted for a blue, floral sundress, layered up with tights and a cardigan. It was not a winning style.

In the kitchen, I pulled a box of Cheerios and a trio of bananas, leaving both on the counter beside a note with my office phone number:

> *There are (Ronnie's) bagels in the freezer. Coffee maker is set up, just turn it on. There are cold cuts and bread for lunch or Mac n' Cheese. I left some old photo albums out that I thought you'd enjoy looking through. Give a call (201) 555-1212 x 331 and let me know if I should cut out of work early. –A*

He wouldn't call, I figured. He would just leave. That was why I pulled out the photo albums, figuring that a walk down memory lane might nudge him to stay for dinner.

I settled into my commute, turning the dial to one of those obnoxious morning radio programs simply to hear if there would be a report on whatever was going on with James Keefner. Instead, the DJs were trying to outgross each other by telling their worst emergency room visits. Then they started flirting with a female traffic reporter, who let us know that an accident had just been cleared on Route 17, which was where I was headed. A nice bit of morning luck.

The parking lot was thin due to the conference coinciding with a sales meeting, and I managed to get a space much closer to the door than I normally would. Inside, there was less bustle, more cubicle loitering, the mood more relaxed with so much of the senior staff gone for the rest of the week.

Pooter's chair was pushed in, and his desk was a neat pile of paperwork he'd left handy for me just so he could get uppity and say, "Did you look in the file? It's right there where I left it for you on my desk."

Though Jamie had asked me not to, it would have been impossible to go through the day without confiding in at least one person. Bobbie would have manufactured some excuse to come over and see him, so I didn't dare tell her. I didn't have Dan's itinerary so I didn't know where he would be staying, but I did have Pooter's. Over the past few months, I had seen no evidence that he had told anyone about Dan and me, so my confidence in his discretion had been reassured.

Though it was only 5:43 a.m. Vegas time, I dialed his hotel and the front desk put me through. The phone rang once, twice, thrice. On the fourth ring, I heard the receiver tumble on the nightstand.

"Wha?"

"Hey there, Johnny Vegas."

"Jesus, why are you calling?"

"Oh, it's not Jesus. It's me, Audrey."

"I'm not even laughing on the inside."

"Sorry. I know it's early—"

I could feel the eye roll from 2,500 miles away.

"Then call back when I'm alive." "C'mon. I have mind-blowing news."

There was the sound of the phone being set back down on the nightstand followed by an elephant-blare of a nose blow, followed by a sneeze, followed by another nose blow. He returned.

"Ugh. I think I'm allergic to hotel linens." He yawned loudly. "What."

"So, I'm at home last night when, at about quarter to eight, the phone rings. You're not going to believe who it was."

"Oh," he said, sounding more interested. "Was she all like, 'You bitch, I am going to make pâté from your entrails and serve it at my next cocktail party?'"

"Ew, no, it wasn't Patricia."

He sneezed again, this time into the phone. "Sorry, that one came without warning."

"I promised I wouldn't tell anyone about this, so you've got to swear to me on everything you care about that this goes in the vault."

"That's fine. But given that you're about to break the very same promise you made to someone else, I'm not sure how committed I need to be."

"You're the only person I trust this with. Not Dan, not my sister—"

"Dan's a cheater, and you told me Bobbie is a big-mouth—"

"James Keefner."

He stopped talking. "What about him?"

"Remember over Thanksgiving, I said I had stalked a celebrity?"

"Vaguely."

"It was him. But it was just a quick encounter. So last night," I lowered my voice, "that's who called me."

"He's on the news, you know."

"You heard? What happened? What are they saying? I haven't been able to find out—"

"No, no, you tell me first."

I told him everything in as little detail as possible so as to hear the media story quicker. He kept interrupting with various exclamations of disbelief, "Really?" "Serious?" "For real?" and then most obviously, "Why?"

"I don't know" I said. "But he was friends with my brother, so there's kind of a connection there."

"Well, here's what I heard on the news during my layover last night. It sounds like he flipped out at a family gathering and punched his wife's brother in the face. Then he took off."

"Oh," I said. "That's not good."

"Doesn't sound like they're pressing charges, though."

"What else did they say?"

"You know how those reports go, 'Sources close to the family say Keefner had been acting erratically.' That's, like, code-word for drugs, right?"

"Maybe. He seemed pretty straight last night, but what do I know?"

A light knock on the wall outside my office sent my heart hammering. It was Rigid.

"Hold on." I put a hand over the receiver and mouthed to her, "Important call, sorry."

Like a caricature of herself, Rigid put a hand on her hip, then walked in handing me a thick file. It was clear she found dubious my claim of the call's importance. I shrugged my shoulders and gave her a simpering smile, and she left with a slight shake of her head. After I no longer saw her shadow outside the door, I returned to the call.

"Here's what I think. Maybe he'd just had a big blowup with his wife's family, then he comes back to his childhood home, but there's nobody there," I said. "His dad had just died the summer before. And it's sad and it's lonely. So, he called someone who was kind of familiar. Makes sense, no?"

"More likely he's an addict. And he's using you for something. What if you go home today and find out that he moved a bunch of crackheads into your condo?"

"I guess I'll find out."

He was quiet for a few seconds. "Just, I don't know. Be careful. He's obviously got some issues. I'm not sure having him in your house is a good idea."

It felt strange that Pooter was being serious, and even more so that he might have a point. Still, I knew if I came home and James Keefner was still there, no way would I tell him to find another refuge.

"Thanks for the advice."

"Yeah," he mumbled. "If I hang up now, I can sleep another forty-five minutes."

"You might as well do that. You're going to be on your feet all day." Then I said, "Remember, you can't tell anyone."

"Who would I tell? Renny? That guy is such a wee-nie. I'll call you later to check in."

He hung up, and I was left with the task of wondering what excuse I could use to leave work early.

If a person mopes in her car, and there's no one there to see it, does it provide any emotional benefit? Jamie hadn't called at all during the day. It seemed a safe bet that his sanity had returned and he'd either found a better option or hopped a flight back to LA to deal with his troubles.

I'd caught a snippet of radio news providing speculation about James Keefner's whereabouts, "The forty-two-year-old actor is believed to be distancing himself from the situation, having traveled to New York yesterday. Sources close to the family will not confirm that he has checked into a rehab clinic."

"That's because he hasn't, asshole."

I wasn't buying the drug rumors. Jamie looked tired, not strung out. Then what, I wondered, had caused the violence? I knew his wife came from a well-bred English family with a lineage of dukes and duchesses, so naturally I assumed Jamie's brother-in-law was like all the British villains I'd seen in movies—a man with a practiced sneer and a penchant for saying things like, "Fetch me my riding boots."

The drive home was completely unremarkable. The kind where you have no real recollection of having traveled from point A to B. My consciousness had failed to notice the usual milestones along the way, and so when I pulled into the lot behind my building, it felt as if I had teleported there. Feeling lonely and a bit blue that my momentary brush with celebrity would be over, I parked the car.

And so, it was as if a dying ember in my chest had started to glow when I saw that the visitor's parking space was occupied by the same car that had been there when I left in the morning. The one with New York plates. Though I reminded myself it could have been someone else's overnight guest, I quickened my pace up the walkway.

For the first time since it happened, I noticed the ceramic planter that had broken when Pooter popped it with the champagne cork on New Year's Eve. I made a note to myself to poke around some night soon to see if I could find the cork. Maybe Mrs. Ass would just think the cold, or an animal broke it. In the meantime, I nearly galloped to the door.

Once inside, I was immediately struck by an unexpected smell. It was sweet and tangy.

Cinnamon, but also something else. "Hello?" I ventured.

I heard a pot clang in the sink. Then he appeared. A vision in jeans, a T-shirt, and bare feet.

"You said it was all right for me to hang out, so I decided to do that for today. Is that still OK?"

I was sure there were sparkles in my eyes. "Yeah, of course. *Mi futon es su futon.* I hope it wasn't too uncomfortable."

"I slept great. Better than I have in weeks."

I went to hang up my coat, then remembered my ridiculous outfit. "I'm just going to go change out of my work clothes."

Heading to my bedroom, I heard him say, "Oh, hey—"

Then I saw my clothes, folded in three neat stacks on my bed.

"They're a little wrinkly, but at least they're not heaped in the closet on my account anymore."

I wasn't sure if I should be pleased or horrified. It hadn't occurred to me that if Jamie chose to hang out while I was at work, there would be absolutely nothing to keep him occupied. And that free rein of my home meant that intimate aspects of my life would be exposed like curiosities on display in a museum exhibit: *Chaos and Conformity: The Modern Life of the Suburban, Single Woman.* And I realized, it wasn't just the catalogs I received or the magnets on the fridge, but also the kind of toilet paper I bought. My tampons. My glow-in-the-dark vibrator. *Oh.*

"Wow," I said. "What else have you been up to?"

He clapped his hands, "Right! Come to the kitchen."

I followed, now recalling the smell I had noted when I first came in.

Jamie was speaking quickly now. "Until today, I've never made anything more complicated than a grilled cheese."

He held out a small, red ceramic bowl like an offering.

"You made...applesauce?"

"Try some."

I got a spoon and took a taste.

"It's good, isn't it? I made it with just apples. Well, some water, sugar, and cinnamon, and pinch of salt. There was a recipe in your cookbook." He added, "I hope you don't mind."

"It's good. Really good," I said, realizing I sounded like an encouraging kindergarten teacher.

"Don't worry, I'm cleaning up right now."

Maybe he *was* on drugs. "Oh, I get it," I said. "You're studying up for a role as a 1950s housewife."

He looked at me, puzzled. "No. It's just, there were a lot of apples."

And so, while a mega-movie star washed my dishes, after having folded my laundry, I ordered some Chinese takeout. I liked this new life.

"Delivery should be here in about thirty minutes," I said. "Oh! You should totally answer the door. Can you imagine the look on the guy's face?"

"No," Jamie said. "Don't even joke like that." He looked at me with weight and seriousness. "You didn't tell anyone I was here, did you?"

I thought fast. "You told me not to."

He put the last spoon in the rack and turned off the water. "I just need breathing room, you know? It was too much."

His expression became pensive. Or was it confused? I wondered if he would ask me what I'd learned from the news, but he simply folded the towel and left the room.

The tall and short food cartons made a neat skyline at the cliff-end of the dining room table. The largest carton hadn't been touched.

"You know, I got that tofu-vegetable stir-fry for you. I thought you Hollywood types were particular about what you put into your body."

Jamie was relishing a fried dumpling and had already consumed a large helping of greasy beef lo mein.

"I'm not in Hollywood." He washed down the food with a satisfied swig of Heineken.

"Welcome to the anti-spa experience," I said. "Eat all the crap you want, sleep in, blow off spin class."

He let out a sigh and stretched a little. "I needed this."

"Mediocre *Chinese* food?"

"Alone time. Time out of the spotlight to just be, you know?"

"Yeah, not really something I struggle with."

I was about to walk a fine line: trying to draw him out without coming across as a gossip-hungry groupie. But I would have opened the same conversation with any other friend. So, I rationalized, I was just being myself.

"The news is saying you beat up your brother-in-law. Is that true?"

"As if truth matters."

It would have been disingenuous for me to argue with him on that. Instead, my silence seemed to leave space for him to elaborate.

"Look, a story is going to take on a life of its own once it's out in the world. And the story is much more compelling if I'm the bad guy."

"Then you didn't hit your brother-in-law?"

"Of course, I did. That's not the issue."

"He might disagree."

"That's exactly what I'm talking about."

"I'm sorry. You're right. People don't throw punches without provocation. What did he do?"

But I could see he had already shut down. He started picking again at the lo mein.

115

"Doesn't matter."

Snarky comments were great conversation movers with Pooter, but I sometimes forgot that most everyone else didn't appreciate feeling judged. This was probably especially true for someone who was constantly scrutinized for every ounce of weight gain, every awkward soundbite.

It seemed best to change the subject. "Hey, did you have a chance to look through those photo albums?"

"No, I didn't. I actually spent a lot of time reading one of your books about Woodstock."

"Here, come take a look. It's OK, bring your plate."

We shifted to the living room where I'd left two large faux-leather photo albums on the side table. I flipped ahead to a section that held scattered images of dogs, now long deceased, and grinning teenagers, their fluffy, fly-away hair marking them as kids caught in the tail end of the disco era.

Jamie stabbed a finger at a close-up of a freckle-faced kid crossing his eyes and looking menacing. "That's Marco D'Amore. He lived two doors down from me. We used to slingshot bottles in his backyard. Killed a chipmunk once. I remember going home and crying all night about it."

He slid his finger over the page. "That's Elaine Prouty and Megan Atherton. I don't know the guy."

"Hume. Troy Hume," I prompted.

"I barely remember him."

"There's Kenny and Owen."

"Oh my gosh, yeah. I totally remember that stupid fishing hat Owen wore all the time. What grade...must have been tenth."

"There's you—"

"With Caitlin Free. Frye. Freebird? Frybern? That was at Homecoming. Oh man, look at that jacket I'm sporting." It was white leather with two big isosceles triangles for a collar. "That's hilarious," he laughed and turned the page.

"Is that you?" He asked pointing to a photo of me and Bobbie wearing matching *Virginia Is for Lovers* T-shirts. My two front teeth were enormous. Kenny used to call me "Chiclet" because of them, though at the time I thought it a term of endearment meaning "little chick."

As we pored over the pages of those awkward candid moments, I thought that there might be something to the belief that a photograph steals a piece of your soul. No, not steals, collects. Keeps. The kids in the photos, we were like pinned butterflies, captured at our most colorful.

Jamie flipped back through a few earlier pages and landed on a five-by-seven family portrait. He turned the book sideways for a closer look.

"This is classic," he said.

And it was. Circa 1973. Dad sported a pair of soul-man muttonchops, while Mom's Aqua Net crown seemed to swirl and orbit around her head. Kenny had on a mustard yellow shirt with a zippered neckline. I was sitting pressed up against Bobbie, her slightly annoyed expression an early manifestation of the scowl line that would later become a prominent feature of her grown-up face. I was showing a forced, almost pained smile that prominently displayed the space where those two Chiclet teeth would eventually grow in.

"I know I said it before, but you really look so much like your mother."

Though other people have said the same in recent years, I didn't quite see it. And it wasn't a matter of not being able to recognize my own features on somebody else's face. That had happened before, when during the first few months of my freshman year at college, I was frequently called "Dana" by people passing me in the quad or in hallways. People I didn't know. Finally, one day, a guy on my dorm floor said his friend's new girlfriend—Dana—was a dead-ringer for me. He was determined to get us face-to-face. A few days later I was eating my lunch in the cafeteria when I saw him coming quickly in my direction, dragging a girl by the wrist. It was a bit of a spectacle as we drew a chorus of "wows" once people figured out what was going on. I had to admit, it was true. Dana looked more like a sister to me than Bobbie did.

When I didn't respond to his comment about my mom, Jamie said, "I bet you miss her."

"Yeah," I said. "It's been five years, but I still forget sometimes when I wake up in the middle of the night. It's like I think to myself, 'Wow, it's been a while since we talked. I should stop by and make them dinner.' And then I remember, and I feel sad all over again, like every time it's the first time I realize she's gone. Anyway though, she'd think it's amazing that you're here."

"Oh yeah? She knew about me?"

I laughed. "You do know there's a petition to rename the town park after you, right? My mom would have had to be living in a bunker to not know about you."

"I mean—" I had made him self-conscious again. "It's cool to me that she was able to see that I got somewhere after I left Jersey. My own dad..." he paused. "I didn't need a whole lot of validation from him, and he never gave it. But you know, if my life were a movie and I came back to clean out my father's house after he died, there would have been a box of magazine clippings, reviews, movie ticket stubs—stuff that showed that even if he couldn't say it, he was proud of my success. But in the real world, there wasn't anything like that. Just a bunch of old tax documents, appliance manuals, car service records. Stuff that doesn't matter to anyone after you're dead."

"I have no doubt he was proud of you."

Jamie shrugged. "Eh, we were never close. You know, I left, and he was alone the rest of his life. I don't think he ever forgave me, and I never felt bad about it, so..."

"You took off right after graduation?"

"I didn't graduate, remember."

"Oh my gosh, I totally forgot that."

He nodded. "I took off right after Christmas break. Hopped a bus to California. Never looked back. It turned out I would never need trigonometry."

"You just knew at that point you wanted to be an actor?"

He finished a last forkful of food and stood up. He held his hand out for my plate. As we walked toward the kitchen he asked, "Were you too young or do you remember the gypsy moths in '73? When they sprayed?"

"Oh yeah. I remember it, just barely. It was my friend Kristina's birthday, and her mom wouldn't let her bring cupcakes to school. I remember thinking that was the saddest thing ever, not having cupcakes in school on your birthday."

"It was weird day for sure."

§

For the first time in months, Jamie felt good. Sing out-loud good. And sing, he did, doing his best Robert Plant because you can't sing "Whole Lotta Love" without a whole lotta attitude. As he weaved his bike along the sidewalk, he tried to catch air wherever the concrete was dislodged, landing on the other side with a small skid on the gritty sand. It was one of those late spring days with bright sunshine and high clouds. The neighborhood yards were full of withering daffodils and faded purple hyacinths.

Things seemed to be taking on a new shade of normal, even though at home, the air between Jamie and his father was still heavy with discomfort and all the things they couldn't say to each other. They didn't spend much time together anyway. His father's commute to the city had him leaving before Jamie was awake in the morning, and rather than come home after school (on the days when he wasn't ditching), Jamie would go over to Kenny's or Owen's to play basketball or watch TV.

Today was a no-ditch day. For the first time in weeks, Jamie would actually be arriving to class on-time with his *The Lord of the Flies* essay, "The Good, the Bad and the Piggy" in-hand.

And while no one, least of all Jamie himself, would mistake this punctuality and productivity as anything more than a happy anomaly, he was planning on savoring the look on Mrs. Prior's face. She would make a fuss, he knew, playfully pretending to be knocked back into the chalkboard by the unexpected delivery of his assignment, on time. He liked Mrs. Prior, even if she could be annoying with her questions that always started with "Why do you think..."

After an unsanctioned shortcut through the Garcia's backyard, Jamie arrived at the backside of the school by the baseball field. Starting at home plate, he took off to first, skidded out his rear wheel and headed to second. Glancing up to see if there were any girls sitting on the steps by the gym, he noticed that there were neither girls nor guys hanging out there. He stopped and straddled his bike. No football players trading homework, none of the gossiping girls hanging in the doorway to the gym. He turned toward the deli next door where there were no burnouts smoking and goofing around in their Stooges and MC5 T-shirts. No one.

Was it Saturday?

Jamie started off on his bike, past the teachers' parking lot, which was empty—even the principal's space was vacant of its ever-present blue Volvo. No janitors with their brooms, no one running on the track. The only movement he could see was the sparrows pecking at a pizza crust near the garbage can. They seemed bolder in the eerie absence of harassing students.

Then, he noticed a girl sitting in the second row of the bleachers. With her gray sweatshirt, she was nearly camouflaged against the metal seats. Squinting, he could see she was flipping through a magazine.

"Hey," he shouted at her. She looked up, startled. He took off his headphones and waved to her, but she didn't wave back. Instead, she returned to her magazine.

Jamie rode over. Now closer, he recognized the girl—Carrie Carlisle, a senior. On any other day, he would have no business talking to her, not just because she was an upperclassman, but as the daughter of the longest seated mayor of the town, Carrie was somewhat of a resident celebrity. She was also a co-captain varsity cheerleader.

"Hey," Jamie said again when he was close enough to be heard without shouting. "What's going on? Where is everybody?"

There was a cigarette in Carrie's hand, which she held suspended away from her body as if it were resting on the arm of an invisible chair. She sneered at him like he was a thoroughly irritating insect.

She took a drag, blew the smoke sideways out her mouth. "They're poisoning the town today."

"What?"

She returned her attention back to the magazine. "They're killing the caterpillars. There's a memo on all the doors."

Now he remembered. In fact, he'd received two notices about the gypsy moth spraying, one that ended up as a football "flick" during detention and the other was likely crushed in the bottom of his backpack.

The gypsy moth infestation had begun the prior year. The wiry-haired caterpillars with red and blue spots made pilgrimages in such volume to the tops of nearly all the trees that property owners painted sticky glue belts around the trunks to keep them from reaching the crowns. But the effort did little to stop the caterpillars from decimating the leaves. And they were nearly everywhere on the ground. Jamie, Pete, Kenny and Owen would ride their bikes over them, both because it was unavoidable and because the boys liked the feel of how they popped like party snappers under the tires. Jamie remembered his mother saying that on windless nights she could actually hear the caterpillars chewing as they stripped entire branches overnight. In summer, they transformed into a nearly constant snowstorm of furry, white moths. With the problem reaching Hitchcockian proportions, the local towns had decided to strike back with pesticides that would be rained over the treetops from low-flying planes.

"Oh crap. We shouldn't be here, right? We should be inside somewhere, right?" As if Carrie were in charge simply because she was two years older. "It's got to be close to eight o'clock. What time are the planes supposed to fly over?"

"Eight o'clock," she said. "School is locked."

It might have been his imagination, but Jamie thought he could barely hear the low buzz of a plane in the distance. His mind went to the photo of the frozen-in-time, agony-filled expression of the napalmed kid in Vietnam. Jamie looked around in a mild panic. They could knock at a nearby house, but there was no guarantee anyone would be home or answer the door if they were. Should they smash a window to the school? Break into the snack shed?

"We gotta go somewhere." He decided the snack shed was their best option. He picked up his bike and turned back to Carrie, "Are you coming?"

Carrie considered a moment. Then she closed her magazine and followed him.

The shed was a small concrete building the size of a cabin. As a September tradition, the seniors would paint and then graffiti their names over the outside: sweethearts next to sweethearts, best friends next to best friends, though by the end of the year many of them no longer associated with each other. There were probably more than thirty years of names covering the cement bricks in fine sedimentary layers of high school history.

Jamie assessed the padlock on the door. Surely the shed had been broken into before; it couldn't be that hard. The hinge was a little rusty, the wood door wasn't new. He set down his bike and his backpack and pushed up his sweatshirt sleeves, feeling a little like a hero in a disaster movie. He took a couple of deep breaths before throwing his shoulder hard against the door once, twice, three times. Carrie, who had been digging in her purse, now stepped between him and the door.

He rubbed his shoulder. "Need a crowbar."

"Or this." She dangled a small, tarnished gold key at him. "Cheerleader privileges."

Now Jamie was sure he could hear a plane. "Just hurry up and open the door."

It was cool inside and there was a strong ghost smell of French fries. After he'd wheeled his bike in, Jamie pulled the door firmly shut behind him. Carrie tugged a string, which caused the fluorescent fixture above to buzz to life. At this time of year, the supplies were minimal but there was a stack of soda can six-packs, the generic kind: cola, orange, and root beer. And there was one small carton each of M&Ms, Sky Bars, Tootsie Rolls, and Charleston Chews on hand for the tennis matches and track meets.

Carrie sat down on one of the tables; she started rummaging through a white leather purse the size of a house cat. Jamie leaned against a support beam. The plane's engine was louder now, and he nervously looked up at the ceiling, relieved that he couldn't see daylight through any gaps in the roof.

"Good thing you knew where the key was."

She nodded.

"So, if your mom is mayor, she must have been in on this whole pesticide drop, right? Pretty funny you forgot it was happening today too."

She pulled a comb from her purse. "Who said I forgot?"

Jamie considered Carrie a moment. He'd seen her in the hallways and noticed her at games mostly because she was a cheerleader who never seemed particularly cheerful. Unlike the other girls in her squad, Carrie's style seemed oddly aggressive at times, as if the appeal of cheering were simply in the yelling, and the purpose to defeat the other team rather than encourage her own players toward victory.

Her strange response hung in the air as the first plane passed loud and low over the wide swath of woods just behind the shed. Carrie started to tease the crown of her light brown hair, which took on an orange tinge in the shed light. She was pretty but her features were sharp: a narrow slope nose, dark, mascaraed eyes, and thin beak-like lips. She hopped off the table. Jamie noticed that her mini skirt caught for a second on a splinter before falling back down to cover the back of her legs. He shifted his eyes to some graffiti carved into the counter, "Daryl is a faggot," it said. Carrie grabbed a bag of M&Ms and tossed it to him. Jamie fumbled a little but managed to catch it. She helped herself to a Tootsie Roll and a root beer.

"I'm Jamie Keefner, by the way," he said.

"I didn't ask."

Jamie opened the M&M bag. Another plane passed over on the opposite side of the football field.

"Wait," she said. "Are you the kid whose mom was in that accident?"

He considered lying but shrugged instead.

"Wow, that must have sucked," she said. "Although most of the time I wish my mom was dead."

"That's a stupid thing to say."

"You don't know my mom."

"You don't know what it's like to have your mom die."

She rolled her eyes, "Whatever."

Jamie thought about Kenny, Pete, and Owen and how they were probably sleeping. He should have been home in bed too, but instead, he was stuck in this dusty, greasy snack shed with a hostile cheerleader. He poured a bunch of M&Ms in his mouth.

"Sorry," Carrie mumbled at him.

"Whatever," Jamie parroted back to her. He didn't want antagonism from her, but he didn't want sympathy either. He just wanted to get out of there. Forget school; he would head to the brook to catch crayfish, maybe build a dam and watch them fight each other. He wondered if the spray would kill them too.

"How long are we supposed to stay inside?"

"Couple of hours. School opens at ten thirty."

On the far wall was a faded, old calendar whose watercolor picture of round hay bales at sunset was fixed in time as October 1967. Jamie walked over to it. Someone had marked the wins and losses in the square boxes for each Saturday. The team did not have a winning record. On a small shelf to the right was one of those dashboard hula dolls. He nudged her with his finger, and she wobbled side to side on her spring. She was standing on a deck of cards. He pulled them out and began shuffling.

"Rummy?" he asked Carrie.

They sat opposite each other on the table and played four games of rummy and one game of war. They spoke to each other only when they needed to, "Your turn.", "Hand me a ginger ale.", "What time is it?".

Jamie stood up and stretched. Another plane, maybe two, hummed a few miles away.

"Hey, remember the game 52-pickup?" Carrie asked. And before Jamie could answer, she threw the deck at him, and the cards tumbled and splayed at his feet. Carrie laughed hard. As if obliged by the rules of the game, Jamie stooped down and began sweeping the cards into a pile.

"Want to see something?" Carrie asked.

She unzipped her sweatshirt. He assumed she was showing him her drama club T-shirt, a red one emblazoned with postcard-like letters that said *Oklahoma!*

"Oh yeah, the musical. Were you—uh—you were in that?"

Carrie ignored his question and pulled the T-shirt over her head. Then, keeping her eyes fixed on Jamie, she reached behind her back and unhooked her bra. Almost shyly, she pulled the strap off one shoulder and then the other.

"Uhm," Jamie said.

She slid off the table and stood, topless over him. "Uh...nice. Thank you?"

"You are such a kid. Stand up."

Jamie stood; they were almost exactly the same height. Her breasts were small, or so he assumed, having only seen breasts before in a few movies and in Kenny's dad's *Playboy* magazines. He decided to try reaching out a hand, which Carrie pushed away.

"You've got to kiss me first."

Which he did, with infinitely more enthusiasm than he ever had for his first girlfriend, Naomi, a sad-eyed girl who moved to town for two months and then suddenly moved away.

Carrie kissed him back surprisingly gently. Then, looping her arms around his neck, she pulled him as she shuffled backwards until she reached the table again. She whispered directions.

"Unzip."

"Kiss me here."

"Not there."

"Not like that. Like this."

Jamie obeyed, confused, and terrified that if he so much as sneezed, she would call the whole thing off and kick him out into the poisoned air. Through it all, he couldn't help but focus on the hula girl figurine and the way she had started dancing seemingly on her own.

As he'd heard it would be, it was over before he was even sure what was happening.

"I'm sorry." Breathless, he kept whispering, "Sorry."

Carrie nudged him a little, which he took as cue to step aside. Carrie plucked up her underwear from the floor and stepped back to the dingy sink. Jamie hoisted up his shorts. He held out her bra and T-shirt, holding on to them a second longer so that she had to tug them out of his hand. Once dressed, they stood side by side.

"What time is it?" Carrie asked.

"9:40."

Carrie stretched, "I'm going to take a nap."

"OK, yeah. Me too."

They lay down on the table, Carrie with her purse for a pillow, Jamie using his folded arm. With her back to him, Carrie reached over and searched for his other arm. Finding it, she pulled it around her. As Jamie dozed off, he noticed that their breathing was in near-perfect sync.

They woke when they heard the school bell in the distance. Carrie sat up and rifled through her purse again. She found her cigarette pack and hammered one out into her hand.

Jamie massaged his arm. Slowly, then suddenly, he felt the painful stinging needles as the blood flowed back into his forearm and fingers. Remembering how Carrie had covered her hand with his own while they slept, Jamie stood up and strained to reach her lips before the cigarette did.

He was knocked back by the full-force of a punch to his stomach. Curled and huddled over his knees, he looked up at Carrie who had lit her cigarette and was turned away from him.

"Jesus," he coughed. "What was that?"

She swung around at him fast and stooped down until she was level with his face.

"If you so much as squeak a word about any of this to anyone, I will beat you blind."

She drew the burning cigarette toward his forehead. Jamie grabbed her wrist, his strength enough to keep the cigarette from getting closer, but not enough to push it away. "Got it, loser?"

He nodded.

"What?" she shot at him.

"Yeah."

Carrie stood up. She grabbed a handful of candy, dumped it into her purse. When she opened the door, sunlight streamed in. She was just a silhouette with a halo of honey-colored hair as she tugged on her shirt and walked straight-backed out of the shed.

It was a couple minutes before Jamie would even stand up. Then, he shouldered his backpack and lifted his bike. He stood just outside the doorway of the shed, blinking and squinting against the brightness outside. There was a stillness, and everything seemed shiny. Shellacked. He touched a finger to the concrete and felt a wetness. Jamie heard a soft "thick, thick...thick" sound. They were falling out of the trees, hitting the roof of the shed.

Handfuls of gypsy moth caterpillars, spilling from the branches and leaves all around him. And the ground was alive with their dying. From where he stood, just a few feet from the snack shed, Jamie could see Carrie's footprints tracking a firm path right through them.

He looked up at the blue sky, shook his head and laughed a little. He thought briefly again about ditching, but changed his mind, wanting instead to find Mrs. Prior, to hand her his paper and tell her that he'd decided to join the drama club.

§

"Oh my God, my dad had *Playboy* magazines?"

"That's not really the gist of the story."

"Right. Of course," I said.

"It's like that Butterfly Effect—"

"Or, gypsy moth."

"If I had remembered about the spraying and stayed home that day—"

"You might never have lost your virginity!"

He did not laugh.

"Apparently, I'm not following your train of thought," I said.

"I joined the drama club because I figured there was a chance I'd get laid again (which turned out to be true). But it also turned out that I loved acting. And sometimes I think to myself, if it hadn't been for that encounter with Carrie Carlisle, I might never have moved to LA. I might have ended up just...normal. Here."

"I can't tell if I should be insulted or not," I said.

"No, I meant it neither in a bad nor a good way. There's a lot to love about LA. But sometimes it's like living with that slick, toxic, shininess that covered everything after they sprayed that pesticide." He continued, "Here, you've got your family, you've got genuine friends. And there's no bullshit in Jersey. Nobody greeting you with one hand, hiding a knife in the other."

"Well, I think it's fair to say I'm not going to stab you in your sleep, but you can't really rule out the rest of the Tri-State area."

I portioned out two bowls of applesauce. We carried them back to the living room and sat on opposite corners of the couch.

"It's more than that," he said. "As far away as I've gone, as completely different as my world is, there's something here that will always feel familiar. The way people act and talk. The bagel shops and liquor stores. The playgrounds. Memorial Day parades."

"The landfills, the traffic..."

It seemed absurd to me that he would ever think fondly of life in the Garden State compared to the Golden one. But as they say, you can never go home again. And fame wasn't something that could be undone. Even if he never did another movie and decided to open a laundromat in Piscataway, he'd still be James Keefner: superstar turned small business owner.

His train of thought seemed to follow my own.

"It's weird," he continued. "I get paid a ton of money to basically play. Acting is work, but it's not like being a cop or hauling trash. And when I'm not working, I get the red-carpet treatment wherever I go. So, it's not like I'd want to give up the life I have now."

At least he recognized there wasn't a whole lot for him to complain about with regard to his life situation.

"Then what is it?"

"Home," he said. "After my mom died, no place ever felt like home again."

10: Cheap Shoes

It was a deep paper cut, the kind that didn't bleed but was clean and painful. It gaped open every time Pooter bent his index finger, closed again when he straightened it out, like the talking mouth of a puppet. In his boredom, Pooter imagined himself as that guy, the Spanish ventriloquist, Señor Whatshisname and his talking hand. That guy, and a guy with a mind-numbing job to do.

He pulled a Milky Way from the box, peeled the backing off a sticker and placed it mostly centered on the candy bar.

"Eets your own fault," said Cutty, the talking paper cut. "You not should have overslept. Dmitri y Laurie needed your help, and you were not there."

Stupid Audrey.

"Estúpido Juan Poudre," said Cutty.

Pooter scanned the exhibit hall. Across and diagonally from the Preston booth was a girl standing on a wobbling plastic case. She was stretching up on her toes trying to clip a halogen light to the top of the scaffold. In the booth with her was a tall, scarecrow-ish guy with a goatee. He was yucking it up with another guy from the booth next door. Pooter saw the woman look at the guy, about to interrupt, then she changed her mind and again tried to fit the light in place.

"Ayuda," said Cutty. "Help her."

Pooter tossed the Milky Way in the "already-stickered" box. He looked both ways before crossing the walkway, having nearly been run over earlier that morning by a speeding, beeping forklift. He wandered over to the carpeted square of booth space. The goateed guy looked up, tossed a head flip at Pooter before turning his back and continuing his conversation.

Not wanting to startle the girl (for she really seemed to be a girl, probably no more than twenty), Pooter waited until she sank back on her heels before asking, "Can I give you a hand?"

She did startle for a second, but then smiled. "Sweet."

She hopped off the case, about to hand Pooter the light. But when she straightened up, it turned out she was about two inches taller than he was.

"Ha!" she said. "Or not. Apparently, we do need Dickhead to do this."

She gestured over at the guy. Sensing he had attracted her attention, he glanced up. He mouthed the words, "Five minutes" and held up his hand to reinforce the promise.

"Why don't I go find a maintenance guy to bring over a step stool?" Pooter asked.

"Eh, forget it," she said. "I'm leaving it for him. It's time he got off his lazy ass. I swear he's been gabbing all fucking morning."

Pooter looked up at the logo sign atop the booth. "Panda Paper," he read. "You make paper?"

"No, we're circus performers," she said. "Who were you talking to over there?"

"I wasn't. Nobody."

"Whatever," she said. "Anyway, thanks for nearly coming to my rescue."

"John," he said. "My name is John."

133

"Well, John, I hate to keep you from your sticker-ing. Looks like Dickhead is done chatting up the neigh-bors, so I'm good from here."

Dickhead sauntered back and stopped at the edge of the foam carpet. He stood, legs apart as if bracing on the deck of a swaying ship. His knuckles were on his hips, and he was scanning the layout of the ten by ten booth.

"Daisy," he said. "The panels are all misaligned. It looks terrible."

Daisy pointed the halogen light in her hand like a handgun at him. "That's because you're fucking cheap. I told you to get the upgrade."

Pooter took a few backwards steps, casually head-ing back to the Preston booth away from them, but he couldn't help listening in to their exchange.

"That money went to pay for your flight."

"As if I wanted to come!"

"Jesus—I told Dad you'd be a hassle. I would have been better off with Hector."

"Great. Here you go then." She forced the halogen light into his gut. "This needs to be hanged."

"Hung—"

"I know what I said."

She picked up her tiny handbag with a flick of her finger and strolled out. Pooter had one foot back in the Preston House space when he heard her address him.

"You coming?"

Pooter hesitated. "I—"

"Bring the freakin' bars. I'll help you sticker."

The convention center's main hallway was mas-sive and long. It had an open layout and a glass façade through which one could see the traffic and street-side bustle. It was easy to feel like a fish in a bowl, thought Pooter. A bottom-feeder on the ground floor among the potted trees and other decorative foliage, while on the upper levels, other fish higher on the food chain were enjoying an executive reception complete with Bloody Marys and mimosas. Pooter and Daisy walked for nearly a quarter mile to get to the nearest food offering, more cafeteria than cafe.

They waited in line behind a group of four middle-aged men, all with the same ex-jock, stocky build, in identical khakis and red golf shirts. Two were taking turns telling about their turbulent flight in last night. The other two countered with their account of trying to get a waitress to meet them in the bar after her shift.

Daisy fixed her eyes on the ceiling. "I freakin' hate these things."

"Cafeterias?"

"Tradeshows," she said. "Dickhead is going to be running the company when my dad retires next year. So, he's pushing to do all this fancy advertising and shit."

"It's a book publishing conference and you guys sell paper. Makes sense."

"Please. These things are so useless."

Away from the echoey exhibit hall, Pooter could hear that she had a lisp: "youthleth." It was a funny juxtaposition, all the cursing against a speech impediment that made her seem childish and innocent. He liked it; it worked for her.

Daisy bought a giant blueberry muffin and tall coffee, then joined Pooter at a tiny nearby table.

"So," Pooter said, "Dickhead. That must be an old family name?"

"Actually, it's Wendall," she said.

"I think Dickhead's a step up."

"As in Wendall Berry," she said. But she pulled the two names together: "wendallberry"—like winterberry, like boysenberry.

"What kind of berry is that?" Pooter asked.

Daisy tried to read his expression to see if he was for real.

"Wendell Berry. The writer-farmer?"

Again, she smooshed the two words together, like potato farmer, as if a writer-farmer cultivated writers, helping them grow and produce digestible work.

"Yeah, our dad is an ex-hippie," she said. "He actually started as a farmer himself, but then needed to support a family."

"So, he started a paper company?" That seemed like a safe thing to interject.

"Yes, but not just any paper. He tore up the corn and beans and shit, literally tore it right out of the ground, in order to plant bamboo. These days, everything's made of bamboo—floors, furniture, clothes—it's not so special, but he was the first to really see it as a source that's better for the environment."

Pooter started back on the stickers. "Oh yeah?"

"Oh man. First, it's the fastest growing plant on the planet. It can be harvested in four years instead of, like, twenty, which is how long it takes for trees to be mature enough for paper. It grows without pesticides or fertilizers, and it takes hardly any water. Not only that, but bamboo produces 35 percent more oxygen than most trees and absorbs four times as much carbon. And, since it consumes a superhigh amount of nitrogen, it can detoxify wastewater and improve soil quality. And, and, and," she leaned forward and poked his arm with each 'and.' "Did you know that bamboo also has natural anti-bacterial and anti-fungal properties? It's like this crazy wonder plant. Plus, it makes really beautiful paper."

"So, you do sales for the company?"

"Hell no." She blew on her cup of black coffee. "I'm a substitute teacher." ("a thubthtitute")

"Shut up."

"I'm a fucking substitute teacher. They love me. I'm their favorite."

"I'm sure you are. You graduated, what, last year?"

"Jackass. I'm twenty-six."

Pooter grabbed another Milky Way bar and placed a sticker on it. Daisy, who was clearly not interested in helping him sticker, leaned back and propped a foot on the chair next to her.

They didn't speak for a moment: Pooter peeling and slapping, Daisy staring with distaste at the loud redshirt guys. She turned back to Pooter.

"So let me get this straight. People come to the Preston House booth for a snack, they eat a candy bar and then, what? They're going to buy a bunch of books? Is that the plan?" she asked.

"I guess," he said. "The big title they're pushing this year is a biology book by a woman named Candy Clark. They were going to go with Clark bars, but then they figured people don't really know what those are anymore. So, they just went with a general candy theme."

"Don't people just throw away wrappers when they're done with the candy? How are your sticker labels going to sell books?"

Pooter shrugged. "Don't ask me, I'm not in marketing."

"What are you in?"

"I'm an editorial assistant for college textbooks in economics."

She threw her head back and pretended to snore. "Don't tell me anymore. You'll ruin my image of you as a dashing purveyor of anthologies of post-structural philosophy."

"Now it's my turn to yawn."

"I see you're a Philistine. Eh, I know a thing or two about economic theory." Pooter supposed she knew a thing or two about a lot of things. "I suppose if it's taught right, econ can be cool."

"These books are more for intro classes, the ones in the massive lecture halls. I don't think—"

"Barf." She downed the rest of her coffee in three gulps and stood up. Palming the muffin like a softball she was about to pitch, Daisy demanded. "You ready?"

She was already on the corridor carpet by the time Pooter had put the remaining bars back in the box. He had to jog to catch up.

Pooter wondered if she had disengaged on account of the disappointing nature of his books or if she just had the attention span of a chipmunk. Whatever the case, she was cute—a word he thought fitting despite her superior height.

He said, "So, I'm supposed to go to this thing tonight with the team, but—"

"Don't ask me to dinner," Daisy said.

"Jeez, I wasn't."

"You were so. Don't worry. It's no big deal. I'd want to go to dinner with me too." She punched his arm and laughed loud enough for the two women in front of them to turn and look.

"Go do your thing with your 'team.' We can hang tomorrow after the show."

"Oh, that's very gracious of you," Pooter said. "But I think I have plans."

"Suit yourself."

She turned toward the exit doors opposite those that led back to the exhibit hall.

"You're not going back to help Dickhead?" he asked.

"Fuck him," she said. "And you can quote me."

She headed out of the building, still armed with the muffin and her little purse. As the door swung open, it offered a glimpse of the more vivid, loud, and bustling world outside the convention center. He was tempted to follow her. Then the door closed, and the tinted glass muted both the colors and the bustling sounds outside, leaving only the white noise hum of the ventilation system inside.

"What do you think, Cutty?"

"I like."

"*Sí?*"

"*Sí.*"

The show got underway early the next morning. Pooter stood politely in the booth, hands folded in front of him. He would smile and nod at the attendees who strolled slowly by, some stopping in front of the booth. They would stand with their mouths slacked open, like trout, trying to process the information on the display posters with headlines like "Tailored learning solutions for higher education" supported by bullet points about the "Latest technology" and "Proven pedagogy." Pooter's job was to hand out candy bars and ask the visitors—mostly other vendors and publishers, some of them competitors, but also a handful of professors and authors looking to make connections—if they would like to learn about Preston House's latest line of textbooks due out in the spring. He would then pass the visitor along to the appropriate editor or sales rep.

The new shoes he'd bought for the show were painful. On the long walk with Daisy between the exhibit hall and the lobby, the stiff heels had rubbed sore spots on each of his Achilles tendons. Plus, his toes were pinched. Pooter finally understood why his nana always said: "Buy cheap clothes, never cheap shoes." He thought about asking Dmitri to cover for him so he could duck out to find a shoe store, but he had still not recovered Dmitri's and Laurie's good graces after having missed the previous morning's set up. Instead, he tried not to move around the booth too much.

He planted himself at a good vantage point to see the comings and goings of the Panda Paper booth, but Daisy had not been back. Instead, Wendall was working the booth alone, shaking hands, flipping through a photo album of the bamboo farm, and handing out paper samples folded into origami birds. While Pooter thought it must be exhausting, Wendall seemed to truly enjoy telling people about the business, the process, the paper. His enthusiasm and sincerity were such a stark contrast to Daisy's (adorable) cynicism that Pooter imagined it probably wasn't easy being her big brother, having to compete for their father's pride and attention.

Though he might have been projecting his own unpleasant familial relationships. Pooter's sister, Kate, had a knack for sucking up the family's energy with her addictions and various dramas, usually involving a crazy landlord or dirty ex-boyfriend. And his mother and stepfather had long ago retreated into their own world of borderline alcoholism and isolation, the lines of which were clearly drawn the day his mother sat him and Kate down, ages eleven and thirteen respectively, to tell them that she was planning to marry Dean—a moody man ten years her senior that the kids neither cared for nor respected.

"You two need to know that this is important to me," their mother said. "I've had one failed marriage and I will never go through another."

"What is that supposed to mean?" asked Kate who was already sneaking cigarettes.

"It means that if you kids try to force me to choose between you and Dean, you're gonna lose."

They didn't try. Eventually, Kate spent more and more time out of the house, no one really asked where.

Pooter blew steam from his soup.

"So, I stole this from your booth yesterday," said Daisy. She opened her big bag of loot and pulled out *Journeys in Economics*, Seventh Edition. "This is your guy, right? Herbert?"

Pooter resisted the urge to push aside a strand of hair that was hanging in front of her eye.

"Yeah, he's probably the biggest name in our roster. There are other authors out there, but yep, he's..." Pooter faded out, having nothing to say that was interesting.

"He's totally out of touch. Old school bullshit."

"I guess that's not surprising. He's about seventy. Been around Preston forever from what I can tell."

He went back to his soup. Daisy leaned forward, palms flat on the table. "You know his views on NAFTA, right?"

Pooter had to make a split-second choice: (a) admit that he wasn't involved at that level of the publishing process, thereby revealing the relative insignificance of his position or (b) fake a certain degree of knowledge in the hope that her superior worldliness would allow him to convincingly riff off what she said.

"Well, I know his wife had some role in the Clinton administration." It was a total fabrication, but a calculated one as he guessed that Daisy would be on the liberal Democrat side of such an economic debate, and he remembered seeing a news clip of President Clinton signing the agreement.

"So what?" She countered. "Langer's all rah-rah NAFTA, kissing Herbert's ass, saying how great it is for the economy without ever mentioning what a shitty deal it's going to be for the American worker, not to mention how it'll totally kill Mexican farmers' ability to make a living."

"I'm sure we'll still get lots of fruits and vegetables from Mexico," said Pooter.

"That's your evidence that all is right in the world? What you can find at your local mega-supermarket?" *Thupermarket*, he repeated in his head.

She took a deep breath and tried to speak slowly as if she were addressing a learning-impaired student, all the while her lisp undermining the zealousness of her lecture: "NAFTA—the North American Fuck-You to America—is going to allow U.S. manufacturers to send jobs down to Mexico where they'll get away with paying crap wages."

She couldn't keep her words from gathering speed and emotion. "Not only that, but the manufacturers that stay in the U.S. are going to lower wages because they won't be able to compete. Do you know how many hundreds of thousands of jobs we're going to lose when our manufacturing companies all move to Mexico? And then...then, then, then when the agreement allows U.S. farm products like uber-subsidized corn to flood into Mexico, their farmers won't be able to compete. Corn, for God's sake! They practically invented the stuff. Tamales made from *Iowa* corn? Unconscionable. Plus!"

"Okay, okay. I get it. It's messed up."

"And your man Herbert is warping young minds into believing this was the best move since the Clayton Antitrust Act of 1914."

"Indeed," said Pooter. "Though I'd like to point out, he isn't exactly 'my man.' In fact, the guy pretty much hates me."

She set her muffin down and leaned forward, her lovely doe eyes locked on his, "Do tell."

"It's no big deal," said Pooter, not really wanting to tell the story, but not wanting to give up her focused attention either. He thought back to the tongue-lashing he'd received from Langdon Herbert that last day of September. And then, like a thought slingshot at him out of nowhere, he remembered the odd conversation he'd had with Audrey yesterday morning about James Keefner, wondering if she was playing a bizarre prank on him.

Daisy was waiting for him to continue. "In a nutshell, Herbert wanted to change the cover image on his newest textbook. I don't remember why. But we were just about to go on press with it. For whatever reason, my boss didn't give the direction to the production team in time, and they started printing the covers. My boss would have been in way bigger trouble than me—"

"I," mumbled Daisy.

"Than *I*. So, I owned it, saying I forgot to give the message."

"Why would you do that? Bosses have all the advantages. Why would you do that?" she asked. "Why would he let you?"

"She, you lousy feminist."

She sat back in her chair. "Oh, I get it, then."

Pooter dug out a last scoop of the watery tomato broth and onion. "No, it's not like that."

He considered explaining—and he thought Daisy would approve—how when Audrey shook his hand offering him the job two years ago, they both seemed to make a silent pact to subvert the cold behemoth that was corporate publishing, albeit in small and completely ineffective ways. Their goal, it seemed to Pooter, was never to care too much about the job, the place, but rather to take it for what it was: a paycheck. He just couldn't see getting caught up in the ego and self-importance of the place so clearly exhibited during the few interactions he'd had with Langdon Herbert. He hadn't hesitated to take the fall for Audrey. It was no big deal to him. But then, she went and literally became a strange bedfellow with the capital-M Man himself, Dan Rayburn.

Pooter glanced at the clock, wanting to make sure he didn't over-extend his lunch break. "I gotta get back."

Daisy looked miffed that she hadn't gotten the rest of the story out of him but folded up the remaining half a muffin in its wrapper.

When they'd returned to the exhibit hall, Pooter handed her Wendall's sandwich and soda. "Do something nice. Take this to your brother and let him go sit down to eat it while you handle the booth for a while."

Daisy smiled sweetly at him. "You're too much, John whatever-your-last-name-is."

"It's Poudre. My friends call me Pooter."

"Well, John Poudre Pooter. I want you to have dinner with me tonight."

Daisy had given Pooter directions to a small Indian restaurant that was a ways off the Strip. But she had the handwriting of a six-year-old, and he found himself fruitlessly searching for Olerg Avenue when it should have been Diego Avenue. Giving up, he flagged down a cab whose driver knew the restaurant and drove him the two blocks to get there.

Daisy was already sitting at a table in a dimly lit nook when he arrived thirteen minutes late and self-conscious that his cotton shirt was sticking to the small of his back. There were a handful of other diners at nearby tables and all around them, thumbtacked to the walls, were several elaborately sequined tapestries depicting scenes of elephants, mystical creatures, fierce battles, and dancers. The wall-hanging above Daisy showed a man and woman—he holding a bejeweled chalice to her lips as she reclined into his embrace; their eyes were all amour.

Daisy was sipping what looked like a peach-colored milkshake through a straw. "What's that?" Pooter asked her.

"Mango lassi."

He'd never been to an Indian restaurant before, never had Indian food. It was no use pretending otherwise.

"You're going to have to help me out here with what to order."

She smiled with big, straight, white teeth. Pooter noted that she was one of those people whose smile, even a casual one, seemed to express happiness beyond what the situation called for.

"Perfect. We'll order a tasting menu!"

"I don't really like vegetables—"

"OK."

"And I'm not too into spicy."

"We can go mild."

"No weird meats, OK?"

"What do you consider weird?"

"I don't know. I read somewhere they serve peacock at some restaurants in India."

"Huh. No, I think it's pretty much just chicken or lamb."

"I guess no burgers with that whole 'cow is sacred' thing?" Pooter shook his napkin out over his lap. "I would have pegged you for a vegetarian."

Daisy shrugged. "I sort of am."

"By definition, that's not really possible."

The waiter arrived with a pitcher of water for them. "Do you have any questions about the menu?" he asked.

Daisy looked at Pooter, "Did you want to ask about the peacock?"

The waiter looked at Pooter quizzically. He motioned to the lassi. "Could you bring me one of those, please?"

Over the course of a full and (Pooter had to admit) really delicious meal, they spoke about pop culture:

movies and TV shows they liked. Daisy seemed to know very little about music, though later Pooter would wonder if she feigned ignorance so he could contribute something to the conversation other than halting questions and puzzled looks.

He talked about how, with just a handful of loud, fast, simple riffs and off-beat lyrics, the Ramones ignited an underground music revolution for kids who wanted to puke every time they heard disco on the radio.

"And it wasn't just here. The Ramones teed up the whole punk scene over in England. Bands like the Clash and the Sex Pistols—"

"Oh, yeah, 'God Save the Queen, she ain't no human bein'!'" Daisy chimed in loud enough to draw looks.

After dinner, they decided to walk back to their hotels, which were on opposite sides of the convention center. On the way, she looped the conversation back to Audrey, and Pooter grudgingly talked about their subversive strategy of deliberately being merely adequate at their jobs.

"Why would you want to do anything half-assed?" Daisy wondered. "What's the point?"

"You don't know what office life is like."

"Maybe not, but it seems like a big, fat fucking waste of time to choose to undermine your own success."

Pooter rolled this thought around in his head and found he couldn't disagree.

"I mean," she continued, "I get needing a paycheck. How else are you going to move out of your parents' house? But you work forty out of like 160 hours a week. That's 25 percent. And that doesn't even include sleep."

Thleep, he echoed silently.

She could tell he was legitimately listening, and she put a point on it. "Find something about your job that inspires you. Or find a new job that does."

"Like substitute teaching?" Pooter said.

"I happen to love substitute teaching."

They arrived outside the revolving door of his hotel. "Do you..." Pooter started.

"Yeah, I'll come up," she said. "I'm not going to sleep with you, but we can fool around."

Daisy was a birthday cake with sprinkles, he thought. She was frosting and gumdrops. And somewhere, someone was singing to him while his face glowed in the light of her sparkly candle flames.

She was so matter-of-fact and easy that he didn't feel the least bit anxious as they rode the elevator to the fourteenth floor—excited without a doubt, but not insecure. It didn't hurt that for the last month and a half he'd been getting steady lessons from Julie Lee in the art of being an attentive lover. He was a quick and eager study, so much so that the week before leaving for Vegas, she had finally shut up and just let him have fun. It was a graduation of sorts, complete with her launching into a nearly tone-deaf version of *Ring My Bell* after they were finished.

Two nights later, however, she was over it and had become seemingly distracted as he was applying his fledgling oral skills.

"Oh my God, Julie, are you doing crunches?"

"What do you care?"

"You know, I'm toiling away down here."

"I'm a master multitasker, Pooter." And she sent him back to work.

Pooter's hotel room was neat. He prided himself on being an atypical bachelor who never strew dirty laundry on the floor and always properly placed trash in the garbage can. Though not fastidious in any sense, he liked things to be tidy. "Everything has a place and everything in its place," was another of his nana's favorite sayings. And he'd adopted the thought as his own.

Daisy went right to the window and pulled apart the wide, heavy curtains. Outside, Vegas glittered like a massive rhinestone pin.

"This city is grotesque," she said. "Do you know they only get about ten centimeters of precipitation a year? And still, people install sprinkler systems to water their lawns. Lawns in the middle of the Mojave Desert! Think about that—"

"I'd rather not."

"Because it's crazy, right?"

"Because I want to kiss you."

She lit up with that big, toothy grin and just about tackled him onto the bed. "You can never have another first kiss, John Poudre Pooter. Better make it a good one."

Pooter could count on one hand the number of first kisses he'd had, so he didn't have much to compare it to, but it seemed pretty excellent to him. Long, slow and lingering in the right places with enough force to exchange passion, enough softness to express tenderness.

True to Daisy's word, they did not have sex. But they did spend time refining that first kiss and peeling away much of each other's clothing. Later, as he was dozing off with Daisy's back curving against the side of his ribcage, Pooter thought that if kissing were a musical form, it would be theme and variation, and that he'd never again hear the Paganini Caprice in the same way.

They had left the curtains open overnight, letting the lights of the city fill the otherwise unremarkable hotel room. Daisy stirred early when the sky started to pale with the approaching morning.

"I have to go," she said in a gravelly half-whisper.

Pooter blinked the grogginess from his eyes. "Can I see you later? I'm flying out at five o'clock."

She shrugged. "Depends on what's happening at the Panda booth. Maybe we can meet for an early lunch?"

"Herbert's giving a presentation late morning. I have to be there for it."

"Where's that happening?"

"No idea. It's on the show schedule, though. I can stop by the booth when it's over."

She slipped out of bed and plucked her bra off the floor. Half-in, half-out of her shirt, she stretched over Pooter and planted a cheerful kiss on his cheek.

"Thanks for the fun. I will see you later."

11: Nature People

E ven her outgoing voice message was efficient, "Bridget Knutson is not here. Your message, please." I made sure to call as soon as I'd woken so my sinuses would be a little congested and my voice would be husky. There was no way Rigid would believe I was truly sick, but I didn't care. Jamie had decided to stay another day, and it would have been inconceivable not to play hooky.

The weather had turned unseasonably warm for mid-February, which gave us the perfect avenue for getting out with low risk of encountering anyone. I loaded my trusty day pack with a large water bottle, a couple of sandwiches, a handful of carrot sticks, and a ziplock filled nearly to burst with trail mix. With Jamie as my copilot, we headed out, responsibilities and cares temporarily fading like the road signs in the rearview mirror.

I always enjoyed driving the Palisades Parkway; it was a travel oasis in a state whose roadways were more typically congested, industrial, dingy and, let's be honest, disturbingly odoriferous. The northern part of the Palisades, the part that crossed from Jersey into New York State, was a strange hybrid of highway and rural state route. Trucks were forbidden, but cars could go highway speed, and the two-lane northbound route was separated, completely hidden at points, from the southbound by narrow sections of woods and brushy slopes. Pressed up against the road on the side were thick stretches of pine, locust, and, in the spring, gold-

152

en-flowered forsythia. This was not the turnpike. Here, when I passed slower drivers, I felt no disdain for their lack of speed; rather they became fellow travelers, and we'd all get there when we got there.

I could feel myself easing into the driver's seat. Jamie, who hadn't said much since we got in the car, steadied his gaze on the fast-forwarding prickly winter landscape.

"Want some music?" I asked.

He shook his head. "I like the quiet." A few beats later, he said, "I sometimes think about moving to the city."

"Not if you like the quiet."

Jamie shifted in his seat, and turned to me, either having not heard or choosing to ignore my comment.

"New Yorkers can be pretty smug, but I'll take that over phoniness any day. Out in LA, everyone's hustling something. It's like you always have to be 'on.' And God help you if you have a moment of 'off.'"

It seemed like an opening, "So, I can't help asking, what actually happened with your brother-in-law?"

Jamie's expression remained unchanged and again, he ignored me.

"Sorry, I didn't mean to pry," I said. "Well, I guess I did, actually, but you don't have to answer. Obviously." I felt embarrassed for having asked and clenched my hands tighter around the steering wheel.

Just ahead, a very large bird with a wide wingspan swooped from one side of the road to the other.

"Whoa!" said Jamie, sitting up. "Was that an eagle?"

"I think it was a hawk. But it was pretty cool. I haven't seen one that close before."

"Where are we going, anyway? Are there, like, bears and things?"

"I've never seen one and they'd probably be hibernating anyway. I'm taking you to Harriman State Park. You must have gone there when you were a kid?"

"I was never much of an outdoors guy."

"Oh, it's nice. Lots of trails, pretty views. And I can't believe this day. It feels like March."

"It's always like this in LA. Even in January. Warmer, even."

Fifteen minutes later, we pulled into an empty dirt parking lot beside a still pond. The surrounding trees with their winter-bare branches appeared both fuzzy and prickly—welcoming and unapproachable.

"The trailhead is across the street," I said as we got out of the car.

"It's so empty," Jamie said. "Doesn't anybody come here?"

"Not on a workday. Not in winter."

I enjoyed exploring places in their off-season. When the crowds were gone, the landscapes—whether sidewalks and storefronts or foot-worn trails—revealed unexpected details and offered an intimacy you couldn't experience when there were people chattering and milling about. But for Jamie, accustomed more to the constant prattle and street noise of city life, the lack of a single other person or car seemed a little unnerving. Looking out across the pond, he picked up a flat stone and sidearmed it into the water. The stone plunked rather than skimmed and cast its shimmering rings outward. A leaf bobbed on the tiny waves like a canoe being gently pushed to the pond's edge.

I locked the car, zipped up the pack. "Ready?"

He took a last, slightly wary look up the road. "Lead on." And we ventured into the woods.

The sunlight filtering through the trees fell on the ground in bright, jagged shapes that shivered when the wind blew. Dry, brown leaves covered most of the ground, but there were also rocks coated with scrappy bits of moss. The trail gently steepened and wound its way beside a rocky stream. Jamie kept catching his sneakers on rocks and exposed roots.

"Son of a bitch," he said after a particularly awkward stumble. "Why do they put this stuff here?"

"Nature People can be pranksters like that."

As we hiked along, the running stream filled in its own chatter. I would normally be listening for birds, keeping an eye out for chipmunks and unusual plants, but Jamie's presence was like a mind vortex behind me. I was no longer totally starstruck, but my attention was still keenly focused behind me. *Is my pace OK? Should I slow down? Speed up? Should I point out the scenery? Do I have panty lines?*

The trail alternated between inclined and flat as we continued to climb toward the ridge line. Eventually, we could see a clearing ahead. "There's a really nice viewpoint coming up," I told him.

We arrived at a rocky outcropping that offered a sweeping panorama of the valley. A few high clouds cast Rorschach shadows over the sweep of forest below, but the distant view was so sharply clear that I could just barely make out the Manhattan skyline. We were like Dorothy and the Scarecrow, I thought, catching our first glimpse of the Emerald City.

I sat down. He remained standing but stretched down over his toes, letting out a full yoga sigh. He unfolded and leaned back in the other direction, facing skyward, before coming back to center. Then he joined me on the rock.

I pulled the sandwiches from my backpack and offered one. "Everything's so brown," he said.

"Only for a little bit. Things will start to go bright yellow and green just a few weeks from now. And come fall, this spot is pretty remarkable—a panorama of reds and golds."

He reached out for the water bottle. I confess, I only brought one so that if I ever had the chance to tell someone, I could say that my lips had touched a surface that had also touched James Keefner's.

"You know, I can't remember anymore what it's like to live in a place that has seasons," he said. "Time must feel like it moves faster when every few months you have new weather and colors."

"Sometimes it feels like it doesn't move fast enough, actually." I was surprised by my own words, as if someone else had said them. And yet, in the moment, it felt very true.

"Wait until you have a kid," he said. "Then time will really fly."

"How old is your daughter now?" I asked.

"Storey is fourteen," he said. "It's weird. The baby stage and the kid stage are so different from each other. It's like they're not even the same human being."

"Yeah, but I'm sure it's a lot more fun now that she's older and you guys can do more together."

He picked up another stone and winged it at a tree. It ricocheted and hit another. "You'd think so, but I couldn't get enough of that little baby. In fact, I got rid of the nanny just so I could have her all to myself when Chloe was working or traveling. Storey would be babbling and climbing all over me, pulling my hair, drooling on my clothes, and I didn't care. I loved it. Those were the best years."

"And now?"

"At the moment, I'm sure she's furious at me for skipping town. I stashed a note in her room before I left, telling her not to worry, but..."

He inhaled another long yoga-like breath and slowly let it out. "Storey's a lot like her mother. They're pretty tight. I feel like a third wheel most of the time."

"I'm sure they don't think of you that way."

"Well, that's a polite thing to say, but you really have no idea about it." It was a scolding tone; he had no patience for platitudes.

"Maybe it's just hard for you to connect. It sounds like you didn't have a good role model."

His eyebrows pinched. "Totally different," he said. "My dad was all grief. He had nothing left to give me. Chloe and Storey have this dynamic. It's like a shell no one else can penetrate. They may fight like hell one minute and be all hugging the next, but that bond...it's a biological thing, I think" he said. "I'm sure you were close with your mom."

Mentioning her brought to mind an unexpected snapshot, not of my mother's face, but of her hands. She had long fingers that reminded me of taper candles, the long, unpolished nails like pale flames. She sometimes played piano when we were very young. I could remember sitting next to her on the bench while she fumbled through scraps of classical pieces she had learned as a kid.

"In some ways, we were," I said, "And not in others." I picked at some lichen by my toes. "I think we'd be close now if she were still alive. But who knows, maybe not."

A breeze had begun to kick up causing the shrubs to shiver a little. "How did she die?" he asked.

"It was cancer."

§

The windows were fogged from steam rising out of the stockpot. Between the humidity and the thermostat being turned up to seventy-three, the kitchen felt like a rain-forest. And though outside, it was below freezing, I was peeled down to a T-shirt and wishing for a pair of shorts.

Slicing tomatoes for a salad, I heard the bell ring from upstairs. That bell, straight out of a bad sitcom. Bobbie had given it to Mom after she came home from the hospital so she wouldn't have to strain herself trying to get her needs tended to. But what the person who has a bell doesn't realize is that no matter when it's rung, that innocent, twinkling chime is always an interruption, an irritation.

"Just a minute," I called out.

The bell rang again. I mumbled a swear as I went to the bottom of the steps. "I'll be there in a minute!"

I heard a muffled two-syllable reply, a question.

"What?" I yelled.

No reply.

I went halfway up the stairs. "What did you say?"

Still no reply.

I knew her game. She was reeling me upstairs like a fish on a line. I could cut and return to prepping dinner, but I knew I would get no farther than the kitchen doorway before hearing another muffled question.

They'd set up the hospital bed in Kenny's old room. The built-in bookshelf still held his video game cartridges and *Rolling Stone* magazines. The day she came home, Mom had been able to climb the stairs with Dad's help, though halting every two or three steps to catch her breath. She'd joked that the only way she was ever going to do these stairs again was when they carried her out. When none of us laughed, she glowered and told us all to "Lighten up."

Three weeks later, she was mostly bed ridden and her moods had become dark. I stood in the doorway. "You rang?"

"Nothing."

"What do you mean, 'nothing?' I came all the way up here."

"I wasn't calling you. I was calling your father."

I bit the inside of my cheek. She had been napping when he left. "He's not here. He stepped out."

"What do you mean? Where?"

Working hard to sound casual, I said, "He's at Finney's, at a birthday party for Alan. Won't be home for dinner. He wasn't going to go but since I was coming over anyway, I thought it would be good for him, you know, to get out, take a break."

Since she had come home, my mother had been keeping my father within a very tight radius. When she couldn't see him, she called out to him, echolocation-style, to be assured he was near. When he went to the grocery store, she squawked if he was gone longer than forty-five minutes. When he was on the phone, she needed to use the bathroom; when he was watching TV, she wanted fresh water.

He was extraordinarily patient and generous with his attention, far more than I was able to be, and I was only there a few times a week. "She's my Dot," he said to Bobbie when she expressed concern. "How could I not give her anything she needs?"

We were instantly shamed for feeling frustrated with her. And yet, the strain of being always on-call was starting to show in his posture and the fatigue in his voice. She forbade visitors to the house apart from me and Bobbie, and very occasionally, Doug and the twins. So, we conspired to find ways to get him out, especially before the illness demanded more hands-on care.

"You thought it would be good for him to get out?" Her eyes were sharp.

"He needs some socializing, Mom. He can't just be chained at home all the time. It isn't good for him." I picked up and folded a towel that had fallen to the floor. "He's got to live his life too."

And with that, she reached out to the night table and swept her hand across everything in reach—a pink rose in a bud vase, a few bottles of pills, a lidded cup with a straw in it.

"Fuck you, Audrey."

I was stunned. In my entire life, I had never heard her use the word. As far I knew, she never had. And her first application of it was toward me? For trying to do right by my father? Fuck me? I made soup!

Trying to put a firm lid on my indignation, I squatted to pick up the broken pieces of vase and mop up the spilled water with the towel in my hand.

"You call that bar," she said, "And tell him to come home."

I shook my head.

"Then bring me the phone and I'll call."

"I won't."

I worried that she might threaten to get it herself, and then what? Would I let her collapse? Would I physically force her back into bed? Restrain her? But she didn't rise.

"That's so like you," she hissed at me.

"What?"

This woman who was my mother, the one who had baked banana bread on Sundays, who gave standing ovations at my school plays. I couldn't recognize her anymore. Couldn't find her through that mask of raw anger and disease.

"You're a do-nothing," she said to me.

Standing, I had to tell myself not to clench my hands around the ceramic shards. There was a familiar taste in my mouth I hadn't experienced since I was a teen. It was brassy and sour: the taste of angst, injustice, frustration. Had I been fifteen, my pitch would have been shrill and doors would have been slammed. Instead, I simply turned to leave.

"I said you're a do-nothing!"

"Go to hell," I mumbled. I hoped my father was getting drunk.

Downstairs, I clicked on the TV and turned up the volume. For the next hour and a half, I channel surfed, switching among *Tron*, CNN, and a nature program about reptiles. Though all along, I gnawed on those words "do-nothing" with no choice but to try to fill them with meaning. What was the something I was supposed to have done? Medical school? Peace Corps? Politics? What did she do? She kept the house clean and chauffeured us around. What was there to show for that?

Somewhere very deep, I understood that her lashing out was not about me at all, and I shouldn't have been so wounded, but I couldn't get there in that moment. By the time Bobbie barreled through the back door with a grocery bag in one hand and a bottle of wine in the other, I needed some air.

"I'm going to the video store."

"Everything OK?" Bobbie asked, pulling out a long baguette and a carton of eggs from the bag.

I considered warning her about the hostility she might encounter upstairs, but I didn't want to talk about it. Bobbie handled Mom better than I did, giving back a reciprocal amount of whatever crap got thrown at her, often with a tension-diffusing laugh.

"The soup and salad are ready," I said. "We can eat when I get back."

I headed to the bathroom as Bobbie went to see if Mom needed anything. I was drying my hands when I heard her cry out.

"No. Oh no, no, no! Mom! Please, no!"

There was a choked panic trapped in the words. And I knew that somehow, while I was sitting stupidly in front of the television, my mother had died.

I swallowed what felt like an enormous stone lodged in my throat. And then, I picked up my keys and quietly left the house. As if I could turn back the clock three minutes and inhabit a world in which I thought my mother was simply upstairs napping.

I drove around the block twice, casting out cold breath smoke signals. I realized that if I returned without a DVD and fell to pieces at the door, Bobbie would know that I knew and that I had left her alone in what might have been the worst moment of her life. I did what I had to do: I went to the video store.

The light was ghastly, overly bright and hot as a spotlight. It seemed entirely possible that everyone in the store knew where I'd just come from, and I could feel their judgment pointed at me, though they were simply looking at the shelf or giving a polite smile as they passed. I was in the comedy section when my eyes zeroed in on a critic's endorsement of *Spaceballs*: "SCREAMINGLY FUNNY!" Which in that moment, was actually screamingly funny, and I had to stifle a choking sob-laugh as I took the video from the shelf and held it tightly to my chest like I thought someone would steal it from me.

Standing in line, my hands felt as insubstantial as cobwebs. As if the wind from someone opening the door could just blow them away. Over and over, I thought, *I will not cry here. I will not cry here.* Meanwhile, three people ahead of me, a woman in dress heels was arguing about her late fee.

"I'm sorry ma'am, that's the policy on new releases," the cashier was saying. I couldn't hear her response, but she was clearly not acquiescing.

Like someone possessed, I dug into my wallet, pulled out a twenty-dollar bill. I jumped the line and slapped the bill on the counter. "Will this cover it?"

The woman was aghast. I pressed the cashier. "Will this cover her late fee?"

"It's seven dollars and fifty-nine cents, so yeah, I guess so."

"Good." I turned to the woman, "Your tab is paid. Could you please step aside?"

Haltingly, she left the line and then made a break for the door. I turned to the couple behind me. "I know I cut, but can I just get this and get out of here?"

She looked appalled; he looked impressed. They both said, "Yes, go ahead."

As the cashier handed me my change and the VHS tape he said, "Good choice. Seems like you could use a comedy."

When I returned home, Bobbie met me at the door and fell on my shoulders, wailing. For all she or anyone ever knew, my mother had a stroke and died quietly in her sleep. Maybe that was true.

§

I couldn't bring myself to look over at Jamie. Instead, I focused on a black-capped chickadee that flew in and landed on one of the shrubs. The branch bounced and swayed beneath him. When he took off again, fat tears, whole handfuls of them, spilled from a deep well that couldn't contain them anymore. Though I relived that day a thousand times, it was the first time I'd ever uttered a word about it.

"Hey," Jamie said in a gentle voice. "People die all the time for reasons that have nothing to do with us. It's not your fault."

Whether it was or it wasn't didn't matter. "I was so shitty, Jamie."

I snatched the biggest leaf I could find and blew my nose into it. Neither of us seemed to know what to do with this unseemly emotional purge. We stared around at the landscape as I reeled my composure back in.

A swath of clouds behind us had pulled in front of the sun, and it was beginning to feel legitimately chilly. I sniffed deeply. "We should head back."

The hike wasn't a loop, so we backtracked along the trail by which we'd come. The stream followed and pulled away, now on our right side, as we took our steps more cautiously to avoid slipping on mossy rocks and wet roots. It was Jamie who eventually broke the awkward silence.

"So. I hit my brother-in-law because he told me I had bird crap on my car."

I stopped midstride. "Seriously?"

He nodded. "Well, that's not exactly the 'why', but it was the trigger." He tipped his chin forward to resume the hike. And we started walking again.

"You've got to understand. Chloe is one of those British blue bloods. I came along and muddied their gene pool. And her family has only made the slightest effort to conceal how they feel about it. And Desmond never tried at all."

"It's not like you're some random Joe from Jersey. You're you."

He sighed. "She already had the red-carpet lifestyle. She didn't need me for that. What she didn't have was a fancy title. Duchess or Dame or whatever they call their old ladies.

"Desmond and his wife Helen were stopping over for a few days on their way to Napa for a charity event. Now, about a month before, I had bought a car. A gorgeous, stormy blue, 1966 Shelby Cobra roadster. Total work of art. Fast, brilliant machinery.

"Anyway, Chloe was telling Des about it and suggested that I take him out for a ride along the highway. It certainly beat sitting around listening to them all gossip about people I don't know, so I was game."

I thought to myself, apparently, even celebrities sting when they're not part of the "in crowd."

"Desmond and Helen waited in the driveway chatting with Storey while I backed out of the garage. Normally, people go ape over the car. But Desmond, he just walks around it with his prissy arms folded. Doesn't say anything until he gets all the way back around to the driver's side. At this point, I've gotten out of the car so he can see the interior.

That's when he says, 'Looks like you've got a spot of bird turd on your grill, mate.'"

Jamie imitated him with a pitch-perfect note of amused condescension.

"For thirteen years they made me feel like the shaggy stray that Chloe brought home. I packed all that resentment into my fist and gave him a fast shot to the jaw."

"How badly was he hurt?" I asked.

Jamie shrugged. "I've done so much fake fighting over the years that at the last second I had the good sense to take a little off, so I don't think I broke his jaw or anything. They didn't say in the news?"

"No, but it sounds like the press didn't have a whole lot to go on, so they're doing a lot of speculating."

"Typical. Her family finds publicity in poor taste. They'd as soon lop off their hands as talk to the media, even if it means protecting my bad behavior."

He stopped talking. A wind was rattling the dead leaves in the high treetops. "Man, I figured we were done with uphill," he said.

It took me a second to understand what he meant, realizing my own breathing had gotten heavier. The trail was on a slow but steady incline. We were supposed to be headed down to the parking lot. Maybe it was just a rise in the hill's contour. But there was no longer a stream chuckling along beside us. I scanned ahead for the blue blazes we were supposed to have been following. A few feet ahead, I saw a marker on a knotty, old tree trunk, but the color was deep red, not blue. My stomach went into a lurch. Overhead, two turkey vultures carved portentous arcs in the sky.

I stopped. "You're right. We actually should be heading downhill, so we probably just took a wrong turn."

"We're lost?"

"Not at all. We just have to backtrack until we hit the blue blaze trail again. It's not far."

But it was far. In fact, I never found it again. We eventually came to an intersection with another trail, but it was marked with a white blaze.

"What the hell, Audrey?" he said. "I thought you knew this place."

"I do...I just. We were talking and I must have gotten off track."

"So now what? It's getting dark—"

"Shh."

"We don't have coats. It's the middle of winter—"

"Shut up."

"You shut up!"

"Jesus, Jamie, I mean be quiet. I'm trying to listen for cars so we can work our way down to the road."

"Then what?"

"Then we hitchhike a ride back to the car."

"No way."

"Jamie."

"Audrey, if we get picked up by someone, it'll be a shit show for both you and me."

I had been so caught up in the excitement and celebrity drama that I hadn't even considered what my complicity in his disappearance might mean.

He spoke calmly, "We are not hitchhiking. So point the way down, and we will walk until we get to the lot, even if it takes all night."

We heard only a few cars, but they were enough to lead fairly quickly to the road with only minimal bushwhacking and thorn scrapes. We came to a rotary, which allowed me to know exactly where we were in the park. Unfortunately, the part of the road we reached was on the far side of where we needed to be.

"Here, I saved the last of the trail mix for you."

I held the bag out to him, and he plucked out a single peanut. "We should ration," he said.

"I think we're going to make it."

"Well, you'll understand if I don't put too much stock in your ability to get us out of here."

"That's a bit harsh," I said. We continued a focused march in the direction of the setting sun, but his legs took on a longer stride, and I struggled to keep up.

"I don't even know what the hell I'm doing here." I heard him say. "I don't belong here. I never belonged here."

I had to jog a little to stay with him as he continued to mutter frustrations. But his words projected forward, so it was hard to hear until he threw over his shoulder, "Doesn't even have a fucking TV."

"Hey!" I yelled.

He stopped and turned, sour-faced.

"I may not have a TV, and I may have gotten us a bit lost, but you know what, Mr. Perfect? Your shit stinks too." After a beat I added, "And I can personally attest to it."

I raised my hand to my mouth, immediately wishing I could take it back. Surely, he would insist that I drop him off at the airport on our way home, and this surreal little adventure would abruptly end.

But then, he started laughing. And it was the perfect cinematic moment, the one where the guy and the girl banter and bicker to a climax, and then the sheer force of their mutual attraction draws them together for that first, unstoppable kiss.

"You're a nut," Jamie said, still standing there, laughing and shaking his head. "Let's get to the car before the wolves eat us."

So much for life imitating art.

Sore-footed, hungry, and exhausted, we arrived at the car nearly an hour later, having not spoken the rest of the way. The daylight was nearly gone, and as we pulled onto the road it started to drizzle, so there was some consolation that things didn't go as badly as they could have.

Jamie fell asleep during the drive back. Whenever a car approached from the other direction, I stole surreptitious glances of him lit up by their passing headlights. With his face unguarded and still, it was easy to recognize the features of that teenaged boy.

And then like that movie reel starting, a long-buried summer memory played in my mind.

§

There had been a fast storm, flashy and booming loud. Running home from the town pool, the raindrops fell so hard they stung my skin like the arm-twisting burns Kenny gave me whenever we wrestled. Arriving home

to find that the downpour had rinsed my chalk draw-
ings into pink and yellow rivulets that flowed down the
driveway, I felt sad and surly.

I changed into dry clothes as the thunder faded.
Bobbie had toasted us some frozen pizza squares and
sliced up a few token carrot sticks that neither Kenny nor I would touch since Mom wasn't there to force
us. The three of us ate quickly, barely even sitting. The
first few partygoers would arrive in forty-five minutes.
Who knew how many kids would come once word got
around that our parents were out of town?

"So," Bobbie asked Kenny, "who of your friends are
coming tonight?"

"The guys. You know. A few girls. Pete's got a new
girlfriend from Mount Ivy, so some of her friends may
show up."

"Like Pete, Owen, Travis, Marky, Jamie, Tommy R?
Those guys?"

"Which one?" asked Kenny.

"What do you mean?"

"Which one are you hoping is coming?"

I knew which one, but not because Bobbie had con-
fided in me. Eavesdropping on the family room phone
was a recent habit I had picked up, carefully lifting and
covering the receiver with my hand and quieting my
breath to hear whatever gossip she shared with Gillian.
Their conversations were pretty stupid, but I listened
to every word because you never knew when some
juicy information would come in handy for bartering
or blackmailing. But this time, I couldn't help myself,
and rather than use the information strategically, I let
out a sing-songy, "Jay-mee! It's Jamie she wants to see."

"Ugh," said Kenny. "Not you too."

"Shut up, you twit," Bobbie snapped at me. "It's
time for you to get out of here, anyway. Are you packed?"

I was being exiled to my friend Tia's for a sleepover, though I'd rather have locked myself in my room. Not because I didn't like sleepovers. I just didn't want anyone using my bed for a make-out session.

"It's not like I'm going on vacation." I bit off a corner of nearly burnt pizza. "Can't I just stay here tonight?"

They both answered in firm unison: "No."

Kenny got up from the table leaving his crummy plate and crumpled napkin. "Oh, Jay-mee! Oh, yes, Jay-mee, yes!" he falsettoed as he headed down the hall to take a shower.

"Hate you," she said, probably to both of us. Then she pointed at me, "Clear the table."

"Why—"

"I made dinner," she said.

"You opened a box and turned on the toaster. I could have done that."

She got up and left me alone in the kitchen. The party mess was going to be way worse than this, and I considered leaving the plates right where they were out of protest. But I became strangely concerned about their welfare, imagining one of the drunk Stacies careening into the table and sending them crashing to the floor. Missing plates would get noticed by Mom who would then ask me about it, and I'd have a hard time lying. I brushed the crumbs into the garbage and figured the plates looked clean enough, so I restacked them in the cabinet.

With the storm clouds gone, the setting sun still had enough heat to cause steam to rise off the asphalt like breathing, and there was a sharp, salty smell in the air, like dirt and driveways. Feeling like a runaway with my sleeping bag slung over my shoulder, I left the house without saying goodbye. Let them wonder if I was hiding out somewhere to ruin their stupid party.

Tia had moved in next door three summers before. We never formally introduced ourselves, just played in our respective yards, eyeing each other with suspicious curiosity for a week before gradually setting up our Barbies closer and closer, until one day, like fashionable plastic ambassadors, our dolls started talking to each other.

Our birthdays were two months apart, but with me having teenage siblings and her having a brother in kindergarten, I always felt a little more like a big sister than best friend— teaching her the myriad uses of the word "fuck" and misinforming her with my sketchy understanding of periods and sex.

It was a nearly full moon that night. Tia and I had climbed out her bedroom window and settled into two adjacent crooks of the crabapple tree. We were supposed to be asleep, so we had on our pajamas in case we had to make a hasty retreat. While the tree's roots were technically on the Wallace's property, the broad, old branches hung over into our yard, offering a prime perch for spying on the party.

This was peak summer. Humid with a thin breeze. Moths like flying scraps of white paper flitted around the porch lights. From various yards in the neighborhood, you could hear the frequent pops and sizzles of the bug zappers that were left on all the time, even when there was no one around. I hoped it was the mosquitoes and not the moths getting fried.

There was a small cluster of teenagers on our deck. Their backs were to us, so it was hard to tell who was there, even when squinting. The stereo was playing loud enough to be heard but not enough to keep Tia's little brother awake, thereby causing Mr. Wallace to bust up the party.

"Can I break off this branch?" I asked Tia.

"I guess. Don't make it too obvious though."

"They'll never see us up here."

I snapped about an arm's length of leafy branch and let it flutter to the ground. Someone turned up the music in the middle of *Born to Run*, right at that line that made me feel all fluttery: "*Just wrap your legs 'round these velvet rims.*" A few of the girls shouted, "Strap your hands 'cross my engines!"

Kenny joined the group on the deck. I could tell by the way the porch light glinted off his glasses. The guys leaning on the railing were probably Travis and Owen, and there was a girl I couldn't identify. They all took big swigs out of their beer cans and sporadically let out loud bursts of laughter plus a couple of croaking boy-belches. The girl rumpled Kenny's hair, then casually left her arm draped around his shoulders.

"Seems kind of boring," Tia said. "Wanna go play Yahtzee?"

"Don't you want to know how to be a teenager? I mean, we're going to be there soon."

The music cut off, and you could suddenly hear the steady buzz-saw sounds of the summer bugs.

"Hey!" Owen yelled out, "Who the fuck turned off the music?"

Someone inside shouted something back, and then a new song came on, Queen or Bowie or someone. Just then, to our left, coming from the front yard, someone was backing through the break in the hedges.

"You should have seen his face—" It was Bobbie. "It looked like this."

A boy laughed. "Oh man, I bet."

He followed her as she turned and walked over, just below us. Tia and I looked at each other with wide eyes.

"It's not like she was actually going to go through with it," said Bobbie. "Bethany just likes to push people's buttons."

Bobbie picked up the branch I had dropped and twirled it around in her fingers. Then she sat down at the base of our tree and rested her back against the trunk. The boy was taller than Kenny, skinnier too.

"Well, he thinks she's crazy now," he said.

Closer, I could tell it was Jamie by his posture: round-shouldered, head tilted forward and to the side, shaking the long bangs out of his eyes without removing his hands from his pockets. He seemed unsure as to whether or not he should sit.

"So..." he said, shuffling a sneaker in the grass a little. "Are you sure? About this, I mean?"

"Yeah, of course."

Spying from a distance was one thing, but Tia and I did not want to be this close to whatever action was going to happen next. We would have to climb about five feet up to get back to Tia's window, and that wouldn't go unnoticed from below no matter how quiet we were. Bobbie pulled something out of her back pocket. I would later find out that it was one of my father's cigars, but in the moment, I was sure it was one of those "things for making you not have a baby," so I panicked and let out a squeal.

"What—?" Jamie and Bobbie tipped their heads up toward us. Tia bolted first, with me scrambling fast behind her. "Go, go!" I shouted.

"You're dead, Audrey!" was the last thing I heard before Tia and I tumbled onto the carpet. We paused to catch a breath, looked at each other and exploded into loud hyena laughs. That brought a firm knock on the door from Tia's father, "Girls! Watch the racket!" Tia just happened to have a badminton racquet under her bed. She pulled it out and pretended to stare at it. This sent us into hilarity again, smothering our giggles with pillows.

But Tia was one of those kids who lacked the stamina for the marathon sleepovers I was used to, and it wasn't long before she was overcome by yawning. Nestled into her bed, she half-listened while I told a ghost story about a drowned boy, during which she fell into a light-snoring sleep.

I lay there a while, watching an oscillating fan scan the room, its electric breeze ruffling a pink feather boa to my left and Tia's squared-off bangs on my right. But the fan's meager breeze was fixed on a plane above my sleeping bag on the floor. I was sticky from the humidity and knew that sleep would be a ways off.

Meanwhile, the party sounds next door had become more muted—Kenny was smart enough to make sure the noise level was reasonable enough to avoid Mrs. Kahn complaining to our parents. Still, the mellow voices and low thumping bass notes from the stereo lured me back to the crabapple tree. I climbed out and into the relief of the cool night air.

Where it was darkest, near the picket fence that marked the edge of the Deegans' backyard, you could see lightning bugs flashing here, then gone, over there—on and off like a visual Morse code. This would have been two years after they sprayed for the gypsy moths and the crabapple tree had rebounded with a bounty of green fruit. Plucking a cherry sized apple from a nearby branch, I took a sour bite and spit it out almost immediately. I settled into the wide Y of the branches and breathed in the smell of damp grass clippings and charcoal barbeques. Looking up at the night sky, I saw Orion, a silent witness to this delicious secret moment that was all my own.

Until it wasn't. I was startled by the sound of cracking branches coming from the hedges—not where the
normal opening was, but near enough to be either
a dumb dog or a drunk partygoer forcing his way
through. *Same difference,* I thought to myself.

From my perch, I felt invisible, invincible—a bemused demigod watching with curiosity as the figure
forcefully broke through, stumbling, then tumbling
onto the dew-slick grass. It was one of Kenny's friends.
But he was hunched over like a shadowy boulder so
it took a moment to make out that it was Jamie, who
had returned, this time without Bobbie. He stood up,
swayed a moment and then sat down again heavily in
a corner where the edge of the hedges met a low wall
that the Kahns had built out of stones excavated for
their wide vegetable garden.

Jamie folded his knees up and rested his forearms
there as a perch for his head. I considered leaping down to
the lawn, Catwoman-style, scaring the piss out of him. Or
maybe just whispering his name so he'd look up and invite
me down to keep him company. But there was something
about the tilt of his head as it rested there that held me
in place, silent and still but for my own shallow breathing.

As a youngest sibling, spying was a natural way to
cobble an understanding of experiences that were considered too grown up for me: fights between my parents
about why my grandparents wouldn't visit; that time
when Mrs. Paxton was sobbing in the kitchen having
lost the baby she was carrying; a kissing exchange
between Bobbie and Charlie Laraway. But Jamie was
totally alone with no awareness of any other presence.
And so being there, it felt different in its invasiveness;
I felt both uneasy and exhilarated.

He just sat there, plucking compulsively at the
grass. He rubbed his nose on his sleeve, and then Ja-

mie Keefner did something completely unexpected. He put his hands together and started to pray.

I knew I should bolt back to my place on the sleeping bag to give him back his privacy but doing so would have robbed him of even the perception of privacy. I sat immobile, waiting, and unable to look away.

I'd known kids who went to Sunday school and had first communions. I had friends whose families always said grace before a meal. But those things didn't seem like religious practices; they were something people just did, the same way they went to the grocery store or brushed their teeth twice a day.

There was no way for me to know if Jamie was actually praying to God, but he was clearly moving his lips, expressing something from within to something from without.

It wasn't long, roughly a minute. Then he stopped whispering and took a deep breath. He seemed to slap his legs a little, as if they had fallen asleep, and stood up. Once on the other side of the hedges, he didn't return to the party. Instead, I saw him—just a shadow at that distance—cut through the Delacroix's yard in the direction of his house.

I never told anyone about the encounter, but the few times later that I saw him, there seemed to be a seriousness that hung like a shadow around his shoulders. And later, as an actor, it was an intangible quality that seemed to hover at the edge of every role he played, a kind of world-weariness that gave even the most lethal superhero a nuanced kind of grace.

§

Back at the condo, and without discussing it, it became clear that Jamie would be spending another night. We kicked off our sneakers and dropped backpack and jackets at the door. I took to the kitchen to scrounge together a skillet of scrambled eggs with herbs, parmesan, peppers, and onions. "Good frittata," he said, which I could only assume was scrambled eggs with stuff mixed in.

Spending the whole day together had drained the well of conversation. But the clanking silverware on the plates made me feel like I was wasting an opportunity to rebound from the day's discord. Without even really thinking about it, I asked, "Do you believe in God?"

There was the slightest hesitation of his fork on its way to his mouth, but then he continued eating, and seemed disinclined to answer.

This time, rather than fill the silence with nervous chatter, I waited him out, not taking another bite of food until he responded in some way.

He took a swig of orange juice, then, "Is this where you ask me to accept Jesus Christ as my Lord and Savior?"

"I swear, I don't have a single religious hair on my head."

"And you think I do?"

After all these years of holding onto that memory in some pocket of my brain, it felt crazy to tell the story aloud, let alone to the person who was the subject of said memory, but I did it anyway.

"When I was about ten, my parents went away on a weekend trip for their anniversary. And Kenny and Bobbie threw a party." I had faint goosebumps on my arms as I recounted what I remembered.

At a certain point in the telling, I could see his eyes change. He clearly knew the moment I was speaking of, and it occurred to me that—even these years later—hearing that he had been spied on might not be well received.

"You were there? At that moment? You were there—what—watching?"

"I was a kid, I didn't know what to do. And I was there first. You just happened to come along. In that sense, you were intruding on me."

He didn't seem to be listening to my defense. "Let me tell you about that night." Jamie picked up our empty dishes and brought them to the sink, giving them a quick rinse. He poured himself a glass of water in the empty orange juice glass, then came and sat back down at the table.

"I drank more that summer than at any other point in my life. Not just beer, hard liquor—probably more than over the course of my entire life. We were about to start our senior year, and it was all that crazy, raw energy of being seventeen. The sex, the alcohol, and the pot...that total freedom of having cars. Going to the city, going to the beach. It was just, everything was so... wide open.

"I remember that night. People were playing beer pong in your basement and shotgunning cans of Bud. At that point in the summer, I had gotten good at keeping a level-steady buzz, but most others were getting bombed. This girl Jessica, puked in the shower. And I do—I totally remember your sister taking me by the hand, out the front door and through the hedges to the side yard. I figured she wanted to fool around." He paused. "It's so funny to think that was you—" He gestured at me sitting across the table. "Back then up in the tree. That was you? So weird how time collapses like that. Things feel like they just happened even though it's been, like, twenty-five years.

"After you and your friend bolted from the tree, we went to the other side of the yard and smoked that cigar. Or your sister did. I just took a few fake puffs. I was kind restless that night, and when we went back inside, I started talking with this girl from another school—Pete's cousin, I think. She was upset about some guy who'd made a joke about her teeth or her eyebrows? And I remember looking up, around the room at everyone just hanging all over each other with their lazy eyes and slurring words. And that girl went on and on.

"It's not like I was bored or mad or disgusted or anything. What I felt was...I was just...done. Not just done with the party, it was bigger than that. I was done with that part of my life. Just like that, ready to move on. Like I had finished the last sentence of the last chapter, came to a period, and closed the book.

"The air started to feel really stuffy, and the noise was too much. I left the house, but I didn't want to go home and see my dad asleep on the couch in front of the TV. I felt like I needed to sit and think. That's when I went to the side of the house where you must have been skulking around in that tree."

He stopped and closed his eyes a minute.

"It had been a long time since I'd let myself think about my mom. I was pretty much still a kid when she died, and I kept this idea that whenever I felt sad about her, I would push those feelings down to an imaginary hollow place in my left ankle. You know, like how you compact garbage down at the bottom of a bag so there's more room to pile other crap on top. I did it so much, there was a time when I actually thought my left leg was getting heavier than my right. Isn't that funny? Probably not the healthiest coping mechanism, but I just wanted to be normal. I didn't want to be the kid with the dead mother. Never even mind the fact that she was gone.

"Anyway. That night, I actually wanted to think about her. I wanted to know what she would say, what advice she would have given.

"You were too young to know my mom, but she was no bullshit. She started her own law practice at a time when all the moms around her were home raising their kids. They didn't know what to make of her, and I don't think she had too many friends. Plus, my mom had no patience for politeness, so that didn't help her much. And she always told me that while it was important to be respectful of others, I needed to always look after my best interests because nobody else was going to.

"She had no idea how prophetic that advice would turn out to be.

"So, there I was in that corner by the rock wall. And I tried and tried but I couldn't conjure her voice or even her face. It had been such a long time. I was at a loss. There was nothing else I could think to do so I put my hands together. It wasn't really a gesture of prayer. Or maybe it was. I don't know, but it helped. I asked the question over and over, 'What do I do now?' And finally, I was able to imagine—at the time, I wanted to think I channeled—her response: 'Pack your things and go find what's next.'

"I didn't tell anyone, but I started saving money, making plans. I figured I would stay with my dad through Christmas and then pack up and head to California."

He slid a penny out from where it had wedged beneath the napkin holder. With a gentle finger, he held it on its side and flicked it into a spin on the table. Signifying nothing in particular, it landed on tails.

When my mother heard that Jamie Keefner was dropping out of school six months short of graduation, she threw a fit at my brother, insisting that he talk some sense into Jamie if his father wasn't going to. Kenny just shrugged and said they didn't hang out that much anymore, and it wasn't her business anyway. She just shook her head with disgust and said, "His mother would roll over in her grave."

Jamie and I turned in early, retreating into some personal space, he with a cup of tea and me with a book that I couldn't concentrate on. Instead, I again relived that long-ago summer night, this time though, replaying the scene through the lens of an unwitting witness to a real-life origin story.

12: Bowl over Beethoven

Saturday morning. I had returned—the triumphant knight completing her quest—with a baker's dozen of assorted fresh bagels in the crook of my arm. L.A. could keep its avocado salads and fruit smoothies; a fresh bagel with its shiny outer crust, its yielding, chewy interior—this was New Jersey's gift to the world.

"Smell this." I held the bag under Jamie's nose. He breathed in the warm, yeasty aroma.

"We have bagels in California."

"With sprouts and seaweed and crap baked into them. This—" I pulled one from the bag, scattering poppy seeds to the floor, "is a true and earnest wheel of carbohydrate perfection."

"It's just a bagel."

"And a Pinot is just a Pinot."

"Please."

I tumbled a handful of bagels into a basket and caught a small wave of joy upon discovering that Jamie had already made a pot of coffee and set out two mugs.

He called out from the couch, "Man, your neighbors across the way were totally going at it last night when I went to brush my teeth. You ought to send them a set of blinds."

He chimed in again. "Oh, hey, there's a message on your answering machine from someone named Joyce.

Sounds like you're supposed to meet her at eleven o'clock today?"

My jaw wrenched open wide. "Oh shit. Shit, shit, shit."

Whatever wan enthusiasm I had mustered about meeting Joyce and Bobbie at the spa dissolved upon arriving at the tiny strip mall in which the Sweet Serenity Day Spa was housed, flanked by a pharmacy on one side and a tax accountant's office on the other.

The girls' spa day had been Joyce's "gift" to us since we hadn't been invited to the wedding. We had tried putting it off, but she gave us so many date options, it was impossible to decline all of them.

Bobbie was standing beside the entrance, pacing to keep warm. "Thank God. I was terrified you weren't going to show," she said as I approached.

"I considered feigning illness just to imagine how long you two would last in a steam room together." I had actually been ready to call Joyce and make just that excuse, but Jamie insisted that I go.

"Does this place even have a steam room?" Bobbie asked.

"Maybe they converted the walk-in freezer from when it was a Chinese take-out place."

As I reached for the door handle, we heard Joyce calling from the parking area, her shoes clacking on the pavement. She carried a big, quilted bag over her shoulder.

"Good morning, ladies!"

"Hi Joyce," Bobbie said.

"Hey Joyce."

She reached us, slightly out of breath. "Our appointments are for eleven thirty, but I brought along a thermos of mimosas to share while we waited." She shook her bag to let us hear the ice cubes rattling. "It's been a long time since we had a chance to catch up. I can't wait!"

Bobbie side-mouthed to me as we followed Joyce into the check-in area, "I hope they have a no-talking policy."

The fluorescent overhead lights and overstuffed couches did little to ease us into what was marketed as a restorative experience. Bobbie and I exchanged looks, a wrinkled nose and furrowed brow, respectively.

Joyce took the lead since she'd booked the appointments. "Hello, there. We're here for massage appointments."

The young woman behind the counter had the complexion of Snow White. "And you are?"

"Tambrough, Beadle, and Rohmer."

"You know, that trippy, prog-rock band from the '70s," I joked. Snow looked at me confused.

"I know we're a bit early," said Joyce, "But I was hoping we could relax in the lounge area beforehand."

"You'll need to be totally quiet," she said looking right at Bobbie and me.

"Score!" Bobbie mouthed at me.

We were ushered through a pair of frosted doors where a short, muscular man with a crew cut led the way. There was a pleasantly wispy, vanilla-musk scent to the air, and a quiet flute playing, leading us like a lone canyon bird. As we followed the dim hallway, I was reminded of the kids in *The Lion, the Witch and the Wardrobe* wandering away from the "Spare Oom" into a transforming landscape of winter wonder.

In the changing room, we slid into plushy, warm, white robes and slippers that felt like pillows strapped to my feet. From her bag, Joyce pulled out three plastic cups and set them on a bench to pour her smuggled Mimosa mixture. Maybe this wouldn't be a wasted afternoon, after all. Even Bobbie seemed pleased.

We crossed to the waiting area where the furniture was as sleek and contoured as the check-in's was lumpy and awkward. We settled in comfortably, allowing a gauzy mellowness to seep in with our breathing.

"A toast," said Joyce. "To our new family."

You would think she'd set off a stink bomb for the sudden change in the room's atmosphere. Bobbie looked as if she'd found a dead fly in her mimosa, and I couldn't muster more than a half-hearted smile. We did not raise our glasses in return but instead sipped at them in silence. Joyce covered her embarrassment by pulling a brochure from the display.

"Did you know they also do mud wraps here? It's supposed to draw out the bad stuff we put in our bodies and replace it with healing minerals."

"I think we're supposed to be quiet," Bobbie whispered.

The mood was stiff and silent as we waited roughly fifteen minutes for our appointments. Finally, the first therapist arrived, half-whispering Joyce's name into the waiting room. When she'd left, Bobbie mouthed at me "Oh my gawd! I cannot deal with her." I shook my head in response.

A moment later, Bobbie was swept away by her therapist, the crew-cut guy who had escorted us to the changing room. My therapist arrived less than a minute later, saying my name quietly, though I was clearly the only one in the room.

She held her hand out to me, "Audrey, I'm Tatum." Tatum wore the thickest glasses I had ever seen, making her expression especially eager and intense.

She escorted me to a golden-lit room where a small water fountain was chattering from a corner table.

"Is there anything you would like me to know?"

"Oh, well, James Keefner is staying at my house. He's taken to folding my laundry and making apple-sauce, but I thought it more important to come here for a spa day with my new stepmom."

The sheer absurdity made us both laugh. "Haha, I mean, any areas I should focus on?"

"Oh, no, I don't think so."

"OK, I'll step out for a moment."

I had had very few professional massages in my lifetime, having found there was a thin, fragile line between feeling OK about being pretty much naked at the literal hands of a total stranger, and being completely freaked out by it. But Tatum had a kind voice and she seemed fascinated by the body's various manifestations of tension. Part physical therapist, part Sherlock Holmes she spoke quietly to me as she worked.

"You're a lefty."

"You spend a lot of time sitting during the day."

"Did you have a bad ankle sprain in the last few years?"

"You should be drinking more water."

Over the course of an hour, she dug into areas that were so unexpectedly and profoundly tight I nearly leapt off the table. And though I wasn't the least bit relaxed, the experience felt liberating. Like ice dams breaking on a river. I nearly cried.

After I'd dressed, I met Tatum in the waiting room. She was holding out a cup of water and a warm towel.

"How do you feel?" She blinked owlishly behind her glasses.

"Wrecked. In a good way. I think."

She smiled, proud of her work.

"I found quite a few trigger points. That's not unusual, especially for someone with a desk job. But there was one area—the left side, behind the shoulder blade that was especially gnarly."

I could still feel an angry pulse radiating from that area. "I seem to recall that."

"In my experience, that kind of deep accumulation of toxins—lactic acid, proteins and stuff—is often related to emotional, not necessarily physical issues."

"Oh, I'm not depressed or anything like that."

She made a thinking face, then decided to explain it differently. "Imagine you're holding a big stone in your arms. It's not super heavy, but you can't put it down. Over time, your body is going to focus its energy on keeping that stone held tight. Your muscles surround it, your spine curves against it, your heart and surrounding organs get cramped by it." She put a hand on my upper arm. "Anger, secrets, worry—those things are like stones we hold onto."

I liked my massage a whole lot more without the therapy. "Oh. Thanks, that's helpful information. I appreciate you taking the time."

"I hate to see people burdened in that way."

"I'm not. Really. I probably just need a better chair at work."

She smiled indulgently and made a slight bow of her head as she left the room.

Joyce, Bobbie and I had a plan to meet at the warm, saltwater pool after our massages.

Neither of them was in the changing room when I got there to get into my bathing suit. That probably meant they were alone together, so I moved quickly.

I followed signs written in an exotic, Asian-style font that read, "To the water." In the Jacuzzi, I did find my sister and—I decided I had better get used to saying it—my stepmother, making (very) small talk. In the larger pool, three other women were huddled around the stairs while an older man in goggles was swimming gentle, tortoise-like laps. I slid tentatively into the hot, bubbling tub.

"For my lower back, he suggested I 'strengthen my core.'" Bobbie was saying. She turned to me, "Me. Doing sit-ups."

"How was your session, Audie?" Joyce asked.

Bobbie and I exchanged a telepathic "eyebrow raise" at Joyce's inaugural use of my familial nickname. Like a person inserting a vocabulary word she just learned into casual conversation, the attempt was worthy, but ultimately unsuccessful.

"I'm not really one for strangers and my skin coming into contact with one another. But she was skilled and knowledgeable."

"Jeez, Audie, you make her sound like a car mechanic," Bobbie said.

"Apart from the horror of suggesting that you exercise, how was your guy?" I asked.

"Too nice," she replied. "I got so tired of telling him to dig deeper, I nearly got up off the table to demonstrate on him. Honestly, if I don't feel bruised the next day, it's not worth the hour of my time."

"Well, I had a wonderful experience," said Joyce. "There was a recording of the ocean playing. The sound of the waves got me daydreaming about the wedding trip with your father in Florida."

I sank to my chin in the bubbling water, letting the heat soak deeply into my tender back muscles. We retreated into our own mental spaces, and I became nearly hypnotized by the slow, rhythmic breaststrokes of the lap swimmer. Though he must have been about eighty years old, he was still lithe, focused with strength and determination.

I was reminded of a photograph of my mother that I hadn't thought about in ages. It was one among a collection of loose prints in an old shirt box that had been stowed in the living room cabinet. The picture was of my teenage mother submerged to her ribcage at the end of a pool. A modest, dark-colored bathing suit flattened her breasts, and a smooth swimming cap was suctioned to her head. She was smiling, ebullient, as she held high a round medal that was ribboned around her neck. Someone, probably my grandmother Luce, had written in loopy script on the back: "Dottie wins! July 22, 1952."

And then my mind leapfrogged to a memory of my grandparents' home in South Carolina and the inground pool they had in their backyard. My Grandpa Leo was trying to teach me to float on my back, but no matter how much he tried to assure me he wouldn't let me sink, I was frozen in a rigor mortis V, refusing to point my chin up or lift my hips toward the sky as he directed. He became frustrated with my willful distrust.

"You know, in her day, your mother was the best swimmer in all of Massachusetts," he said. "Smooth and fast as a shark." He lifted me up out of the water and set me on the cement. "You should try to have a little more of her in you."

Five months before my mother was to go to the nationals at the age of nineteen, she met Louis Rohmer, a quiet young man who was just starting out his career in broadcasting. He bought her a drink, he brought her to Brooklyn, and they were married just before she would otherwise have competed. And as far as I know, she never swam a lap again.

My thoughts were interrupted by the opening of the door and a subsequent wave of chilly air. Joyce told us the woman entering was Brynn, her massage therapist. Brynn neared the pool and called to one of the women there. Joyce gave her a wave and she smiled warmly in return.

Joyce shouted to her, "I'll drop off a copy of that recipe on my way home from work on Monday. Your husband is going to love it."

"I don't want you to go to any trouble," the woman said.

"It's no trouble. It's right on my way."

"You're so sweet," she said. "Thank you, Joyce."

Brynn's next client got out of the pool and dried off as the therapist waited patiently by the door. When they'd left, Bobbie said to Joyce, "You just have to make friends with everybody, don't you?"

Joyce pursed her lips a little. There was a beat; then she seemed to make a decision.

"You know, my plan today didn't include either of you," she said. "This was going to be my day. My indulgence in a few hours of luxury. I didn't want to spend it with you any more than you wanted to spend it with me. But your father asked me to invite you. And do you know why I did? Because that's what you do for people you care about."

She stood suddenly, and the water splashed around us.

"I'm going to the sauna," Joyce said. "Please don't join me." She snatched up her towel and dried herself briskly.

Bobbie looked at me in mock sheepishness, "What was that about?"

I watched Joyce walk off, straight-backed and calm. "I think she's tired of us pointing out the bird shit on her new car."

I waved away Bobbie's confused look with my hand. "It's just an expression I heard recently."

For the next couple hours, Bobbie and I followed Joyce's request and avoided the sauna by alternating between the hot tub and the saltwater pool. With my massage therapist's counsel in my head, I danced at the very edge of telling Bobbie about Dan. Instead, I asked if she had ever thought about cheating on Doug while they were married.

"Of course, I thought about it," she said matter-of-factly. "You're married to the same person for seventeen years, the idea is bound to come up." She dunked under the water in the pool and rose again, wiping the stream from her eyes and nose.

"About four years ago," she said. "There was this guy—his name was actually Guy. He used to come into the bakery every Thursday at nine thirty for a Morning Glory muffin, a cappuccino and a molasses cookie. He was really sweet to me. Seemed honestly interested in what I had to say. And every visit, he made it his mission to get me—this grumpy, frumpy, middle-aged mother—to laugh out loud. It made me feel young again."

She stopped speaking, her fingers tracing a small crack in the cement floor. "One morning when Marcella was in the back, he asked me to meet him at Gillespie Park after my shift was over."

This was a rare, calm candidness for Bobbie. I didn't want to speak and pop whatever strange and luminous bubble was blooming.

"It was this cloudless, perfect blue-sky day," she said. "I think it was April. He was sitting on a bench feeding pieces of bread to the ducks when I got there. He said he was surprised that I came, but glad. We talked a bit about our lives.

"He was from Montreal but had married a woman from upstate and became a citizen. When his job got transferred to Hoboken, she didn't want to move, so they split. I told him about how I had always wished I'd moved to California before I got married. I talked about Doug and how we'd met in college. I told him about the twins and how I know I'm sometimes not a good mother to them."

She stopped talking again and didn't seem inclined to resume. "What happened?"

"We kissed—just once, though. It was strange and exciting and scary. And then I told him he probably shouldn't come back to the bakery. He never did again."

I wanted to hear more. I wanted to ask what precisely kept her from making a different choice. Was it simple adherence to what was moral? Was it ultimately an abiding love for Doug? Was it a fear of the twins finding out? And now that her marriage was officially ending, did she regret sending Guy away? Would she try to find him?

But Bobbie was already scooting toward the steps. "I'm turning into a prune," she said.

While her back was turned, I felt a flash of impulse to keep that tenuous thread between us intact just a little longer. I was a dime-thin moment away from blurting out, *Jamie Keefner is staying at my house!* Instead, I pinched the flesh on the back of my upper arm, hard. Because letting Bobbie in on that particular secret would have created a nightmare scenario where she would insist on "just stopping by" with or without my collusion, and either way, Jamie would feel cornered and worse, betrayed.

I left the spa day still holding my stone of secrets in a vice grip. And now, there was a new burden: figure out an olive branch that Bobbie and I could offer to Joyce with some sincerity.

§

It was a muscle memory long buried: the lowering of the driver's side window (back then, it was the hand-cranked kind), the light heft of the quarter pinched between the thumb and forefinger, and the artful, arc-toss into the yawing mouth of the toll basket. Five toll baskets, to be precise, that stitched together the Garden State Parkway from Bergen County down to the shore towns and Exit 82 for Seaside Heights, affectionately known as Sleazeside.

Now, almost twenty-five years later, in an ever-green air-freshened rental car, Jamie had settled into the easy pleasure of driving for its own sake. No company, no schedule, just the mostly open road ahead, and passing signs calling out the names of towns he'd long forgotten.

It seemed like someone else's life—a character in an old movie—remembering those summer treks to the shore with Kenny and Owen and Pete. Easy, delinquent days spent bodysurfing and playing volleyball. Chasing the high-haired girls in half-shirts and cutoffs. They would scam and steal their way along the boardwalk, in and out of the arcades, and party crawl into the night. If they got back to their homes by three o'clock in the morning, it was an early night.

Jamie angled into a parking space and cut the engine. He looked out at the wide, empty beach and the waves rolling in, dragging out. He walked along the boardwalk with his coat collar turned up, thankful for the knit cap and a scarf he'd pilfered from Audrey's coat closet.

Though an unfair comparison in the middle of winter, the Jersey shore couldn't be more different from the Malibu beaches. The light cast everything in varying shades of concrete, and the air wasn't just cold, it was salt-stinging, toothy and vicious. This part of the eastern coast might as well have been the dark side of the moon compared to SoCal's teal hues and coppery warmth, the lean palms doing their slow hula along the shoreline. He felt a twinge of homesickness and a craving for a fresh-squeezed carrot-ginger-apple juice.

But this strange, forced vacation had been an unexpected gift. A chance to make a kind of peace with the ghost of Ernest James Keefner. Being back in New Jersey for more than a few hours had allowed Jamie to ask himself questions like "What kind of father would I be to Storey if Chloe died suddenly?" Ernest James Keefner asked in return, "What kind of father are you to her now?"

Brined and brittle, the boardwalk planks groaned below his feet. He approached the strip of bars and arcades and rides, all shuttered and empty, their carnival signs unlit and dingy. If not for a lone jogger in the distance, he might have found the whole scene post-apocalyptic, as if he might round a corner and find the Statue of Liberty buried waist-deep in the sand.

But for all his thinking during the drive (and several quiet moments of curious domesticity over the past couple days), Jamie still felt like there was something deeper and more profound that he was missing. Something just out of his mind's reach that a more nuanced thinker would have figured out. About how to feel grounded in the "real" world when everything around him was superficial and illusory.

He sat down on a wooden bench overlooking the wide Atlantic. There was this girl, he remembered, from the summer before his senior year. She was a local who lived upstairs from the laundromat that her family owned just a few blocks from the beach. She had dark, shaggy, Joan Jett-style hair and went only by her last name, Crenshaw. They'd had a condom break the only time they had sex, and for the next several months, he braced himself for a letter saying she was having his baby.

From a few feet away, a boy on a bike came wheeling hard around the corner. He wore a red, white, and blue Giant's ski hat with a big pompom on top.

A wind gust grabbed hold of Jamie's scarf, nearly unraveling it from his neck. The kid had circled around and was passing now from the opposite direction, this time slowing down to look at Jamie. Jamie lowered the hat over his eyebrows and glanced away at the rusty, frozen Ferris wheel.

When the boy came back a third time, Jamie figured he'd better find somewhere else to go. As he was about to stand, the boy came to a stop a few feet away.

"Aren't you supposed to be in rehab?"

"Who said that?" Jamie asked testily.

"My mom. That's what she heard."

"Do I look like a drug addict to you?"

"I dunno. Maybe with that beard," the kid said. "And anyway, why are you here?"

"That's the big question, my friend."

The boy rolled his eyes. "I mean, why aren't you on some remote tropical island instead of this hole."

"I spent a lot of time here a long time ago." Jamie picked at a flaking piece of gray paint and tugged it gently, managing to pull up a long, narrow strip. "It was a fun place, fun time in my life." He tossed the paint aside. "But I bet you can't wait to leave, can you?"

The boy shrugged. "I go to my dad's house in Michigan every summer. I only get to live at the beach in the shitty seasons."

"Well, someday, you'll have the freedom to live wherever you want. The hardest part will be figuring out what it is you want." His voice trailed off full of dramatic wistfulness.

Once again, the boy rolled his eyes. It was irritating. "What is that?" Jamie asked. "What's with the disdain?"

"I dunno. Seems like someone like you wouldn't have too much to complain about."

"Here's the thing about the good life—what's your name?"

"AJ."

"See, AJ, the more you have, the more you have to lose. It can all disappear like that," he snapped to punctuate the point. "That day when the shit hit the fan back in LA? I had gotten a call from my agent telling me I lost a part that was practically written for me. They gave it to some asshole ten years younger who has no depth of experience."

AJ nodded slowly. "I hear ya. I got cut from the soccer team when this hot shit new kid, Damon Wright moved in from Tom's River."

"No offense, but Damon Wright didn't short you out of a $10 million soccer contract." Jamie flicked an ant that had climbed onto his jeans. "And that's not even the point."

"What's the point, then?" said AJ.

"Exactly."

The boy gave a puzzled look, squeezing and releasing his brakes a few times. The two of them regarded each other like one generation trying to discern a trace of itself in the other.

"I gotta go meet my friend Savion for a science project."

"Listen, don't tell anyone I was here, OK?"

The boy thought a moment; it was a good story that would, no doubt, up his social cachet considerably.

"Or...just keep it to yourself for a week?" Jamie said.

"Pretty sure you can afford to bribe me."

Jamie opened his wallet and pulled out a couple of twenties. "Best I can do."

The kid grabbed the bills and cracked a winning lopsided grin. He could easily have been cast in a movie. He stuffed the money in his pocket and gave a little salute before pedaling away.

Jamie called after him, "Hey, your last name isn't Crenshaw, is it?"

§

I didn't get home until after four o'clock. Jamie's car was not there, and I went into a slight panic, run-walking from the lot. If he had truly gone, Joyce would become the scapegoat for my dismay, and I might never forgive her for something she had absolutely nothing to do with.

Rounding the corner, my momentum was stymied by the forbidding presence of Mrs. Ass. Here's the extent of what I knew about Mrs. Ass. Her ass was flat. Flat like Kansas. Flat like old roadkill. She was a sheer cliff from head to heel without a single dip or curve on her. Her shoulders were as narrow as her waist, as narrow as her hips, and her legs were the narrowest. Clad in green corduroys, her build reminded me of a standing cartoon frog. In that moment, she wore a fuzzy wool hat on her head and gloves on her hands as she scratched at her perennial beds with a rake, pulling dead leaves and sidewalk salt (and perhaps some pieces of a broken ceramic planter) into a small heap beside her sensible shoes.

Turn. Turn around and look at me, I thought at her. *Why won't you look at me?*

She remained a willful wall of disengagement. I flipped her off, hoping she could see me reflected in her window. I wouldn't even have minded if she turned and flipped me off in return. At least it would be some interaction.

Once inside, I tossed my keys onto the counter and went straight to the guest room. The futon was precisely made, but in the corner were a pair of brown suede shoes, neat and patiently waiting their owner's return. Nearby, his black suitcase was propped open, the contents folded and stacked in three rows. If a sigh could be gleeful, mine surely was.

I went back to the hallway to hang my coat and found a note in Jamie's masculine, blocky print: "Went for a long drive. Don't wait on me for dinner."

Not the best news, but not the worst, either. With nowhere to go and nothing to do, I settled into the couch with a month-old *New Yorker* that Dan had left behind. I wondered when he was getting back and if I would hear from him before Monday morning's staff meeting. I flipped through all the cartoons first, then went back to an article chronicling a controversial death-row trial.

My body worn out and logy from the spa, it wasn't long before I closed my eyes and started to doze. I had been out maybe forty-five minutes when the phone wrenched me awake. Disoriented with my heart pounding, I was desperate to get to the receiver and make the blasted ringing stop.

"Yeah. Hello."

"Hey, it's me, Pooter."

He never called me at home. I wondered if I was still asleep.

I stretched into my words, "Was napping. What's the matter? Are you still in Vegas? Are you in jail?"

"Why would you think I'm in jail? No, I got home last night. But I need to talk to you. Can we meet up?" He sounded tense.

"It's Saturday. This is the first alone time I've had in days, and I was really looking f—"

"I wouldn't ask if it weren't important."

I gave a slow, leaky grumble but wouldn't commit. There was silence on the other end.

He knew I found phone lulls unbearable and waited me out. "Fine," I said.

"Thank you."

"Meet me at the bowling alley on Delano Avenue."

"I just want to talk, I don't want to bowl," he said.

"I'm hungry, and they make a good burger. You're buying this time. Be there in twenty."

Weekend afternoons at Pinny Lane were a zoo of kids' birthday parties, but at six o'clock, the leagues practices started, so the parking lot was nearly full when I got there, and I struggled to find a space.

The alley's previous incarnation was the Bridgetown Bowling Center. Back then, your typical bowler was a middle aged, paunchy guy who bore a striking resemblance to Barney Rubble. A few months after I moved to the area, though, the owners sold the business to a gay couple from Boston who gutted the dusty, faded interior and rebirthed the whole venue with a Beatles theme. The alley now featured four sweetly nostalgic sections, each decked out in its own distinct Fab Four era.

Pinny Lane's grand opening invited bowlers and non-bowlers alike to attend in retro attire or actual Beatles costume. And they showed up in masses, totally game for the festivities. It was a karaoke extravaganza with bowling. Not only did "Bowl Over Beethoven" become an annual event, but it also transformed the league into a hip, fun scene. The "Barneys" were still reigning champs, but now they were competing against ambitious career women, recent college grads, the occasional local politician—all showing their bowling pride with clever team names, monogrammed shirts, and customized balls.

It took a few seconds for my eyes to adjust to the dim lighting. I had seen Pooter's parked car when I arrived, so I squinted around the center aisle from which all the alleys radiated. I only spotted him when he was just ten feet in front of me, carrying a cardboard tray with a few items, including a couple of Happiness Is a Warm Bun cheeseburgers and a Hippy Hippy vanilla shake for each of us.

Pooter pointed his chin in the direction of a far lane behind me that was out of order, empty and unlit. Meanwhile, all around us were the loud crashes of scattering pins, like cartoony exclamation points popping up every time a strike was struck.

We sat down on a high-backed vinyl bench. Pooter looked tired. In fact, it seemed as if the volume had been turned down on his very being. He took a slow slurp of milkshake and flattened his palms on the table on either side of the cup. As I waited for him to speak, I dug into a basket of Glass Onion rings.

Finally, he opened with, "I really want to hear about your celebrity guest, but first I need to tell you about what happened at the conference." His eyes were full and serious.

"OK."

He shook his head slowly, "I think they're going to fire me."

"You dragged me here to tell me that?"

"Please don't joke."

I softened my tone, but I still couldn't fathom what could be so grave. "Preston doesn't fire people. It just lets them get bored and waits for them to move on or retire. I'm sure whatever happened is not as bad as you think."

Another laden pause, then Pooter started talking about a girl he met—a woman, he corrected himself, named Daisy.

"Oh, come on, that's not her real name—"

"It is. Her brother's name is Wendall. Her dad was a farmer. But I don't..." he said helplessly. "It doesn't matter. That was her name."

He told me about his first encounter with Daisy—a crazy-smart substitute teacher who seemed to know everything from eighteenth-century German clock-making to competitive paintball strategies. Pooter had clearly been smitten.

"We got to know each other over the course of the show," he said. "Wednesday night, we went to dinner at an Indian restaurant. There were these yogurt drinks that were really good—not alcoholic or anything."

I tried to be patient, but I could feel my left foot bouncing up and down. Jamie might be getting back at any moment. All around us, the bowlers bowled, their dainty, leg-sweep follow-throughs more akin to ball-room dancing than launching a fifteen-pound polyure-thane ball at a bunch of precarious pins.

"So, we ended up spending the night together."

He tried so hard to make it sound casual, knowing it would never sound casual coming from him. What shined through instead was an endearing mix of bra-vado and bashful awkwardness. I couldn't muster any enthusiasm for a condescending comment, so I ate my burger and let him continue.

"Oh. I should probably mention that Daisy has pretty passionate stances on certain issues. Like cor-porate America and you know, NAFTA."

"Are you getting to the point about why you're get-ting fired?"

"Potentially."

"You're potentially getting to the point?"

"Potentially getting fired. That's why I called you."

§

Pooter had overslept again. Daisy had left three hours earlier and his dreams were thick and murky, but vaguely pleasant. Eventually, the sound of the radio alarm seeped into his slumber, enough to pry open one eye and aim it at the clock.

He quick-showered and dressed. No time to neatly pack his suitcase for checkout, he tossed dirty clothes in with the clean and swiped his toiletries, including the hotel's travel size bottles, into a bag. He had just fifteen minutes to pick up a stale danish and coffee before he was scheduled to be at the booth.

The rest of the team, likely hungover, were not there. So, Pooter turned on the halogen lights and began straightening posters, stacks of books and brochures, all with fingernail precise edges. He restocked the pyramid of candy bars, and as he did, he thought back to his fumbling introduction to Daisy. Then he thought about the scattered freckles on her shoulder, and how they rose and fell gently as she slept. And then he thought about how breathing was like the ocean along the shore coming in, going out.

The Panda Paper booth was agonizingly dark. The exhibit hall hadn't officially opened, but it would soon, and he madly hoped Daisy would appear.

Pooter was replacing the Band-Aid on his heel when he saw a trio of Preston House people: Renny Culpepper wearing an impossibly pretentious blue bow tie; Dan being all Danly with his sporty stride and stupid-perfect hair; and a man Pooter only recognized from the photo in his author bio, Langdon Herbert. The three men were approaching the booth.

Pooter stood, shoving Band-Aid wrappers into his pocket before locking his arms to his sides in an awkward "attention" stance. He nearly felt compelled to salute.

Dan and Herbert were in deep conversation; Renny kept crisp pace with them, nodding as if whatever they had just said, he had already thought the same exact thing. Their shiny shoes reached the booth carpet's edge.

"Ah, the man manning the booth," Dan said to Pooter. He addressed Herbert, "I don't know if you've met Audrey's editorial assistant?"

"Ah, Peter," said Herbert, extending out his skillful handshake.

"Pooter, actually," Pooter said.

"That's right. I had always wondered why that wasn't a typo."

"Yes. Well, we have a nice prominent display of your book here in the spotlight spot," said Pooter.

"Let's hope such a prominent presentation delivers the goods. Sales, I mean," Herbert said with a tiny wink. Renny laughed.

Dan chimed in, "Hey, I want to introduce you to Rod Howler over there. He's at UConn now."

Before he left the booth Herbert said to Pooter, "My presentation is at eleven o'clock. Would you please see there are sufficient copies of the book there?"

"Yes, of course," Pooter said, though he realized he had no idea what amounted to "sufficient."

The attendees at Herbert's talk were mostly men sporting ties and jackets, toting notebooks and briefcases. They sidestepped to their seats in the first three rows of the lecture hall. Pooter sat behind them, keeping his attention forward for signals from Renny, who had already had him fetch a pitcher of ice water and a glass. Off to the side of the stage, Herbert was speaking with Dan and an exceptionally tall, round-shouldered man.

The title of Herbert's talk, *"Cracking the Code: Creating an Academic Best Seller"* was printed poster-sized and propped up on an easel next to the podium. Herbert had retired from active teaching two years prior. And while Pooter didn't necessarily dispute the man's academic bona fides, he had to wonder how much of Herbert's best-selling success could be attributed to an inflated sense of his own importance. An "If you act it, they will believe it" kind of strategy.

Herbert moved to the podium and tipped the microphone up toward his face. There was a white-light glare reflecting off his bald head, and Pooter took a small bit of satisfaction from the indignity, even if the man himself wasn't aware of it.

Herbert tapped a set of index cards on the microphone a couple of times to quiet the audience before he started speaking.

"Good morning to you all. It is still morning, yes?" He welcomed friends and colleagues, fellow academics, current and future authors.

Behind Pooter, the hall door opened. He turned, and there she was, dressed in a flowing fuchsia dress, looking like a strange and beautiful sea anemone that had suddenly swept into a school of mackerels. Heads turned and craned momentarily, and Herbert himself glanced up from his notes to watch her glide into the seat next to Pooter.

She smiled largely at him. Pooter smiled largely back. As Herbert resumed his talk, Daisy nudged Pooter's attention forward to the presentation.

But he couldn't concentrate. She was a giant mind-magnet sitting next to him. Though his eyes were on Herbert, and Pooter's ears could make out words like "curriculum" and "compendium", "sizzle" and "preposterous," and though he pretended to laugh when the audience found something funny, the rest of his being was tuned to Daisy and a steady vibration he imagined he felt in his skin—an energy filling the space between their nearly-touching arms. When her pinky curled around his, the vibration exploded into sparkles.

Overhead slides were projected, points were made. The talk lasted precisely twenty minutes. Pooter had no idea if there was any substance to it, if would-be college textbook authors had indeed been handed the code to writing their own best sellers in art history, computer science, nursing, world finance. By the time the Q&A portion had begun, all Pooter could think about was convincing Daisy to change their return flights for one they would take together to a place they randomly selected on the map. From there, the two would be metaphorical leaves on a river, going wherever the current took them.

"Can you speak to the ways in which multimedia will impact how students will be learning in five, or even ten years from now? Do you see a time when textbooks will be quaint relics of a bygone era?"

Pooter had heard a lot about multimedia in recent months. It seemed every new title needed an interactive CD-ROM, and even older titles were getting new editions just so they could be packaged with one.

"The short answer is no," said Herbert. "Multimedia is merely a supplement, just like a study guide is a supplement. The marrow of real learning remains grounded in words that can be read and digested via paper. Electronic bells and whistles will never replace that experience."

One of the few women in the group stood to ask a question. Renny passed her a microphone.

"I was wondering if you or one of the other gentlemen representing the publishing industry could speak to why there aren't more women authors represented in today's catalogs."

Look around the room, lady, thought Pooter. If the schools hired more female professors, they would write more books. Maybe it wasn't quite that simple, but maybe it was.

Dan fielded the question and deflected it by citing a handful of female authors on Preston House's roster and saying that the publisher welcomed book proposals from thought leaders without consideration of their gender.

"That's exactly the point," the woman pressed. "Gender should be given consideration, especially in the math and sciences. It's essential that we hold up good role models of women in academia."

"I see your point," said Dan. "And I assure you, we are making strides in that area. The truth is, we would love to see more female authors and certainly, I encourage you and your colleagues to reach out to us."

From anyone else, the words would have felt like a brush-off, but Dan was Dan and with just the most subtle glint from his eyes and timbre in his voice, he disarmed the woman and she countered not with a skeptical tone, but a flirty one.

"I will if you will."

The audience chuckled, and she took her seat. As she did, Daisy stood. Pooter figured she was headed to the restroom or was going to ditch the rest of the Q&A session. But then, to his horror, she was gesturing to Renny for the mic.

"No, no no no no," Pooter whispered forcefully, "Daisy, don't do thi—"

Herbert looked appreciatively at the girl in the flowing fuchsia dress. "Yes."

"Mine's more of a comment than a question," she began. "I just wanted to say that I find your perspective on NAFTA—as reflected in your book—to be not only misguided, but unconscionable." The statement, most notably the last word, was loaded with speech impediment, but there was no mistaking the bluntness of her message. It seemed as if every face in the audience had its eyes on her.

Herbert looked over at Dan who looked equally non-plussed. Pooter sank in his seat. The whole room seemed to hold its collective breath waiting for a reply to the odd young woman in the back of the room. Finally, Dan kicked into gear and stepped to the podium.

"I can't comment on his perspective, but this forum isn't intended for that kind of debate."

"Then let him."

"Pardon?" said Dan.

"You can't comment, but he can. He's the one teaching the youth of America—"*(Oh God, Daisy*, thought Pooter, *"youth of America?")* "that it's perfectly fine to snatch away good jobs from our loyal citizens in order to pay crap wages south of the border—"

"Miss," Herbert finally cut in, "I hardly think you're qualified—"

"As an economist, you have to know there are ramifications."

"Really, this is a publishing forum, not a protest venue," said Dan.

"And you must know those jobs are never coming back," she shouted.

Pooter sank low in his chair. When he looked back at Herbert, the man was shooting furious eye daggers not at Daisy but at him, as if Pooter were the one on verbal attack. Renny came out from behind the curtain and mouthed "Get. Her. Out. Of. Here." His expression was crazed. Pooter stood and practically hip-checked Daisy in the direction of the aisle.

As Pooter herded her toward the exit, she yelled even louder, "Did you even consider the environmental impact of doing business in a virtually unregulated country?" They were suddenly cast out into the bright lights of the empty hallway.

Though he couldn't pinpoint exactly why, Pooter ended the story here when he told it to Audrey, despite the exchange having continued when the door clicked closed behind them.

Daisy shrugged Pooter's hand off her elbow and faced him.

"You're welcome," she said.

The adrenaline was flash-flooding through his bloodstream. His arms flapped wildly as if trying to disconnect from his body.

"You are crazy. You are totally fucking nuts." He took three stormy steps away from her. "I'm so done. Herbert's going to have my head. I'm going to get shit-canned because of your stupid, useless protest."

Daisy was calm and even a touch bemused. "Not if you don't want to."

He glared at her, both furious and so completely conflicted by her adorableness that he had to turn away. "You may not know this, Miss Substitute Teacher, but in the business world, when you're fired, losing your job isn't optional."

She came over to him and put a hand on his cheek before kissing him with honey sweetness.

"You'll figure it out," was all she said before turning and walking away from him.

As he watched her geeky-long stride carry her down the hallway and around the corner, Pooter felt his anger dissipate like smoke from a candle that had just been snuffed out. It was replaced by a fist-sized knot in his stomach when the lecture hall doors opened and spat out the session's attendees.

In a moment, Renny's blue bow tie was in Pooter's face.

"Mr. Herbert was not amused by your little stunt, Pooter. I don't care where you go, but I don't want to see you anywhere near the booth today."

But Pooter had no choice, he had to go back into the exhibit hall to get his suitcase. Thankfully, the only people in the booth were Dmitri and Laurie.

"Where are you going?" Laurie had snagged him. "You can't cut out—you're on break-down."

He ignored her. They would find out soon enough, Pooter thought. Then, if he were fired at least he wouldn't have to deal with their continually disgruntled attitudes. Pooter grabbed his luggage and left.

Wendall was in the Panda Paper booth just beginning to pack things up. Pooter paused, wondering if he should go over to say goodbye. But he knew it wasn't about saying goodbye to a guy he barely knew; it was about getting a message to Daisy, whom he knew would not be returning to the exhibit hall. Yet when he thought about what he wanted to say, Pooter's mind was empty, unable to synthesize anything meaningful. So instead, he turned and headed toward the exit signs, pulling his roller suitcase behind him as if it were a sullen and obedient dog.

§

Like a balloon with a slow leak, Pooter had sagged down in his seat, defeated, his head resting on the vinyl.

"I can't believe she did that to you," I said. "What's the point? Did she think she was going to change Herbert in some way?"

"I spent a long plane ride asking that," Pooter said.

"Maybe it's not as big a deal as you think."

"Trust me. It is." He sat up and leaned forward at me, "That's why you have to talk to Dan."

"Nope, no way." I stood up to throw away the wrapper in a nearby garbage can. "I'm happy to talk to Renny for you."

"Renny can't do anything. Renny won't do anything. He was so livid he nearly burst his bow tie."

"You're asking me to use my personal relationship with Dan for a professional favor."

"That's exactly what I'm asking."

I shook my head. "We don't do that, Pooter. Those two worlds are totally separate."

"I don't believe that for a minute. You're not capable of compartmentalizing."

What was it with people telling me to compartmentalize? As if compartmentalizing were as simple as putting your feelings in different shoeboxes. Experiences and emotions have about as much respect for boundaries as watercolor paint on a wet canvas. Asking Dan to intercede was not simply a matter of blurred boundaries, it was a request that would otherwise have had no reason to be elevated to his level of seniority, and it crossed an uncomfortable line.

When I didn't answer, he tried a different tack. "Audrey, this may never have been my dream job, but it's the first chance I ever had to prove that I could succeed at something. And some days, I actually feel like I am better than mediocre at it. I don't want to give that up. Not now."

His wide and earnest eyes were fixed on mine. His expression was anxious, vulnerable. Two words to me that I wouldn't have imagined ascribing to Pooter. "I can't make any promises. All I can do is talk to him."

He nodded. "I know."

"I'll see if I can duck in his office first thing on Monday."

As we left the bowling alley, the parking lot was awash in the bright white light of a full moon. We walked together to my car.

"So, is your 'asylum seeker' still present?" Pooter asked.

"Yeah, it's been crazy. He went somewhere today, just left a note not to wait for him for dinner. I can't imagine he'll stick around much longer."

"What's he like?"

"Normal, I'd say. Dealing with his shit, just like the rest of us."

"Huh," said Pooter.

We stopped by the bumper of my car.

"Are you going to stay in touch with this Daisy?"

Pooter shrugged. "No. Maybe. I don't know. Anyway, thanks."

And then he opened his arms and hugged me fully, chest to breasts. After two years of working together with barely an accidental hand-brush let alone a hug, Pooter had breached an unspoken clause in our friendship.

It had always seemed to me that the population could essentially be divided into huggers and non-huggers. I was of the latter camp, though I often found myself forced into an awkward embrace that was either anemic on both sides or completely lopsided in the degree of effort. My tendency was to use a few backslaps as a way of covering up my discomfort. But, given the situation, I did my best, scrunching up my shoulders in a poor imitation of a squeeze and saying, "It'll be OK. Just, please, stop being so...ew."

13: We Were

From deep within a cocoon of comforter and pillows, I was awakened by a smell, sharp and acrid. The clock said 9:37 a.m.

"What the hell?" I croaked, trying but failing to be heard. Whatever Jamie was cooking this time, I wasn't eager to try it. But pulling the blankets further over my head made me feel like I was suffocating. That and curiosity compelled me to get up.

Groaning into a stretch, I examined myself in the mirror. There was little I could do to minimize the sleep film and rumpledness, but I raked my fingers through my hair, dug a gritty speck from my eye, and scrunched and released my face a few times to jumpstart some circulation.

As remarkable as it was having Jamie around, I had to admit, I was starting to miss living alone with its corresponding freedom to fart with impunity and eat Cheerios for breakfast, lunch and dinner.

Opening the bedroom door brought a rush of that smell. Vinegar. From the end of the hall, Jamie looked up. The parquet floor leading to where he stood gleamed shiny and wet.

"Don't step!" he said. "I'm just about finished."

I nearly burst out laughing. For all the lackluster and morally questionable choices I'd made in life, this was an absurd gift. I leapt across the wet floor onto to the living room carpet.

"Had a hell of a time finding a mop," he said. "It was way back in the closet." I didn't even recall owning a mop but didn't say so.

"And there was no floor cleaner that I could see, so I just used vinegar and water. It's what the help use at home."

Right, "the help."

Jamie emerged from the kitchen, holding up his pink, rubber-gloved hands. "These could totally ruin my reputation."

"Given your current situation, they might actually improve it."

"Funny," he said, but was shaking his head to say, *not funny*.

The piles of magazines and books beneath the coffee table were neatly stacked; the throw pillows artfully arranged. My home had been neatened as well as cleaned.

"Maybe housekeeping is your true calling," I said. "I hear they make, like, twelve bucks an hour." I flopped to the couch and put my feet up. *Why not,* I thought, *if a celebrity is going to do your chores?*

"I was up early and had to do something. There's no TV. Plus, the place really needed it."

"I hear hotel rooms have TVs. And they're cleaned every day, so you wouldn't have to."

"You should meditate," he said. "Might soften that sarcastic edge."

"Sarcasm never broke anyone's jaw."

He gave a grim nod. "I fully acknowledge that I have work to do, Audrey. Do you?"

"I bet you miss your therapist," I said. "In the meantime, do you want breakfast?"

"I had some applesauce and a cup of tea. Have to get my diet back on track. No more Chinese food and bagels."

It struck me that I had no idea what to do with the day. The weather had turned wintery again, so another hike was out of the question (for other obvious reasons, as well). I flipped open the Sunday paper to the entertainment section, wondering if there was something going on in the city that Jamie could get into incognito. He hadn't shaved since before he'd arrived, so he already had some camouflage. Perhaps I could dig up other elements of disguise.

I turned to the movie section. Maybe we could sneak into a theater late and leave early while the lights were down. Too bad he wasn't in any movies playing at the time—how surreal to watch a James Keefner movie with James Keefner.

It was even more surreal to notice that just to the left of the movie times table, in the celebrity gossip column, there was a short blurb about him. "Keefner Still MIA" read the headline. There was a short entry saying that "Sources close to Chloe Philips say that other than a brief phone call from Keefner telling her that he 'needed some time alone,' she has not heard from her husband since the physical altercation with her brother, Desmond Philips. According to Keefner's agent, the actor 'Is taking time to deal with some personal issues. We are all here to support him when he is ready to come home, which I can assure fans, will be very soon.'"

"Do you want to read this?" I asked. "It mentions you."

"I don't know, do I?"

"Doesn't really say much of anything."

He thought for a moment. "Then no."

If celebrity, by its very nature, was a manifestation of public perception, it seemed a brave move for Jamie to decline reading what was being said about him, especially during a public relations crisis.

I folded the newspaper and flopped over on a couch pillow. There was a sudden, startling knock. Jamie and I looked at the door and then at each other. His eyebrows raised in a question. I shrugged my shoulders.

Jamie mouthed, "Don't answer." I OK'd with my fingers. Another knock, this one louder.

"Hey, it's Dan."

Jamie stood perfectly still like a Madame Toussaud's figure of himself in jeans, a sweaty T-shirt and those absurd pink rubber gloves. I barely breathed as I tried to will Dan away from my door by simply thinking at him.

Another loud knock came, "Audrey? You there?"

We held our frozen positions, ears sharply attuned. But there was no subsequent knock.

He must have given up and gone back to his car. But then I heard a rough scrape and realized with a panic that he had pulled out the key hidden in the loose brick. He was about to unlock the door. I bolted upright, slamming my pinky toe into the table hard enough to bring tears to my eyes. Locking a hand on my mouth to hold back a string of curses I shoved Jamie into the guest room. I was hobbling toward the entryway, pretending that I was already on my way to answer the door, just as Dan swung it open.

"Oh, hey, I'm sorry," he said. "I saw your car out back and figured you were just out for a walk or something. Are you OK? You're limping."

"Yeah, just caught my toe on the table leg."

He offered up a box tied with red and white bakery string. "I wanted to surprise you with some pastries."

"I'm definitely surprised."

Holding the box out sideways, he slid his other arm around me and drew us together.

For a second, the thrill of being with Dan after nearly a full week of not seeing him was overwhelming. He was there, and he was warm, full of breath and kiss and stubble. But then my sock soaked up a puddle of vinegar and I flinched.

"What's that sour smell?" he asked looking around.

"Vinegar. The floors got mopped."

"Wow. What prompted that?" He started to slip off his sneakers.

"Hey, why don't we go out? Give things time to air out."

"Nah, it's fine. It's nice you cleaned up the place. Wow, it looks great in here. I don't think I've ever seen it this neat." He nudged his shoes next to mine, then took two quick, cat-like steps to the carpet. "It was a long week. I just want to be with you."

He sat down and untied the bakery box. "Come have a pastry."

"Well," I said. "I actually have plans. A childhood friend is in town, and we're hanging out."

"Oh." He looked disappointed, then tilted his head and asked, "Didn't you want to go out just now?"

"I did. I do. That way I can be out and meet up at the place we're meeting up at."

"Oh," he said again. "Well, just sit with me for a little bit. I missed you. Plus, I need to talk to you about something that happened at the conference."

Pooter. The realization sent me into a whole different panic. My mind was running hard trying to keep its mental plates spinning. James Keefner was a silent prisoner in the guest room; Pooter was a pain in the ass; and Dan was probably looking to get laid.

I sat down cautiously next to him. Pulling out a cherry danish, I asked "Does this have to do with Pooter?"

He nodded. "He spoke to you."

"He's pretty upset."

"So is Herbert." He paused a beat. "I need to let you know; he's insisting that I let Pooter go."

"Herbert's a baby."

"I don't necessarily disagree. But he generates a lot of revenue, and I can't ignore him," Dan said.

"Dan, the man was a lecturer for thirty years. He can't handle a little criticism from a twenty-year-old girl?"

"That wasn't the forum for it."

"Who cares? It could have been an interesting debate."

Dan wiped the crumbs from his hands onto a napkin. He leaned back into the couch corner and crossed an ankle over his knee. He paused, then said. "Audrey, Herbert didn't write this new edition."

"He didn't?"

"It was ghostwritten by a young professor out of Northwestern."

"He had a ghostwriter?"

"We needed the Herbert series to get a little more modern, leverage multimedia opportunities to go head-to-head with the competing titles coming out this year. But CD-ROMs? PowerPoint? Herbert thinks that stuff's just stupid magic tricks. His mind simply doesn't work that way." Dan stretched his arm across the cushion behind me. "The more we talked about it, the more he started to consider retiring altogether. But we weren't ready for that. Our forecasts had already factored in sales of a twelfth edition. We needed his name on a significantly updated book.

"So, we drew up a contract that stipulated that this edition would be revised and updated by Shem Wolcott, an economist who's gaining a lot of respect in the academia circles."

"Herbert let someone else update his book and publish it under his name?" It was hard to imagine.

"It was the best business decision for everyone. After this one, the next edition will be 'co-authored.' Then Herbert will officially retire, and Wolcott will step in fully." Dan wiped a crumb from my chin.

"OK," I said. "Fine, he didn't do the edition. That's still no reason to go apeshit at Pooter."

"When that girl started slamming Herbert for his stance on NAFTA, he felt ambushed—I'm not sure he even has a stance on NAFTA. Herbert assumed Pooter knew about the ghostwriter and was putting the screws to him for it."

"That's ridiculous."

"Herbert doesn't think so. Remember when Pooter didn't give you that message about the cover—"

"Good grief, he's still going on about that stupid cover?"

"He believes it's a pattern of willful disrespect."

"Dan, it was me. Pooter was covering for me not passing along the message."

He sighed and reached over to my hand, holding it tightly. "Even if that's the case, it's moot at this point."

"Pooter didn't do anything wrong. In either situation."

"I'm sorry. I truly am."

"Maybe if I explain to Herbert."

He shook his head. "I can't afford to keep straining that relationship. We're already asking a lot of him."

"For which I'm sure he is being well compensated."

"Pooter is a bright, funny guy. He'll land on his feet. You can give him a great recommendation. I can even reach out to some of my contacts."

I was heartsunk. It never occurred to me that the termination would actually go through. I figured there would be a warning, a probation, something that would enable me to protect Pooter until the incident blew over.

Selfishly, I thought about what Pooter's leaving would mean for me. Life at the office was generally frustrating, predictable, tiresome, sometimes even bleak, but having Pooter there to eye-roll and snicker with made it tolerable and some days, almost like fun.

"Dan..."

"I know."

"It's unfair."

"It's business."

"It's shitty business."

"Audrey—" I could hear a note of impatience creeping in his voice. "Your paycheck, my paycheck, probably thirty people in our division's paychecks are carried to some degree on the back of Langdon Herbert's reputation. I'm accountable to those people, and I'm not willing to risk their livelihoods in the service of playing fair with Pooter. Herbert wants him gone, and sadly, that's where we are."

I was out of words. I took back my hand. Dan was pragmatic, utilitarian. But I couldn't pretend to feel OK about it. The clock in the kitchen ticked more loudly than it should have been capable of. Pooter was going to be devastated.

As if reading my mind, Dan said, "I know you're upset, but I need you to promise me that you won't tell Pooter what I just told you. In fact, you can't tell anyone; that was part of the agreement. I shouldn't have shared it with you, but I thought you deserved an explanation. And I trust you." He looked at me with full weight and seriousness.

"What am I supposed to tell him then?"

"All he needs to know is that the incident in the lecture hall set Herbert off, and that the matter is being handled by HR. They'll take care of the rest."

I didn't answer. "Audie?" Silence. "Audrey."

"Fine."

"Thank you. I know this is really hard. I know it."

He pulled me into a one-armed embrace and kissed my eyebrow. We sat quietly as the news settled in my head. He waited a requisite minute or two before moving on. "Hey, let's just hole up and stay in bed and watch movies all day. We can read to each other, have breakfast for dinner. Come on. Cancel your plans today."

It took a second to remember the plans he was referring to. I hadn't heard so much as a floorboard creak from Jamie.

Had I known in that moment that it would be the last chance I would have to have sex with Dan, I would have led him to my bed. I would have opened his shirt, one button at a time, and delivered a bittersweet kiss everywhere an open button revealed his skin. I would have kept the shades wide open, Mrs. Ass be damned, so I could commit to memory the way the contours of his body formed a shadowy landscape rising from the rumpled bedsheets. I might have imagined Dan's fingers as paintbrushes leaving washes of color on my collarbone and ribcage, and firm thumbprint marks on my knees and hips. I would have stranded James Keefner in the guest room to die of boredom, or else get thoroughly disgusted and head back to Hollywood. But I didn't know it would be the last chance. We nearly never know when it's the last time. And that's probably a good thing, otherwise we might never pry ourselves away. And we might be more careful with the things we say.

"I can't," I said simply.

We chatted a little more about Vegas, about the booth bimbos and the promising new connections he'd made. I chimed in with encouragement to keep him talking while a dull sadness settled over me. Eventually, Dan realized he wasn't getting my attention back.

"Well, I don't want to keep you from your date."

"It's not a date. It's just old friends."

I sent him off with hug that I hoped conveyed that despite my utter disappointment, I would eventually see and understand that he was only doing what he thought was best. His return hug seemed to convey that, despite how low I was feeling now, it was all eventually going to be all right.

After he had gone, Jamie emerged from the guest room.

"Who knew publishing was so full of drama?" he said. "You're sleeping with your boss?" It was a question that sounded like a statement.

"Not today, thanks to you."

I tore into a croissant and compulsively ate it piece by piece.

"Don't worry, I won't cramp your style much longer. I'm working on a re-entry plan."

"Yeah?" I was relieved that I wouldn't have to ask when he was planning on going home. At the same time, I could already anticipate the funk I would feel after he had left.

"Yeah, this has been good," he said. "Really good. I spent a lot of time thinking yesterday. Staring at the ocean seems to be good for that. For the first time in a long time, I feel like I have a clear head. I mean, don't get me wrong, I'm not proud of what I did and I'm going to have to eat some hefty crow, but I'm going to come back and get on top of my game."

Amy Klinger

He opened the louver doors that hid the wash-er and dryer. Pulling an armful of dried clothes, he came over and dumped them on the couch. "Here's my three-point plan. One: Have a man-to-man with Des-mond. Apologizing, yes, but also making it clear that I shouldn't feel like an outsider in my own family. Chloe married me, we have a child together, and it's about time they got over it."

He snapped out one of his T-shirts. Laying it flat on the cushion, he folded it meticulously like a Gap store manager. "Two: I'm going to take Storey away for a long weekend, just her and me. Try to rebuild those bonds, you know? Maybe I'll bring along her old baby album so she can see how much fun we use to have."

Without any hesitation, he retrieved a pair of blinding white boxer-briefs. "And three: Start looking at scripts that offer deeper roles—get away from this tough guy, hero stuff. I'm getting too old, and it's start-ing to bore me. I want to do something more. Some-thing serious where I have to get physically invested. Lose a lot of weight. Or maybe gain a lot of weight—that would be more fun."

He looked at me full of earnest optimism.

"That's great, Jamie. It sounds like you're in a good mindset."

I admired his clarity. Simple, focused objectives to get him where he wanted to be. He had a plan. I had no plan. And, I thought with a queasy feeling, I was about to lose Pooter.

"You know what that guy Dan was talking to me about?" I asked Jamie.

"The author or the Pooter...is that his name?"

"The Pooter."

"The one who's getting fired?"

"Yeah. I have to call and tell him." I gnawed at a hangnail. "It's going to suck."

"I didn't mean to eavesdrop, but it sounded like your boss said to leave it alone."

"You remember *Old Yeller?*"

He nodded. "I get it. You want to be the one to put him down."

Once again, Jaime banished himself to the guest room so I wouldn't be distracted. He took the laundry pile with him as well as a book from the shelf, as if he wouldn't be eavesdropping again, and closed the door.

I flipped through the white pages, scanning for Poudre. Pulling the phone to its full extension, I sat down on the couch, figuring the more comfortable I was physically, the less stressed out I would sound. But it didn't work. As soon as Pooter's mother answered the phone, I stood and started pacing.

"John—" I heard her shout. "Phone!"

He picked up from another room, "Got it." There was no reciprocating hang up. "I said I got it!"

Still no click from the other end. "Ma, would you hang up the fucking phone?"

She hung up with a slam.

Perfect, I thought.

"Hey, Shane?"

"No, it's Audrey."

"Oh, sorry, I was expecting another call."

"Right." I hesitated, at a loss for how to begin. "What's...up?"

I coiled the phone cord around my finger, uncoiled it again. "Dan came by this morning."

"Whoa, did he see Jamie?"

"What? No, no. That was not an issue. Anyway, he totally caught me off guard."

"So then, you didn't talk to him about me?"

"No..."

"Seriously?"

"No, I mean no, I didn't not talk to him about you."

"That's a lot of negatives."

"Yeah."

He waited for me to continue. "Audrey?"

"I couldn't fix it, Pooter. I tried, but Dan says he won't change his mind."

"Who won't change his mind, Herbert or Dan?"

"Both, neither. Dan says he has to abide by Herbert's demands. And he demands that you be let go." What a lame euphemism, I thought, as if Pooter were a helium balloon. Better words not approved by HR: cut off, amputated, terminated.

"I don't...did you explain? Didn't you tell him that it wasn't me? I was just..." He gave a thick sigh of frustration.

"I tried, Pooter. I think there might be extenuating circumstances at play, and you just got caught in the crossfire."

"What does that mean?" His voice was getting pinched. "Do I even need to say that I wouldn't have been on Herbert's radar screen if I hadn't saved your ass last year?"

"No, I know it. And I told Dan."

"I can't believe this."

"He said he'd put out a few calls for you, make some connections. And you know I'll give you a great—"

"You must be one lousy fuck."

It was quick and quiet, a knife to the ribs. "Wha— oh. Did you just—?"

I heard him bash the phone receiver four times, each successive strike becoming more forceful. Then he hung up. I listened to the hiss of dead air until it switched over to that terminal dial tone. I returned the phone to its cradle.

I flopped onto the couch so that my back was on the cushions and my legs were hanging over the arm. I just lay there, breathing, trying to calm the pulse that was hammering in my ears. *It wasn't my fault,* I thought. *Dan didn't leave me any room to negotiate.* And yet there it was, the nagging feeling—prompted by Pooter's accusation—that I simply hadn't tried hard enough. My mother was wrong, I wasn't a do-nothing; I was a barely-do-anything. And in some ways, that was worse. Truly doing nothing required a deliberate and contrary willfulness against doing something. It was way more effort than simply going with what you're told.

"Are you done?" Jamie had opened the door. "It got very quiet out here."

"Yep."

"Didn't go so well?"

"Nope."

"Sorry." He came and sat next to my head. I smelled a wave of dryer sheets coming from his jeans, and briefly wondered, if they were my dryer sheets and my dryer, why didn't my clothes ever smell that way? I raised my eyes to see upside down Jamie. For the first time since he'd arrived, I didn't feel awkward or self-conscious openly looking at him. It was as if the inverted angle diffused the full force of his good looks, like seeing an eclipse through a pinhole camera.

"I am one of very few people to have the dubious privilege of looking up James Keefner's nose."

He turned away. Then turned back again. "Lucky, you get a front row seat to the boogers."

"Ew, I'm not actually looking. I do see though that you've got a few grays in your beard."

He sighed. "I hadn't missed a day of shaving in about two years. I didn't even know they were there until I saw them while I was washing up yesterday."

"Don't get all mopey," I said. "You can pluck them out and no one will know."

"They know. Even if they don't know, they know."

I could hear that unreasonably loud clock again and vowed to confiscate its batteries. My thoughts were pulled back to Pooter, and the deep and true anger he'd launched at me. I considered calling him back. But I knew he would let his mother answer, and then he would tell her to tell me to fuck off. And she would pretend he wasn't home even though we both would know that he told her to tell me to fuck off. And that would make me feel worse.

"So, what do you want to do today?" Jamie asked.

"Crawl under a rock and sleep through the rest of winter." I sat up. "Or, let's go see a movie."

There was an art house about forty-five minutes away that was showing a foreign film, so the matinee was almost guaranteed to be empty. But just in case, we arrived at the theater during the previews so that the house lights would already be dimmed. Jamie waited outside the theater hidden behind his beard and a lowered baseball cap while I got the tickets. Then he came in and briskly joined me, in stride, as I handed our tickets to the bored attendant.

The film, a Polish one, was called, "Byliśmy" which translated to "We Were." It was a funny and dark and sad story about a middle-aged man who comes home one night and startlingly finds a woman reading a magazine in his bed—a wife he has no recollection of, though she, in total bafflement, insists they have been married for nineteen years. There is no explanation for how the situation had come to be, no vague references to amnesia or Alzheimer's or con artistry. And narratively, there was no real effort to determine whose version of the story was true. Instead, the film seemed to be a simple exploration through dialogue, body language, and facial expression of what it means to love and want to be loved; the ways in which we are defined by our relationships (or in the lonely hero's case, the lack thereof). The ending held no clear resolution either. Instead, the audience was left to imagine a way forward for these two people. Stay together, drift apart. But either way, the effect seemed to be turning the lens on us to consider the tenuousness of our own connections.

"Well, that was weird," Jamie said as we discretely exited the theater.

"I kind of liked it."

"Was it supposed to be a dream, do you think?"

"Maybe."

"Or a parallel universe?"

"I don't think the writer meant it to be that literal. I feel like he was taking the very concept of relationships and stripping it down to two extremes, total strangers and intimate partners, in order to explore what makes us...I don't know, human?"

"Oh." We had reached the car. "You were one of those smarty English majors, weren't you?"

"I've been known to appreciate a good bildungsroman."

"Right, me too."

I pulled onto Route 17: the crowded, speed-limit-be-damned state route on which I first learned to drive. It seemed terrifying now to think about Mr. Garafin, my stoic Driver's Ed teacher, putting his life in the hands of hundreds of freaked out teenagers who stepped too hard on the gas and braked much later than they should have, all the while being passed left and right by double-long tractor trailers.

In the passenger seat, Jamie eyed the fleeting strip malls and used car dealerships. "Let's not go back yet," he said.

"Where would you want to go?"

"I don't know. I just want to stay in this bubble a little longer. Sitting in that theater and walking around outside anonymously—it was like stepping outside myself for the first time in forever. It felt light and new. You know?"

"I'm not sure where we can keep you incognito." It was too cold to hang out at a park. Museums and libraries were closed. "There's a small diner a little north of here. I don't think many people will be there at three o'clock on a Sunday. But it's still really risky."

"I'll make myself invisible. It'll be like an acting exercise."

We stopped at a CVS, picking up a newspaper and a pair of weak reading glasses as additional camouflage.

I was right, the Gaslight Diner was empty save for a school-aged kid sitting by herself on a stool at the counter.

"This is a massive menu. How can they possibly make all this stuff?" Jamie asked.

He'd been away from Jersey too long to realize that here was the quintessential diner experience, complete with faux Tiffany lamps hanging over our heads like dusty jewels. And the wide booths upholstered in deep red vinyl, each one featuring its own tabletop jukebox.

"Check out the juke!" Jamie started flipping through "pages" of songs that were a disordered mix of contemporary and nostalgic. Dave Matthews Band beside Madonna, Seal beside Styx.

"I don't think we should play—"

But he already had a quarter out of his pocket and was putting it in. He pressed a letter-number combo and Van Halen's "Panama" came on as the waitress approached.

"Quick," I said, "What do you want?"

He flipped back to the menu, "I don't—"

"You ready to order?" the waitress asked. Even she was an aging diner icon with her heavy eye makeup and half-moon glasses poised on the tip of her nose.

"Yes, he'll have the Greek salad and a Diet Coke, and I'll have a Denver Omelet with home fries and wheat toast. Iced tea, please."

I handed her back the menus and she walked away.

"I hate feta," he said. "You could have just said we needed another minute."

I leaned in. "I'm trying to minimize your interactions with people. You could try making it a little easier."

"Hot shoe, burnin' down the avenue," David Lee Roth sang. The kid at the counter started swiveling the lower half of her body in time with the music. She was hunched over a loose-leaf notebook. I reached over to the juke and punched the button twice to lower the volume.

Through a wide rectangular window behind the counter, I could see the cook pull the slip of paper from the rack. He had sandy hair and his forearms were covered in tattoos. He gave a wink to the kid before starting on our order.

The waitress returned promptly with our drinks and a couple of straws. She was thankfully not chatty like another waitress I'd had there before.

After she was back at the counter, Jamie leaned comfortably into his seat. "So, what's the deal with your boss?"

"He's not my boss; my boss is on very long-term maternity leave. He's my interim boss."

"Sounds like the same thing."

"Well, it's not."

"Are you guys open about it?"

"Definitely not."

"You shouldn't get messed up in stuff like that. It never ends well."

David Lee Roth gave a final *"Panama!"* before the jukebox clicked off. I picked up a pink packet of Sweet-N-Low and spun it on the tabletop. It stopped, spin-the-bottle style, short ends pointed perfectly at Jamie and me.

"You don't know the half of it," I said.

"What else?"

I scrunched up my nose and shook my head.

"It can't be that bad." Then he added, "Unless he's married."

I glared at him. "You don't get to be all judgey like that. You don't know the situation. His wife might be a crazy woman living in the attic waiting for just the right moment to burn down the house."

He looked at me blankly.

"It's an English major thing," I said. "The point is, extramarital affairs happen too often for them not to be a legitimate part of the human experience. Maybe marriage is an unnatural state of being, and we just fool ourselves into thinking it's the ultimate gesture of love."

"Said the woman who's never been married."

"Said the guy who gets paid millions to make out with gorgeous women who aren't his wife. How is that not infidelity?"

He held up his hands helplessly. "It's acting."

"Maybe marriage is 'acting.'"

"Now you're just trying to deflect the conversation."

The sun was dropping lower in the sky and a bright beam of gold light streamed so brightly onto our table it seemed like you could reach out and hold it. Over at the counter, the waitress delivered a plate of fries to the

kid and said something that made her laugh. There was
something about the kid's profile that looked familiar.

Jamie propped his elbows on the table and leaned
in. "You're right. I don't know the situation, except for
the fact that the guy is not only married, but he's also
your boss. Interim boss. That's sounds like a lot of power dynamics." Behind the cheap reading glasses his
green-gold eyes were big and brightly locked on mine.
"What do you get out of it, Audrey?"

Were you supposed to get something from being
with someone, or was that just the perspective of a guy
whose very being was a commodity?

"I don't know: companionship, laughter, thoughtful
conversation, great sex. We're just like you non-adul-
terous human beings that way."

Out in the parking lot, a car pulled into the space
next to mine. "As for power dynamics, I have never felt
manipulated or coerced. In fact, there hasn't been a
single moment when I thought I couldn't simply walk
away."

"That's exactly the point!" He raised his hands em-
phatically. "Don't you want a marriage of your own? A
family?"

I didn't want to answer that question. I was ambivalent: both intrigued by and dubious of the concept
of marriage. And children were even farther from my
mind. But I had no interest in saying so and stayed
stubbornly silent. He picked up the newspaper. I resumed spinning the sweetener packet.

A bell dinged from the kitchen, announcing our order was ready. The waitress abandoned her own folded
newspaper to pick up our meals.

"Can I get you anything else?" she asked as she slid
our plates respectively in front of us. Jamie seemed
about to reply, so I jumped in, "No, we're all set, thanks."

He took a fork and nudged the little squares of feta to the edge of his plate. The gesture reminded me of Pooter. I felt another pang and tried to displace it by pounding the bottle of ketchup over my home fries. We ate quietly for a minute or two while I did a little more mental prodding at Jamie's question. I was ready to answer.

"My father remarried last month," I said. "It's the weirdest thing to me. To have had this long, full life with one partner. They met in their twenties, had kids. Raised them up and out of the house. Then retirement, sickness, and suddenly he's a widower. Five years later, here's someone completely new, somebody who wasn't there for any of it. She's a postscript, Jamie. An epilogue. And as a daughter, I don't know what to do with her.

"I don't even know my point. Except maybe it's this: getting married isn't a specific objective of mine. So, if the man I'm involved with doesn't seem too bothered by the fact that he has a wife, then why should I be?"

The door to the diner jangled and a woman in a long coat and colorful scarf blew in like a pile of wind-blown autumn leaves. She smoothed her hair and greeted the waitress with familiarity while the girl at the counter shoveled her books into a backpack.

"I'm not sure what to say," Jamie said. "I think you deserve better is all."

It made me flush warmly to know that I held some regard in his eye. That he had made a positive judgement about the quality of my being and what I did and did not deserve.

My attention was brought back to the counter where the woman was chatting with the waitress. The cook leaned out to speak to the girl. "Make sure you tell your mom what you told me about that boy at school.

He can't talk to you that way." He waved a spatula at her. "I mean it, Ruthie."

In a near parody of an exasperated kid, Ruthie sighed heavily and mumbled, "It's no big deal."

"Marla!" the cook leaned out the window. "Make sure Ruth tells you what happened at school on Friday. You might want to talk to her teacher."

Marla shifted her weight and braced a fist against her hip. "Oh, I might? What about you?"

I pointed in their direction and said to Jamie, "Then there's divorce. Tell me again about what I deserve?"

As the kid got on her jacket, I looked at her mother's irritated face again. And then a name popped up like a flashcard in my brain: Schimke. The kid's mother was Marla Schimke. It was Bobbie's neighbor. A woman I only saw annually at the Chestnut Street Block Party. The one who had once held me verbal hostage talking about New Jersey's "astronomical" property tax rates.

She must have felt my eyes on her. I was too late in glancing away.

"Crap," I whispered and felt my heart tick a few beats faster. She started blustering over to our table. "Make yourself invisible. Fast." Jamie looked confused for a second, but must have heard Marla's boots clacking toward us. He snatched up the newspaper, rested his cheek in his hand and turned to the window.

When I was a kid, I had a picture book about a giraffe that inexplicably wanders into a suburban neighborhood and befriends the story's seven-year-old protagonist. While all the kids from the block flock to the scene in excitement and awe, the grown-ups—pre-occupied with grown-up matters—don't even notice the fifteen-foot-tall giraffe in their midst. They simply rush off on their commute, clutching their umbrellas and briefcases.

So seemed to be the case with Marla Schimke, who gave a polite nod, but no actual glance at the astounding presence of James Keefner. She had something to say to me.

"You're Bobbie's sister, aren't you?"

"Marla, right?"

"Mmhm," she said. "Hey, I wonder if I could ask you about something."

Next to the register, dropping her backpack at her feet and unzipping her jacket, Ruth settled in for what seemed like a familiar kind of waiting.

"Well, I'm—" I said.

"Last summer, Bobbie hired Andy, my fifteen-year-old, to mow her lawn once a week."

Oh, I thought, I know what this is about.

"He's a responsible kid. Always showed up the next day if it had rained. He cut that lawn smartly, getting the very edges, and cleaned the mower when he finished—"

"Marla, I really don't—"

"Then one day, out of the blue, Bobbie tells him not to come back. Says she doesn't need him anymore. Meanwhile, the lawn is growing and growing. Now this isn't a neighborhood where you can do that kind of thing without people talking. So, I asked Andy what happened."

"This sounds like it's between Andy and Bobbie. I really don't know anything about it."

"I think you do, though. And Andy certainly thinks so. He said that you told Bobbie to fire him. Why would you do that?"

I glanced at Jamie working hard to compress himself into nonexistence. This was a bad turn and I needed to do something before we had a much bigger problem than a chatty real estate agent getting on my nerves. I felt a surge of momentum lift me from my seat to stand nearly eye-to-eye with Marla Schimke.

"OK, since you've asked. You're right, I did tell—no insisted—that my sister fire your creepy son. And I'll tell you why, because apparently she was too afraid to."

I started walking her backwards away from the table. "I caught him mowing over a bog full of frogs—on purpose."

I'd managed to get her back near the register. "That's not true!"

"Ask him."

"You must have mistaken what you saw."

"You should get that kid some counseling. Cruelty to animals is often a gateway to psychopathic behavior."

She presented such a horrified look that I almost felt bad.

"Now," I said. "I'd like for you to let me enjoy my lunch, and we can simply part ways. OK?"

Marla sucked in a breath. "You are terrible. I am going to tell your sister what a rotten person you are." She reached a protective arm around Ruth who had the smallest hint of a satisfied smile on her face. I nearly winked at her but was too close to getting out of the situation to risk it. Marla shuttled her daughter toward the door.

"Bye, Daddy," Ruth shouted over her shoulder.

I glanced over at the cook who actually gave me a lopsided grin and thumbs up. It's quite possible that I sauntered a little returning to the table.

I slid into my seat. "That takes care of that," I said.

Outside, Marla had gotten into her car. I couldn't see her face, but her hand shot up at me, middle finger raised in a silent shout. I looked at Jamie and the two of us broke into fits of laughter.

"Shh, shh," I said, still laughing.

"Was that true?" he asked.

"Mostly. I did see a couple of mowed-over dead frogs and told Bobbie about it." I sighed. "And anyway, the kid really was creepy."

"I'm not sure I feel entirely comfortable with you slandering a fifteen-year-old, but I'm glad she's gone."

I hadn't noticed the waitress come over until she was standing right beside us. She set the check down and then braced two hands on the table.

Looking squarely at Jamie, she said, "Listen up. For an autograph on this check and a healthy tip, your secret's safe with me."

The waitress made a fifty-dollar tip on a four-teen-dollar tab that day. We could only hope that she'd be true to her word, or at least give us enough of a head start to get back to the relative safety of my condo.

14: Dizzy

D an Rayburn was dreaming about a cat. The cat he'd had as a kid. A fat-bellied, orange tabby that had been dead for nearly twenty-five years. But not in the dream. In the dream, the cat, Dizzy, had been left outside. Who knew for how long? Maybe months. It was nighttime. It was snowing. Through the open door, he was calling "Di-zeee, Di-zeee!" The stoop, which simultaneously was and was not the stoop of his childhood house, was covered with several inches of snow, but just past the bottom step, it was blackness. Like a night ocean. Like space. Then, out of the blackness, came Dizzy on halting, geriatric (dead) legs. Relieved to see the cat had returned safely, Dan knelt to pick him up and bring him back inside. Inside, there was a ringing sound. Then it stopped. And then he was in his car. The ringing happened again. And stopped again. He was at a party. Above them an airplane was trailing a banner with a slogan whose words made no sense and kept changing.

The bedroom door opened with a gust that startled him awake. Patricia strode in. He hadn't even heard her come home last night, and here she was fresh and flushed from her morning treadmill. She was religious about her "Daily 5K." He glanced at the clock: 6:23 a.m.

"Jeez, Tricia, I have seven minutes left." His throat was dry, his eyes unwilling to focus no matter how many times he blinked.

"You have no idea," she said. "You're sleeping and you have no idea!"

"What." It sounded like a croak.

Patricia seized the remote control from his night table and turned on the television. "You seriously have no idea."

"You keep saying that."

It had always been a habit of hers: the staging of information, holding it just out of reach for heightened drama. He used to think it flirty and playful, but lately, it just made him want to interrupt, insisting that she get to the point. Especially when he could have otherwise been sleeping.

Pressing the remote through various channels, Patricia lowered herself to the bed, nudging him over to a colder spot. Dan sighed gruffly, but she didn't appear to notice.

"Earthquake?"

"It's got to be on somewhere." she mumbled. She pressed, paused, and pressed again. "There."

The screen showed one of the morning talk shows. A reporter with a halo of black hair and heavily painted eyelids was standing in front of a brick building he seemed to recognize. She was tilting her head with gravitas at the camera.

"*In hiding for nearly a week after an altercation with the brother of his wife, model Chloe Philips. Though no charges were pressed in the case, Keefner left his family's home in Santa Barbara under cover of night.*"

Dan shook his head, "This is what you woke—"

"Shh."

"*The superstar was believed to be in a precarious mental state.*"

"I don't really care where they found his body."

Patricia waved her hand at him and turned up the volume.

"Received a tip that Keefner was hiding out here in Maybrook, New Jersey, at the home of an old high school flame, thirty-five-year-old Audrey Rohmer."

Audrey's senior portrait flashed on the screen. Her hair was shoulder length and '80s feathery; her face was rounder, her smile wide and eager. The photo changed to one presumably taken over the weekend, a more familiar, profile shot of Audrey getting into her car.

The pieces weren't making sense. Why was Audrey on the television? And why was an encounter with James Keefner sounding familiar? His pulse ticked up with the next question that had formed. Had Patricia made some kind of connection to Audrey?

"Wow," said Dan. "She works in my division." He felt unhinged and unsteady, like he was about to enter a street fight drunk and unarmed.

Patricia turned to him with a dry look. "She does. In fact, she followed me around the grocery store last month. I can't imagine why she would do that. Can you?"

Damn it, Audrey.

The reporter continued, *"Indicating that Keefner had been there since last Wednesday evening. Our exclusive source also revealed that Ms. Rohmer has been involved in an ongoing affair with another man, forty-three-year-old Daniel—"*

There was the punchline. Dan tried to grab the remote from Patricia, but she pushed his hand away.

"The current husband of Patricia Ripley, who viewers may recall is the ex-wife of disgraced Senator Chasen Baylor, whose own infidelity—"

Now Dan did manage to grab the remote, and he immediately turned the TV off.

"Did she ever mention to you that she had dated James Keefner in high school?" This was not the question he was expecting.

"She? She, Audrey? No. She never did mention that."

"Seems like something that would come up at some point in conversation," Patricia said. "Assuming you two discussed things."

He couldn't bend his mind around all these revelations. The less he said until he had some space to think, the better.

Patricia popped up like a loaded spring. "Well, this totally screwed up my timing this morning. Sorry, but I'll have to jump in the shower before you."

She peeled off her workout clothes and carried them to the hamper in the closet. "Oh, by the way, I did us both the courtesy of unplugging the phone."

Her bare, beautiful rear smirked at him as she headed to the bathroom and shut the door. Out of everything in this *Twilight Zone* morning, Patricia's dismissive calm was possibly the eeriest.

The alarm clock clicked on. "Forty-one-year-old star was apparently—" Dan slapped the button to shut it up.

Was he really to believe that Audrey was having a fling with James Keefner? Was that what that bagel story was about? James Fucking Keefner?

He wasn't convinced this wasn't some colossal misunderstanding. Audrey had a habit of stumbling into awkward situations from which it was difficult to extricate herself. That probably included their relationship.

Dan turned the television on again, but abruptly shut it off when Patricia opened the bathroom door and simply stood there in her towel. She looked otherworldly—a superhero or an alien—as, behind her, the shower steam was drawn up and away by the suck of the ceiling fan.

This is it, he thought.

"You know, Dan. I assumed we were both smart enough to keep our activities discrete." Backlit as she was, he couldn't see her face clearly. "All that work I did to regain my dignity the last ten years. You just pissed it away with some insipid little piece of ass. Yet another nobody who has taken a wrecking ball to my life. Sleeping with you and James Keefner? That is some hilarious horseshit."

Patricia shut herself in the bathroom again. He heard her tear the shower curtain aside and sweep away the shampoo and body wash bottles, sending them tumbling into the tub.

Through the door, she said, "I'm going to my sister's. I want every last inch of you out of here by the time I get back on Saturday."

§

The media called it a "Love Rectangle." They even built graphics around it with faces in each corner: Jamie's and Chloe's, Dan's and Patricia's. There were hearts, and then the hearts cracked and half-dangled. At the center of the rectangle (or "epicenter" as one reporter called it) was a photo of me that had originally appeared in the local paper two years earlier during my hometown's week-long bicentennial celebration. Of all the pictures taken of me through the years, this one was uncharacteristically winning, and thus more successful in pushing the double-homewrecker story they had manufactured. Though it still strained plausibility that I, Audrey Blair Rohmer, could have ensnared James Keefner in a sordid, week-long love affair, the look captured in the photo was one of intentional mischief and knowing secrets. I should know; I had been about to launch a water bomb at the police chief (the older brother of one of my classmates). But the context—that is, the massive water balloon—had been conveniently cropped out.

Of course, I didn't see any of this until later. The morning the story broke, I had been awake since 4:17 a.m., restless and edgy about having to face Pooter. Or worse, not having to face Pooter because he'd already been escorted out of the building. I decided to go into the office early, as much to have a little time to myself as to ensure I had the chance to at least speak to Pooter and try to bridge some kind of understanding before he got called in to HR.

As I was finishing my breakfast, Jamie came in, barefoot and bed-rumpled, looking far sexier than he did in any red-carpet tuxedo getup.

"Sorry, I tried not to wake you," I said.

"It's OK, I have a lot to do today."

Jamie had decided to go back to his father's house in the late morning to do a walk-through in case there was anything he wanted to save. After that, he would simply hire someone to get rid of the rest. He aimed to put the house on the market by the end of the month. And then, I thought morosely, he'll never have a reason to come back.

"I'm going to crash here one more night and then call Tyson in the morning to set up an afternoon press conference. I'm ready to go back, but it's going to be on my terms." He poured himself a cup of coffee. "Hey, maybe tonight, you can work with me on my statement? Help me say things the way I mean them, make it all sound grammar-smart?"

"Of course," I said, again with that disquieting mix of relief for getting my quiet life back and disappointment for getting my quiet life back.

It was 6:03 a.m. If I left in ten minutes, I'd get to the office by seven fifteen, which gave about thirty minutes to myself before people started filing in.

"OK, I'm headed out."

I'll chalk it up to the realization that he would soon be leaving, but I had an unstoppable impulse and kissed him on the cheek. It surprised us both, like I had broken some kind of unspoken rule. I wished I could take it back. "Um. Give a call to the office if you need anything."

I didn't know the reporter and her cameraman were there until I was more than halfway to my car. And, ambushing me from behind, they had blocked the sidewalk, strategically preventing me from bolting back in the building. When I heard, "Miss Rohmer, I'm [Perky Name] from [Blah-blah News Organization]. Can I ask—"

I took off running. I got in my car and locked it. They gave chase and pressed right up against the window as I started the engine.

"No comment!" It's what people said in these situations, right? That, and "I'd like to speak to my lawyer."

I popped the car in reverse and tore out of the lot. The reporter didn't follow. I learned later that she and her cameraman had gone after the bigger fish, Jamie, in the condo. They led him to believe that the knock at the door was me having forgotten something.

It was a different vehicle that had pulled out behind me, a gray SUV with two men. *FBI?* I wondered in a panic. I took turn after turn, the most convoluted way I knew to get to the highway. It took three lefts to confirm that I was, in fact, being followed, though in a non-aggressive kind of way, which gave me time to think. I would go to the office as quickly as possible, rush inside the main entrance where our security desk would prevent them from following me into the building.

Then I could call Jamie and warn him.

Plan in place, my thoughts turned darkly to Pooter: *he must have tipped them off.* However pissed off he was, that kind of betrayal of confidence was vindictive. So mean-spirited, in fact, that I had to pause to consider whether he was actually capable of it. But how else could the news have gotten out? Then I remembered the waitress and determined she must have been the source. But how would she have known where I lived? She couldn't. It had to be Pooter. He was the only other person who knew.

I reached the highway with a fresh head of incredulity. The SUV was still behind me, keeping up at a safe and steady two-cars' length distance.

Then again, the waitress could have pulled my name off the credit card and called in a tip. A news organization would have been able to track me down. Anyone savvy enough to use a phone book could have tracked me down.

Glancing in the rearview mirror, I saw a car slide in between me and my tailers. Here was my opening, if not to lose them, then at least to put enough distance between us to ensure I got in the building unmolested. Channeling my inner Julie Lee, I pressed down on the accelerator and broke ahead. That's when the red swirling light and siren alerted me to the fact that I was about to be forcefully escorted to the shoulder.

The police officer looked about seventeen years old and had a soft, golden mustache that brought to mind a fuzzy baby duck.

"Ma'am, may I please see your license and registration?"

Even his voice, which had a sotto voce, Casey Kasem quality to it, lacked any authority. "Yes, of course, Officer."

I opened the glove compartment and silently prayed the registration was up to date. It took a little rifling through oil change, maintenance invoices and a nest of other years-old receipts, but I found the slip, and deferentially handed both pieces of documentation to Officer Dawlish, as his name tag indicated.

As he walked back to his car, I adjusted the rear-view mirror to see what had happened to my pursuers. At first, I couldn't find them, but then angling the mirror a bit farther back, I could now see the SUV had pulled over, as well, at a distance that kept them fairly inconspicuous if you weren't looking for them. Whoever they were—and I guessed now that they were more likely a different media crew, not the FBI—they seemed disinclined to encroach, but not necessarily to let up either.

I sat, painfully impatient to contact Jamie, and having a sinking feeling that he had already been rooted out. I wondered again about the possibility that I would be in legal trouble. *Would I be found to have been harboring a fugitive?* Unlikely since Desmond hadn't pressed any charges. Still, what if the media had alerted the police and there was an APB out for me? Was that why Officer Dawlish was taking so long?

When he finally strode back with one hand on his belt and the other holding my papers, it was no surprise to hear him ask, "Do you know why I pulled you over?"

When I got my driver's permit, Bobbie gave me two pieces of advice for when you get pulled over: first, say you were speeding because you had to pee really bad; and second, never admit you did anything wrong; otherwise, you can't contest it in court, which you should always do. I looked at Officer Dawlish with his total lack of gravitas and made an instinctive, friend-or-foe assessment: this young cop had probably been under-estimated his whole life. I needed to strike a balance between respecting his authority and eliciting his sympathy for a fellow underdog.

"I do, Officer. I was speeding."

"You were speeding," he said as if he hadn't heard me. "Do you know how fast you were going?"

"I don't, sir, but, if you'll allow me the opportunity to explain why I was speeding, I'd really appreciate it."

"Let me guess, you just suddenly had to pee like crazy."

"Well, I'm sure you've heard that lots of times. But no," I said. "Here's the thing, I'm being followed." He tilted his head as if to ask what kind of fool I took him for.

"If you turn and look about 500 feet behind us, you'll see a gray SUV."

Without realizing I was going to, I told Officer Dawlish the story. And not the Cliffs Notes version, the whole bizarre, convoluted story. He stood there, arms folded over his narrow, Boy Scout chest and just listened, eyebrows raising and head nodding at the appropriate moments.

It felt as if I'd been talking for thirty minutes though it barely amounted to six. It was a great unburdening of guilty conscience, insecurities, and little conspiracies. I felt lighter and more animated just in the telling.

"So you see, Officer Dawlish, I have to get to the office. Not to call Jamie, James—it's already too late for that—but because I need to try one more time to save Pooter's job."

Those last words bounced back at me, and they were a revelation to myself. *Yes! That was what I needed to do.* I would go straight to Dan's office and tell him that if he fired Pooter, I would resign. It would be my redemption, not just in doing right by a friend but in ridding myself of that do-nothing heaviness I'd been dragging around like an old suitcase for the last five years.

"Please." I appealed to young Officer Dawlish. "Can you simply let me go?"

His expression was a mix of dubiousness, perplexity, and, I was sure, a glimmer of sympathy. He took a breath in and let it out slowly. I could see now, he was closer to my age and likely not as naive as I had initially assessed him to be.

"Wait here," he said.

The idleness of the next few minutes was maddening. Now that I had my ambition set, the need to move was imperative. Every second wasted made it more likely that Pooter would be called in and pink slipped before I'd even had a chance to park my car. Finally, Officer Dawlish returned.

"Ms. Rohmer. Your story apparently checks out. The news is reporting that James Keefner has been found, and he's been positively linked to you."

It felt as if a big stone had dropped into the well of my stomach, sending out queasy ripples.

"I think you've got one hell of a day ahead of you." He shifted his weight. "Here's the thing. I can't keep those media folks from following you—freedom of speech and all that. But I can help you get to where you're going without them harassing you too much. That might give you some time to save your friend's job, but frankly, I think you've got some bigger problems on your hands."

And so, we got back on the highway: me, Officer Dawlish—no siren, but lights flashing— and the gray SUV, all driving at a perfectly cruise-controlled fifty-five mph. Before long, other story chasers had joined the procession, and because the media love nothing more than a good case of déjà vu, there were helicopters overhead filming the slow chase, OJ-style, to the offices of Preston House.

The whole time, I masochistically listened to what was being said on the radio. It was then I learned with another agonizing kick to the gut that Dan—and, oh Christ, Patricia—had been dragged into the sordid story the media was constructing.

It was then I knew, without a doubt, that it had been Pooter. And raw hurt turned to anger, not just at having my utmost confidence betrayed, but at having been duped into wanting to put my own livelihood— nay, my career—on the line to save his job. I seethed and boiled, and still needed to drive with meticulous, law-abiding care, which incensed me even more.

By the time we rolled up to the parking lot, I was desperately hoping that Pooter had not yet been called in to HR. Only now, it wasn't because I wanted to reconcile, it was because I was ready to confront.

It was 7:55 a.m. The sweet spot of Monday morning arrivals. Cars flowed in and jockeyed for the closest space to the door. Anyone who hadn't already heard the news reports was at least treated to the intrigue of seeing me escorted into the building by Officer Dawlish, at his insistence.

Even at my mother's funeral, I hadn't felt as exposed and vulnerable as I did walking through those glass doors, my chin tucked, my eyes on my shoes, concentrating on the simple act of placing one foot in front of the other.

We stopped just in front of the security desk. I raised my face to Dawlish's. My voice was a vocalized whisper. "I'm really grateful to you. You're very kind."

His neck turned a little blotchy and red. "You can thank me by sticking to the speed limit, ma'am."

I'm not sure what it was with impulses that day, but I reached out and gave this skinny stranger an emphatic, nearly desperate hug.

"You take care of yourself," he said quietly to the top of my head.

The elevator doors were daunting and massive. They yawned open to swallow a waiting group of a dozen or so employees. I took a bracing breath and joined them, shuffling myself into the front corner, away from the buttons. Jamie's Jedi mind trick of invisibility proved fairly ineffective, as there were people riding up who had no doubt seen my escorted entrance. Clearly not everyone had seen, however. Because from the opposite side of where I stood in the elevator, you could hear a voice in mid-recount.

"Since he'd gone missing."

"Omygawd. Who is she?"

"She's in biz texts. Friends with Julie Lee. But that's not all—"

There's already something inherently awkward in being in the confined space of an elevator with a bunch of people. You're standing closer than is normally acceptable, brushing arms, collectively experiencing smells, and being a captive audience to any inane conversation happening nearby. This was a whole new, excruciating level of uncomfortable. And not just for me, but for everyone around me who knew I was there. You could almost feel this great pressing in the air. It was wholesale embarrassment on my behalf combined with borderline hilarity, everyone trying his or her best to hold it together.

But when the speaker started in on "her boss," a barely perceptible game of telephone was initiated by a guy behind me clearing his throat, which I imagined triggered an elbow, followed by a head tilt in my direction, leading to a fast chain of tacit communication that finally reached the talker who was interrupted mid-gossip.

"For like a year, maybe lon—"

"[Undecipherable whisper]"

"What?" she said, followed immediately by a sharp intake of breath.

We rode the next two floors in colluding silence. I turned my back to everyone, facing the corner like a classroom troublemaker, and focused on what I would say to Pooter: The nerve, the absolute disregard for the other lives affected, those who had nothing to do with his petty vendetta. It was time for him grow up. *You can either blame everyone around you, or you can own it and make something better, but you don't take people down with you. People who tried to help. People who thought they were your friend.*

I rehearsed words to that effect a couple times before we arrived at my department's floor. Pushing my way out into the hallway, I took long strides toward my office, buoyed by indignation and the determination to ignore the heads popping up from cubicles, like prairie dogs scouting the horizon for a coming storm.

I turned the corner to our department, marched to our workspace. But my resolve faltered when I saw that his desk had already been cleared of everything except a lamp, a jar of pens and pencils, and the calendar blotter pad with a cartoon Mighty Mouse he'd drawn on it.

But he wasn't gone yet, just merely bent over, arranging his personal items in a cardboard box. When he realized I was standing there, he sat up, wiped the dust from his hands on his jeans. We looked at each other for no more than two seconds. And then. He laughed. It was a full, unabashed laugh, confusing and humiliating to me. I was so stunned that all the declarations I'd prepared scattered from my mind.

Desperate to respond in some way, I grabbed the jar of pens and pencils and overturned them with a mighty force. Which is clearly relative, when speaking of writing utensils. They fell and rolled like a game of pick-up sticks. This made him laugh even harder. I was at a complete loss. Now that the anger rug had been pulled from under me, everything came in tsunami style: Jamie facing an even bigger PR catastrophe, the affair with Dan forced into the glaring light for all our friends and colleagues to see. Patricia scandalized yet again. I backed into my office and quietly closed the door.

On my desk, the red light indicating voice mail messages had transformed into something menacing, glowing brighter and dangerously insistent the longer I looked at it. It seemed as if Hell itself were calling. Before it could ring, I snatched the receiver off the hook and left it lying on its side like a wounded animal.

Pulling my chair out, I folded myself into the cave-like space beneath the desk. It was one of those oversized wooden executive desks recycled from an era when a woman would never have had the privilege of sitting behind it. And probably the only reason for a woman to be beneath it, the way I was, would have been either to clean up a spill or to service her boss.

And then, speaking (or rather, thinking) of bosses, there was a discrete knock on the door: "It's Dan. Can I come in?"

Inconceivable, I thought, *I cannot face him. Not now.* He came in anyway and closed the door behind him.

"I wanted—" he paused, confused by my missing corporeal presence. "Oh. Come on out. It's bad, but it's not hide-under-your-desk bad."

He waited, patient, as always. But I was paralyzed and willful in my silence. "Or maybe it is."

He sat down, settling in for what I determined would be a one-sided conversation.

"You know, I had actually planned on coming in this morning with some better news for you. I managed to find a place for Pooter with the humanities team. Unfortunately, he had already submitted his letter of resignation to me and to HR. It looks like there's a letter on your desk too."

Dumbass Pooter, I thought.

Dan went on. "When I left your place yesterday, I couldn't shake the feeling that I lost enough of your esteem to make this whole thing of ours unravel. Apparently, there were other things working to make that happen." I could imagine him shaking his head, baffled. "But in that moment, I just felt really sad. I wanted to make it right. Not for Pooter, for you. I wanted to fix it for you."

Keenly focused just on his voice, I could hear for the first time, the whisper of a twang from his midwestern roots. A harsher short-a in "unravel", a short-i instead of e in "again."

"I know I haven't been fair to you. I pulled you into a situation you'd never imagined yourself in. And I kept you there as a fix for something that was broken.

"But you were good. Better than I was at keeping things light and casual. Funny how we both thought I was the one who was better at compartmentalizing."

He stopped speaking for a moment. The ambient noise of an active office on a Monday morning came into sound-focus. The percussive rhythm of the copy machine, the distant ringing of an unanswered phone, laughter (gossip), the elevator bing. It was the din of a corporate rainforest.

"I know it's easy to say now, but I would have done it if you'd asked me to," Dan gave a sigh. "Leave her, I mean."

His words were a camera flash, lighting up everything and blinding me for a few seconds before the burning afterimage slid slowly, achingly downward. What was I supposed to do with that? Unfold my body and rush to him, tears in my eyes—the daft heroine crying, *"She's out of our lives, Dan. We can finally be together!" I had just needed to say the magic words?*

Simply put, a future with Dan—without Patricia— was never even part of the equation for me. From our first kiss, I beat it into my brain that there was an expiration date. Savor the days, I told myself, don't get attached and always be prepared to move on.

How had we left the biggest of things unsaid?

"Audrey?"

Would it have been different? Would *I* have been different? In that moment, all I could say for sure was that I was a junkyard of emotions—mortification, bafflement, anger, anxiety, devastation.

He sighed, "It's like talking to a desk. Ha." But his "Ha" lacked any trace of funny. "Would you come out, please? I have no idea what to believe. I have nothing to go home to. I need you."

With my thumbnail, I had gouged a small divot in the soft wooden underbelly of the desk. If it was stubborn that I wouldn't come out, it was cruel that I wouldn't even speak. I was already letting him go.

"I guess you need some space." Then, just shy of an edge in his voice, he said, "In fact, why don't you take some time off. Leave of absence or whatever." He stood up abruptly and left, closing the door behind him.

Or whatever. I let out a long, slow breath. Without Dan in the room, it felt like that short reprieve after you've puked your guts into the toilet; you know there's more to come, but in that moment, there's nothing but holy gratitude for being in a state of not-puking.

I was suddenly overwhelmed by fatigue. I stayed like that, fetal-curled in the womb of my desk. Not moving, not even really thinking. It wasn't long—no more than twenty minutes—but enough to have sent a sharp cramp to my back. It took slow effort to unfold my body and stand. I needed to pee.

I could hear the office was still bustling. Work carried on. It seemed plausible that Dan was holding his Monday morning staff meeting, though how he would face them all knowing what they knew, I couldn't imagine. I climbed up onto the filing cabinet and stood on tiptoes to peek out the high glass window of my office. All trace of Pooter was gone. There were some sales team members near the elevator, a couple of admins walked by, but the time seemed right to make a dash for the bathroom. From there, I could duck into the staircase and go home. No, not home, but somewhere.

The bathroom was mercifully empty. In my old stall, the one I'd avoided after my conversation with Pooter, the scratched writing had been painted over. In fact, the whole inside of the door was now just a shade off from the tomato soup red of the partitions that surrounded it. I ran my fingers over the surface and was able to find, like brail, the ghost words "You are so shitty." *So be it,* I thought, *but isn't everybody in their own way?*

Washing my hands, there was no hiding from my face in the mirror. If a person could look lopsided—like a painting hung just a little off-center—that was me. My cheek had a small round indentation where I'd been leaning against a bolt-head, and my hair was matted and tangled on one side. I splashed my face and dampened my hair with cold water. If I was going to be photographed running to my car, I wasn't going to look a wreck. Turning to the hand dryer, I caught a horrifying view of the parking lot, packed nearly bumper to bumper with news crews and other gawkers: a tailgate party, sans coolers and frisbees.

Just at that moment, the bathroom door swung open behind me. I turned, deer-in-the-headlights, to see Rigid lumbering in. She looked at me, purse-lipped for a moment, not sure what to make of me standing there.

"You sure know how to whack a bee's nest," she said. I think my chin started to quiver.

"Don't be ridiculous. You get those emotions under control, or they will make a meal out of you."

"Bridget, you don't know, you haven't seen..." I pointed over my shoulder to the window.

"Oh, I know." She pointed a hooked finger at me. "I just got in from the dentist's and had to throw elbows just to get to the door." She folded her arms. "You are lucky they aren't letting anyone in without an ID badge."

I sat down heavily on the radiator, and took slow, steadying breaths to get "my emotions "under control."

Bridget set her hefty purse down on the sink and leaned in close to the mirror, baring her teeth like an angry gibbon. "She damn near pulled a crown off with that scraping and picking. Telling me I need to floss more."

Could I wait them out? Go back to my office and just stay sequestered there? Or would that mean I'd have to suffer another mortifying moment with Dan? What would happen if we left the building together?

I whispered, "I've got to get out of here."

Bridget straightened. "Just hold on."

"No, Bridget, I mean it, I've got to go."

"I said hold on."

She went into the "you're so shitty" stall. I turned back to the window, unable to not hear her peeing for what seemed like a very long time. The toilet paper roll, the flush, the zip of her khakis. At the sink, she scrubbed her hands red, while my patience seeped. Then she pulled apart the mouth of her purse and dug around, pulling out random items: a pair of batteries, some fishing line, a lint roller, a single domino. My foot started tapping impatiently. Then, triumphant, she pulled the largest collection of keys I'd seen on anyone who wasn't a janitor.

She selected one and held it up for me.

"Now. You take the stairs down to the cafeteria. Go into the kitchen, tell Alma I sent you and have her lead you to the delivery door. Take a left from the loading dock. That'll put you behind all the rubberneckers. Stay low and out of sight until you find the green Oldsmobile Firenza, plates GVN-23L. Say it."

"GVN-23L."

"Drive out the south exit. They'll never see you leave. You call me by noon and tell me where to pick it up." She unloaded the fistful of keys on me.

My chin must have started quivering again. She snapped her fingers just in front of my nose.

"I floss," she snipped.

"I never doubted it, Bridget."

15: Just Add Water

It was the official end to summer, a Labor Day weekend that was humid and hot. There was no hiding the fact that the quality of light had noticeably changed and the colors were fading from vibrant to tired. I was sitting in my parked car with a peach-blackberry pie as my passenger. Twice I put my fingers back on the key in the ignition, ready to call later with a fabricated excuse, and twice, I forced my hand to let go. One breath in, two breaths out.

Approaching on the sidewalk was a couple with a baby in a sling, the father carrying a bottle of wine and some flowers. If I was going to go, they seemed as good coverage as I was likely to get. So just as they passed, without taking another chance to stall, I slid my hand under the pie and ventured forth, staying close, but a few paces behind them.

From the bottom of the driveway, you could hear live music playing, presumably The Cock Asians. The house was a squat, bungalow style, perched at the top of a freshly mowed and meticulously landscaped low hill. There were streamers and white balloons strung around the porch pillars, but a sign blocked the walkway. "This way to the party!" it said in loopy Julie-script with an arrow pointing behind the house.

The yard was compact, made all the smaller by the crowd of people and the four-piece band, assembled in front of a garden shed. Long strings of white lights had been looped along the fence perimeter, interrupted by a big, hand-painted banner that read, *"Julie + Blake Got Hitched!"*

Though it was late afternoon, the sun hanging just above the horizon was still bright enough for an excuse to keep my sunglasses on. Most of the guests were strangers, but I recognized a few faces from Preston House, and warily kept a discrete distance.

I delivered my pie to a table that featured desserts of every shape and confectionary type: lots of brownie variations, a tall strawberry shortcake, and more elegant additions like pretty petits fours and a tower of profiteroles. I had no sooner stepped back from the table when I received a straitjacket hug from behind.

"You came! I'm so happy you came!" It was Julie, rosy-cheeked and wearing a curve- flattering, red dress. She held a fizzy glass of champagne loosely, like a chic accessory.

I hugged her back and said, "Look at you, all married."

She grabbed me by the wrist, and we bulldozed our way through several conversations to reach a tall and trim man whose wavy blonde hair and tanned complexion immediately brought the word "golden" to mind.

"Blake," she interrupted him mid-sentence, "here's Audrey, my friend, Audrey."

Blake turned to the couple with whom he had been speaking and said with a cheery Australian accent, "Pardon me. My bride has someone she would like me to meet."

I avoided looking making eye contact, still trying to keep a relatively anonymous presence. "It's so nice to meet you, Audrey. I've heard a great deal about you."

I shook his hand with more confidence than I felt, "Well, this is definitely one of those cases where you shouldn't believe everything you hear."

He hesitated a moment and then jumped in, "Oh, I just meant that Julie thinks the world of you. She has missed you terribly."

"No, it's...I shouldn't have." I stumbled, making a mental note to stop stepping on my own toes. "Anyway, so you guys got married? That's amazing."

Blake put a long arm around Julie's shoulder. He was well over a foot taller. "We did, indeed. Hopped a flight to Prague and didn't tell anyone our plans, lest they try to talk us out of it." He side-squeezed her to him.

Behind us, the band cranked up its speakers. "Oh, that's not going to work," said Julie. "Your grandmother is going to have a heart attack." She turned, doe-eyed and pouty, to Blake, "Would you? He never listens to me."

"I see, I get to be the big, bad brother-in-law."

"It's inevitable," said Julie. "Damon doesn't need an excuse to dislike someone."

As Blake peeled off toward the band, Julie hooked her arm through mine and walked me to the periphery.

"Is this OK? I mean, are you OK? I'm sorry. I gave up leaving messages for you. I don't even know how you're doing."

"I'm totally fine. Actually good," I added. "But today isn't about me. I want to hear more about this charming husband of yours. Hand up, let's see the rock."

She lifted her hand in front of her face and waggled her fingers. A healthy-sized diamond ring sat atop a thin, shiny wedding band.

"So, we met two months ago—"

"Seriously?" I interrupted.

"I know! It was one of those preposterous romances you hear about. We were scheduled on the same flight from Miami to JFK. There was a major storm that grounded everything. Hotels were all booked, except I had a VIP card that got a suite at the Hilton."

I tried to listen, but as the first real social outing I'd been to since the media storm, I had trouble focusing. The ambient and visual noise felt foreign and disorienting. But I still knew how to use the right conversational cues, and Julie was rightfully enthralled with her own story, so she didn't notice my lack of attentiveness.

"And a few days later, I proposed. Or more like, insisted."

"That sounds about right," I said.

She asked what I was up to, and I gave a brief recount. I had moved back into my old house with my father and Joyce and would stay there until I figured out what was next, quite possibly a move to another part of the country. I told her how I had been working as a prep cook at a diner for the last several months.

"Really? That's just so...unexpected," she said, a small wrinkle in her nose.

"I know. But it's actually been a good change, the right kind of bridge to whatever comes next. I started just by chopping vegetables and preparing salad dressings and soups, but the lead cook has been letting me apprentice on some of the baking lately. There's a pie over there that I made this morning."

The diner in question was the same one I had taken Jamie to. The day Bridget helped me escape the office, I was at a loss for where to go. I didn't want to bring reporters to my dad's house, I couldn't go back to mine, so I drove to the diner.

Thankfully, a different waitress was handling the few occupied tables that day, while the cook, Ray—ex of Marla Schimke and father of Ruth and frog-mowing AJ—was doing double duty at counter service and cooking. He seemed to have recognized me, not from a sensational news story, but maybe from having verbally steamrolled his ex-wife just a few days earlier. Like a good bartender, he was able to sense my hovering turmoil.

"Pie heals all," was what he said. And he served up a slice of "Mile-High Merengue Pie," with its massive white cloud topping and sunshiney, sour-sweet curd. I eventually learned the line was a schtick he used to sell more pie, but at the time, I was hopeful there was some truth to the claim.

During that first month of my "recluse period," I returned to that counter so many times during the diner's off hours that Ray started asking my input on a couple of new pasta recipes he was developing. By May, I was in the kitchen helping out and enjoying being productive while having the comfort of staying behind the scenes in the back kitchen.

"That's great," said Julie. "Blake and I will have to come by some time."

I neither encouraged nor discouraged the idea. In fact, somehow, I knew this would be the last time Julie Lee and I would see each other. I would get Christmas cards, birth announcements, but whatever strange dynamic had brought us together was now past.

"You've got so many guests. Why don't you go mingle and we'll talk more in a bit."

"OK, but just one question, I hope you don't mind my asking?"

"Go for it," I said, knowing perfectly well what it would be.

"Are you still in touch with him?"

Being deliberately obtuse I said, "Dan? Not really. We got together for dinner once before he moved back to Minnesota. We've spoken a couple times on the phone, but there's no real reason for us to keep up anymore."

"No," she said, "I mean THE him."

"Oh, you mean James," I said. "No."

This wasn't entirely true. Two months earlier, I had received an unsigned postcard from Geneva where I knew he had been on-location. It read:

> *The best feedback I've ever received was when a good friend reminded me that my shit stinks too. Thank you. For that and everything.*
> *—J*

In the days that followed the scandal, I avoided the TV and radio. The only coverage I managed to see was a Daily News cover showing that same photo of me getting into my car with the emblazoned headline, "Tawdry Audrey!" But I did tune in for Jamie's press conference that aired from Newark Airport that fateful Monday night. He gave a simple, brief statement.

"During my time away, I sought to meditate upon my recent bad behavior toward my brother-in-law, Desmond Philips, while also allowing myself time to mourn the passing of my father, Ernest James Keefner. Audrey Rohmer is a dear friend who was kind enough to welcome me into her home during this time. Our relationship is strictly platonic, and I urge you to give her the space and privacy she deserves.

"It is with humility that I return to my family. I am deeply regretful of the pain and worry that I have caused. After a short respite with them, I will eagerly rejoin the cast of *Vengeance City* to begin work on the fourth installment in the *The Malevolants* franchise."

He took no questions, claiming a need to get to his flight, at which point James Keefner's publicity manager took over the damage control. Jamie looked down as he turned to go, his shoulders slightly rounded, his mouth set and serious.

Not surprisingly, the status of Jamie's marriage was a ripe cover-story subject in the checkout tabloids. "Chloe threatens murder to James' co-star mistress!" "Marriage in crisis: James walks out again!" But for all their cry-wolf reports, Jamie and Chloe continued to confound the divorce predictions. It was impossible to know how Jamie's relationship rebuilding with Storey was going, but insiders reported that she was going to have a supporting role in one of his upcoming films.

I saw *Vengeance City* four times in the theatre, each time relishing the fact that I had held his undivided attention for a brief period of time, and in that sense, there would always be a tiny part of James Keener that belonged to me and only me.

"I still can't believe it," said Julie. "I've got a million more questions."

"I'm sure you do, but I think your husband is looking for you."

A whole head taller than most of the guests, Blake was wading through the crowd, arms up, holding a fresh pair of champagne glasses. Julie went all dopey-grinned.

"I'll be back," she said and patted my shoulder before peeling off to join him.

I was eyeing the buffet table, considering the feasibility of putting together a to-go plate when The Cock Asians teed up a song, written just for the occasion, about the sudden nuptials of Julie and Blake.

"And so, for my pit bull of a sister and her judgmentally impaired...I mean, dashing new husband, here's a new tune called *Just Add Water.*"

Amy Klinger

Far from a love ballad, the tune was rough and rowdy. A tongue-in-cheek send-up about an instant romance consummated on the beach with sand in all the wrong places. Most of the guests were oblivious to the music, let alone the lyrics. The exceptions being a woman in a gauzy, flowered skirt dancing with two young children, and to her left, head bopping to the fast beat was Pooter. He was standing next to a girl who seemed unsure of what to do with her arms, though she less vigorously nodded her head to the beat. He leaned over to say something to her, she gave him a thumbs up.

When the song had finished, Damon announced that the band was taking a set break, to which someone in the crowd responded with hearty applause.

"Yeah, bite me, Dad," Damon said, then cracked a smile, "Just kidding, I know you're my least-biggest fan."

Pooter and the girl turned toward the buffet table, which left me clear in his line of sight. I clasped my hands together and dove headfirst into conversation.

"Hey, I remember you."

He didn't quite look at me, more at the space beside me. "Yeah, I wondered if you might turn up."

"It's Julie, you know," I said. "She won't let you decline an invitation."

The girl at Pooter's side reached out an eager hand, "I'm Mandy."

"Audrey."

"Yeah, I know."

"Pooter and I used to work—"

"I know that too."

"Well, you are certainly well-informed."

Pooter chimed in, "We were on our way to get some food." He did not invite me to join them.

"Pooter, I'm not going to stay long, but since we're both here now, maybe we could talk just for a few minutes?" I demurred to Mandy, "If that's OK with you."

"I can go fix a plate for us," she said, giving his arm a squeeze before she left.

Without speaking, we walked away from the crowd along the driveway. Bypassing the "Party's this way!" sign, we walked single file to the porch steps and sat down. I took off my sunglasses and fumbled for a way to begin.

"I've never seen you wear sandals before," I said, feeling embarrassed to have called attention to his feet.

"People do that in summer."

I tried a safer conversational entry: "What are you up to these days?"

"Things are rolling along. I'm working as a marketing and events coordinator for a non-profit called Spokes People. We take in old bikes, fix them, and give them to kids in low-income communities."

You could hear a note of pride in his voice.

"I guess what they say about the closing and opening of doors holds true," I said. "That sounds really great."

"It was actually through one of Dan's connections I ended up there. He passed along my resume to the executive director, who gave it to the hiring manager. It's pretty great being there. Everyone's super passionate and...yeah." He trailed off, politely tamping down his enthusiasm. "How about you?"

I told him about the small freelance editing job I had done for an instructor at the local community college, and I offered sparing information about working at the diner. I didn't want to go too far off on a tangent, away from the talk I'd decided in that moment to pursue.

As the early evening settled, the cars passing on the street now had their headlights on. There was a light breeze fluttering the leaves in the nearby maple tree, and a family strolled by, each member holding an ice cream cone.

"I didn't expect to see you here," I said.

"Yeah, well Julie and I have kind of a short history. It started at your house that New Year's Eve. We kept a casual fling going until just before she met Blake. No hard feelings, though. Actually, I think we were both kind of relieved when she found someone that suited her better."

This new information tripped me, "You and Julie Lee? Oh my gosh, I had no idea."

"And you thought I couldn't keep a secret." He pulled a handful of shrub and started picking it apart. "It wasn't me, Audrey."

I nodded. "I know. That's what I wanted to talk to you about."

§

It was nearly three weeks after the scandal before I went back to my condo. Hiding out at my father's house offered the comfort and quiet I needed to wallow in my mortification. Dad was a formidable barrier against the press, and I was surprisingly well cared for by Joyce, who had very little reason to do so. In fact, she and Bobbie seemed to bond over their shared objective of pulling me out of a a serious funk (though it took nearly a week for Bobbie to be willing to speak to me).

I had decided to sublet the condo. Though I would leave it furnished, I still had to clear out my clothes and personal effects. When I first returned, however, what took immediate precedent was the refrigerator with its exquisite and horrifying collection of mold-entombed leftovers and toxic vegetable sludge; the reek was profound. I donned the rubber gloves—the precious, pink rubber gloves that Jamie's hands had graced—and got to work.

It took so much time, in fact, to tackle the fridge that I decided to stay overnight, taking the evening to finish up packing. In the morning, I would load up the pickup truck I'd borrowed.

Without my dad's late-night pacing and puttering, and Joyce's up-with-the-roosters rise and shininess, my sleep was thick and luxurious. It was nearly nine thirty the next morning when some voices outside my window translated into a vivid dream about a scolding high school teacher displeased with the essay I'd written.

By the time I'd fully awakened, there was more commotion outside. If a reporter had somehow found out I was there, I would be armed with a foul mood and an ego that had sufficiently recovered to stand up for my privacy. I dressed quickly before launching out onto the stoop.

The first thing I saw was the ambulance parked on the road in front of our complex, the lights still swirling. Then, coming up the walkway was an EMT just finishing up a conversation on her radio.

"What's happening?" I asked.

"Are you a friend of Mrs. Gargiulo?" She gestured at Mrs. Ass' condo.

Learning her name (and perhaps seeing an ambulance) changed everything. For a year and a half Mrs. Gargiulo lived right beside me, yet our worlds had never intersected. Who cared in this moment why that was; all that mattered was that failure to connect.

So many questions instantly flooded my thoughts. Where was Mr. Gargiulo? Were there Gargiulo offspring that lived far away and never visited? Had I cruelly mistaken sadness for willful unfriendliness? I suddenly lamented the stories we never shared. The moments never spent in each other's company with tea. The recipe trades and political debates we never had. Oh, Mrs. Gargiulo, we could have been more than neighbors, we could have been acquaintances!

"Yes, I live next door," I said, somewhat obviously. "Is she all right?"

"She'll be fine. Seems like she may be experiencing a bit of a panic attack."

From loneliness, I thought to myself. I may not have been engaged when I was there, but at least I was a nearby, benign presence.

The EMT continued. "We're going to take her to the hospital so they can do a few tests, make sure everything is OK."

I nodded, on the very verge of offering to go with her, but hesitant. "Can I speak to her before you go?"

"I think that should be OK," she said.

Moments later, the EMT was at the front end of the stretcher, easing it over the threshold while a burlier EMT was keeping it steady at the other end. Between them lay Mrs. Gargiulo, propped up, an oxygen mask over her nose and mouth. Her wispy, yellowish hair was mad scientist wild, her cheeks seemed flushed, but she was alert.

They halted the stretcher on the walkway and pressed the brakes down to fix her in place. The first EMT said, "Try to be quick. She's stable, but we do want to get her checked out as soon as possible."

They stepped aside to let me near.

Mrs. Gargiulo's eyes were bright blue and cartoonishly large. She was staring at me, taking in my face for the first time, as I was hers. She lifted a crooked hand and urged me closer. And closer still, until I was stooping over. That was when she reached out and snatched a hunk of my hair, using it to reel me in toward her face. I was so startled, I figured it was simply the action of a scared, sick person wanting to make sure she was heard, "Tell my grandson I love him" or "Please feed my cat." With her other hand, she pulled aside the oxygen mask. By then, her grip on my hair was severe and starting to hurt.

"You hooah," she whispered, short of breath. At first, I thought she was saying "You-hoo" as if she wasn't sure she had my attention. But it quickly became clear that she simply had a thick New York accent and meant something else entirely. "How dare you come back," she said, venom in her voice. "I got rid of you, you filthy slut!"

I gasped and tried to pry my hair from her hand, but her tenacious, weed-pulling grip was unbreakable. In pure self-defense mode, I grabbed a wild lock of her hair, and started to pull with equal force.

"Let go, you crazy—"

The EMTs leapt into action and had to forcibly break up our tug-o-war stalemate. When they did, Mrs. Ass feigned hyperventilation, which incensed me, and I lunged at her again. The bulky EMT wedged himself between us and pushed me backward onto the grass.

"What is wrong with you?" he said.

Gently, almost lovingly, he replaced Mrs. Ass' oxygen mask. Three pairs of angry eyes glared as they wheeled past me toward the waiting ambulance. Just before the end of the walkway, Mrs. Ass pulled her mask off again, and her shrill voice rang out: "Don't you ever come back! Geranium killer!"

§

Pooter had to wipe laughing tears from the corners of his eyes. "Oh man, I'm sorry." His laughter was light, no undercurrent of schadenfreude or sarcasm or irony. "I can just picture your face."

"I seriously contemplated throwing a brick through her window. Thank God I didn't. My sister looked her up and says she's the cousin of one of the main guys in the Lucchese family." I touched a finger to my nose meaningfully.

"Damn, you sure know how to pick them."

"No joke."

Our laughter faded with tired sighs.

"So, she was the one who tipped off the media?"

"Not exactly."

"Oh."

"She was the one who told the reporters about Dan when they came out that day, that he was my boyfriend or whatever. At the very least, I know she gave them his license plate number. It was in the guest parking often enough."

"So how did they find out about Jamie?"

I plucked a loose thread on my dress. "I'm not sure."

This was true; I wasn't certain. But in the weeks that followed the scandal, I kept circling back to one thing: the advice Jamie's mother had given him, specifically to look out for his own best interests. The more I ran over events in my mind—and I rewound and replayed them over and over—the more I suspected that it had been Jamie himself who had anonymously called in the tip. It was just the kind of hyper-scandal that could reboot the popularity, and therefore marketability, of a star whose career was rumored to be on the wane. Though I was fairly certain he hadn't set out to create a scandalous scenario by attacking his wife's brother, it at least seemed plausible that when there was an opportunity to leverage it to his advantage, he took it.

And I tried to get angry about it. If true, it was an outrageous disregard for the only person who had been his ally. But at that point, my capacity for extreme emotions had been exhausted. And strangely, assuming it was true, I admired the bravery of such an act, how Jamie would have understood what mattered most to him and made sure it wasn't taken away without a fight.

"But you thought it was me who leaked to the press," Pooter said.

I nodded. It was just about dusk. From the tall grasses bordering the yard, the crickets and katydids were kicking up a racket of chirps and scritches. As if in accompaniment, a raucous drum solo kicked off The Cock Asians' next set.

"Why did you laugh that day, Pooter?"

"Did I?"

I stood up, ready to abandon the conversation if he was going to play dumb. I had a dense collection of lousy feelings that had settled over time like murky silt to the bottom of a pond, but they were just waiting for a tossed stone to churn them up again. I wouldn't let this be it.

"Hang on, Audrey." I felt him catch the hem of my sundress to keep me from leaving. I stopped. We both eyed the weirdness of him hunkering at my ankle like a seamstress.

He let go, then gestured to sit again. I reluctantly sat back down.

He rested his forearms on his knees, then folded his hands together, as if to keep them from gesturing the way they always did when he talked. "I don't know. I'd only be able to guess at this point."

"Try."

He held his palms up as if in surrender. "Because I'm an asshole. I don't know. Because you and I were

271

sharing this perfectly timed moment of mutual disgrace. I thought you would find it funny too. Which makes me even more of an asshole."

Here was the piece that had been missing during those months at my father's house as I returned to the events leading up to and during the scandal. Even after I knew that Mrs. Ass had been the one who tipped off about Dan, I couldn't understand Pooter's reaction, figuring there had to be something malicious behind it—a retributive glee at witnessing the spectacular ending to a relationship he found repugnant.

It made more sense, though, his explanation.

"And I'm sorry," he said. "I'm really sorry for what I said to you on the phone that day."

I hadn't forgotten that part either.

"Are you going to say something?" he asked.

"I miss your company."

"My company," he repeated.

"Yeah. I miss your company, Pooter."

"You saying that...it makes me feel like I was just the office clown, making you laugh so you could get through the work week."

"Well, what am I supposed to say?"

"I don't miss your company, Audrey. I miss you."

"I do too. I miss you."

We were both looking straight ahead, not so much as a sideways glance at each other. The neighborhood kids were biking and running along the sidewalk, giggling and shouting at each other. They were reveling in this penultimate summer evening, poised on the cusp of a new season—one of buses and cafeteria trays, rules and detentions, homework and crushes.

Sometime soon, their mothers would lean through the open screen door, and call them home. I remembered so clearly what that night felt like that it made my heart hurt.

I reached over and lightly took Pooter's hand in mine. We were still and quiet while I tried to get a read on the simultaneously creepy and intriguing newness of the moment. And the way this awkward holding of sweaty hands somehow seemed more intimate than a first kiss.

I took my hand back. "You've got a girl waiting on you. And I have no interest in resurrecting my bad reputation."

"I have a feeling this thing with Mindy—"

"Mandy."

"Mandy. This thing with Mandy won't go for any relationship records."

"You'd stand a better chance if you actually knew her name."

He offered up a classic Pooter shrug.

Behind the house, Julie's brother let out a primal scream before launching into the next song. The bass kicked in, then drums in a fast, galloping beat.

"C'mon, I want to catch the rest of this set," Pooter said, popping to his feet.

"You go ahead. I think I'll head out."

"Stay."

I shook my head, "I'm still not used the whole 'being around people' thing."

"But you'd be cool with a one-on-one sometime?" he asked.

"Sure, I'll have my dad call your mom to set up a play date."

"Not anymore. I moved out last month."

"Look at you all grown up."

"You should try it," he said.

And here was exhibit A: John Poudre, the very model of an individual for whom an unfortunate series of events had brought about change for the better. Work that was meaningful and satisfying, independence and self-direction. Overall, he seemed calmer, less thorny. I wasn't there yet. Not because I hadn't been transformed by the sudden collapse of the things that had been stable in my life; I was. But it was still raw. And perspective takes time.

Two months earlier, I had agreed to do an interview with a former college friend who had become a writer for *Skyline* magazine. I carefully recounted the story of that week for her—that shocking initial call, the applesauce, the hike, all of it. Before we wrapped up, she asked what I wished I had done differently. And the answer I gave was quick, "Nothing."

People interpret the expression "Shit happens" to mean that bad things will always come along. I think it means that if you're alive—whether you're climbing Machu Picchu or sitting on your front porch—events take place, stories move forward. *Shit happens*.

My time with Dan was happy, fun, and meaningful in its own way. Was it honest, right, fair? All I can say is that it was human and real. And for both of us, it filled a void. Bobbie, having thrown herself into therapy so she could focus on "self-care," was convinced I went headlong into the relationship with Dan precisely because he was unattainable, that I had commitment issues. Personally, I think I just had trouble taking anything seriously. And sometimes, you need to.

With Jamie, I had five strange and wonderful days holed up with a secret friend who was both a living connection to my roots and to a glamorous world I could only imagine through magazine spreads and Oprah interviews.

I was grateful for both of these experiences, and would return to them often, savoring each like a butterscotch candy, sweetly rolling around in my mouth. But to say that I didn't believe in mistakes wouldn't be entirely true. Because if I had the chance on that February evening that my mother died, I would pile on my parka, stuff my feet into a spare pair of winter boots and hike down to Finney's to tell my father to come home. Or maybe not. Maybe what I would do is pull up a chair beside my mother's bed and ask if instead we could play a game of cards and listen to music together until he came home.

Behind Pooter the party had livened a bit. Now fed and booze-loosened, several guests had started dancing to the fast funk beat. Pooter was walking backward toward the festivities, still urging me to join. I made a simple hand-lift in a wave of goodnight. He mirrored the gesture.

The sun had taken the earnest heat with it, and I found myself wishing for a sweater. Still, I continued past my car, strolling along the sidewalk. I relished the familiar summer smells of damp grass clippings, honeysuckle, and from somewhere in the neighborhood, a thin veil of cigar smoke.

Here was a new neighborhood full of wide-open windows and unguarded lives casually carrying on within. But instead of stealing glimpses, I kept my eyes fixed on a flat stone I kicked ahead of me every few feet as my thoughts turned to Pooter and the evening's encounter. After all of the ground-shaking events of the past year, this pleasant reconciliation—let's just call it that—was the most unexpected of all. I smiled to myself, wondering at how strange and yet completely normal it felt.

Acknowledgments

Thank you to The Story Plant and its founder and publisher, Lou Aronica, for taking a chance on this first-time author (and for answering a bazillion questions); and to associate editor, Allison Maretti, for her encouragement and ever good guidance.

The initial motivation to write this story came from the campfire readings with Nathan Hartswick and The Old Hoteliers whose laughter in all the right places made me want to give these characters more things to say. Cheers and thanks, also, to Vermont Studio Center for hosting their annual Vermont Week retreat, which helped me gain traction on the story at a critical juncture.

To my beta readers, including Craig Campanella, Dale Fornoff, Dawn Hayward, Martha Marciel, Leigh Samuels, Heather Schoppman, and Marc Sherman, I'm sorry I put you through that and am grateful for all your smart and kind feedback. My dear friend Eli Scheer wasn't only an insightful reader, they patiently developed cover design ideas with me and brought this quirky version to life. I can't overstate how much Mike Keren's patient tutelage on navigating the query/publishing process (and beyond) has been a driver in getting this book born.

I feel so lucky to have a day job with Bolder & Co. Creative Studios, a team that's the best in the business in all the ways that matter. I'm hugely grateful for my writing partners, Suzanne Loring and Benjamin Roesch, who challenge and encourage me to always tell a stronger story. Alan Michael Parker gets big props for being my earliest and most enduring influence and inspiration.

I come from a small family so I'm going to take the liberty of expressing gratitude to all of them, as each has played a part in supporting my creative spirit: Bernie and Carol Cohen (your refund of a year's worth of rent as an MFA down payment is finally offering a return on investment!); Arlene and Arthur Cohen; Laura, Rob, Matthew, and Zachary Ciampa; Mary Ellen, Itzik, and Daniel Yochay.

More than anyone else, my daughter Sonya has taught me that if you're excited by something, you find a way to fit it into your life. And to my husband, Roger, thank you for always being my biggest cheerleader, my tough-love critic, and my most devoted fan. Books brought us together, and your faith in this particular writer fills me up.

About the Author

Amy Klinger spent 20 years working in a range of office settings that provided both exasperation and inspiration for this book. She has an MFA from the University of Utah and lives with her family in Vermont.

Reading Group Questions

In Light of Recent Events was written in small increments over the course of a decade, during which I worked in both corporate and non-corporate environments. As such, I've come to understand the book as a kind of personal (albeit wholly fictional) time capsule.

There's been so much social upheaval in the 20+ years after Audrey's story takes place that, for me, the story's biggest questions juxtapose our current world against hers, particularly in thinking about how society has progressed and where it has disappointingly regressed. In this sense, the closing line of The Who's "Won't Get Fooled Again" will always feel spot-on and stubbornly timeless: "Meet the new boss, same as the old boss."

—Amy

1.	A lot has changed in the workplace since the 1990s when Audrey's story takes place, but what has stayed the same? In what ways are today's workplace cultures better? In what ways worse?

2.	Similar to Audrey and Pooter's dynamic, many people report having a "work spouse"—a close collaborator and confidante in the workplace. If you have or had a work spouse in the past, what were they like? What made the relationship special? If you no longer work together, do you keep in touch? Why or why not?

3.	In many companies, there has been a shift toward allowing employees to work remotely, often from home. What has been gained? What has been lost?

4.	Audrey's role at the publishing company is considered middle management. Though an essential function within most organizations, the term generally has a negative perception. Why do you think that is? Is it a fair judgment?

5.	To what extent do you think Audrey's apathy is her own versus a product of her environment, both in her work and personal life?

6.	While James moved away from the area in which he grew up, Audrey stayed. How do you think each one's choice influenced who they became as adults?

7.	How do you feel about Audrey and Dan's affair? Does seeing it through the contemporary lens of the Me Too movement affect your perception?

8.   Why does Daisy sabotage Langer Herbert's session? Was it the right thing to do? Was it effective?

9.   How would James Keefner's publicity crisis be different if it were happening in today's world? In what ways do you think the outcome would be different?

10.   What do you imagine is ahead for Audrey and Pooter both within their relationship with each other and as individuals?